FIRST VICTIM

FIRST VICTIM

A Novel of Suspense

DEBBIE BABITT

SCARLET
NEW YORK

FIRST VICTIM

Scarlet
An Imprint of Penzler Publishers
58 Warren Street
New York, N.Y. 10007

First Scarlet edition

Interior design by Maria Fernandez

Library of Congress Control Number: 2022902495

ISBN: 978-1-61316-302-3
eBook ISBN: 978-1-61316-303-0

10 9 8 7 6 5 4 3 2 1

Printed in the United States of America
Distributed by W. W. Norton & Company

To Ted

Vengeance is in my heart, death in my hand.
Blood and revenge are hammering in my head.
—William Shakespeare, *Titus Andronicus*

Do you believe everything happens for a reason? That our lives are predetermined before we're born?

Or do you believe in karmic destiny? That we're the masters of our fate and our actions have consequences none of us can escape?

What goes around comes around?

This wasn't part of some preordained plan. Nor was it an accident of fate. No great cosmic mistake or tragic misalignment of the stars. Only a savage vendetta of violence that was the result of human thought and cunning.

Violence that shatters lives and drives good people to commit bad acts.

To do evil in return.

Is that justice? Or revenge? The instinct that reduces us to our most primal impulses. Exposing us for the bloodthirsty beasts we are. Isn't the evolution of our brains what separates us from the animal kingdom?

Our ability to think. To reason. To make choices.

There's always a choice.

And a cost.

She hears it now.

Under the sound of the water.

It reverberates in her head, drowning out everything else.

A plaintive wail that rips at her heart.

There is another primal impulse.

A mother's need to protect her child.

She looks down.

She doesn't have much time.

There won't be a second chance.

She thinks about karmic destiny.

What goes around . . .

Slowly, she lowers the gun until it's level with his heart.

1

PART I
CRIME

ONE

"All rise. Part Seventy-One to come to order. Please put away all reading material and turn off your cell phones. Case on trial. *The People versus William Henry Young.* Indictment number 02954-19. The Honorable Alice D. McKerrity presiding."

Alice waves everyone back into their seats as she takes the bench. She detests pomp and circumstance. Bad enough judges still have to wear robes, a throwback to some archaic custom. But she has another reason to dispense with formalities.

Time.

The original judge on the case was hit by a car and is in critical condition. As one of the few trial judges working in August, a notoriously dead month, she agreed to help out. On one condition. That the trial be moved to her courtroom, which at the moment is erupting as prosecutor and defense attorney simultaneously leap to their feet.

"Your Honor, I have a matter before the—"

"Due to an unforeseen circumstance, the People request—"

Alice holds up a hand. "One at a time." Her tone is sharper than she intended. But lately, she's been finding it increasingly difficult to hold on to her patience. She takes a breath, turns to the defense attorney, a man she hasn't seen in her courtroom before.

"Mitchell Laszlow. Legal Aid Society for the defendant. I am requesting an adjournment. I was only assigned this matter late yesterday afternoon and my client's former attorney hasn't sent me the case file."

Which means he hasn't seen *Rosario* material, the discovery documents all attorneys are entitled to before trial. "What happened to the defendant's prior attorney?"

"He asked to be relieved."

"Do you know why?"

"No, Your Honor."

Maybe he couldn't work out a deal for his client.

William Henry Young was charged with first-degree murder for killing a woman during the course of committing two other crimes: rape and torture.

What complicated the case was the fact that the victim was pregnant. Before New York enacted the Reproductive Health Act, the defendant could have been charged with double homicide. But the bill gives a woman the right to choose, which effectively removes abortion from the state's penal code. The bill also means that unborn babies are no longer recognized as potential homicide victims.

With abortion a hot-button issue, the Manhattan DA tried to pacify pro-lifers by releasing a statement that the charge in this case was still murder one, and her office would be asking for the maximum—life without the possibility of parole. Which the jury will be likely to vote for after they find the defendant guilty. Then it will be up to Alice to either sentence the defendant to the maximum or find for mitigating factors and reduce the prison term. Not likely with a defendant who committed the ultimate offense against women, one that strikes at the very core of who they are.

God help him if there's a female majority on the jury. Not that a God exists who would ever answer his prayer.

". . . I'm only asking for a couple of days, Your Honor. To meet with my client and get up to speed on the case."

"You and me both, Counselor." Then Alice realizes what Laszlow just said. "Didn't you see the defendant before court this morning?"

Attorneys typically meet with their clients in the interview room on the thirteenth floor of the courthouse after the defendants are brought in from Rikers Island. New York City's maximum-security jail, Rikers sits on four-hundred-plus acres in the middle of the East River between the Bronx and Queens. But not for much longer. It's projected to close over the next few years, to be replaced with smaller prisons scattered throughout the boroughs.

"I didn't see my client today, Your Honor."

"Why not?"

"He wasn't there." The prominent Adam's apple in Laszlow's neck bobs furiously as he talks. A strand of hair flops over his forehead despite his efforts to brush it away. He doesn't look old enough to shave, let alone defend a brutal rapist-murderer.

"Tom." Alice addresses the court clerk, who's seated at his desk against the far wall. "Is the defendant on your list?"

Tom glances at his sheet. "Yes, Your Honor."

Which means he should have been on the bus that transports prisoners from Rikers to 100 Centre Street.

"So where is he?"

"If you'll allow me, Your Honor, I can explain."

Alice looks over at the prosecution table. Katharine Forster is senior assistant to the bureau chief for the sex crimes unit. She's a good lawyer who has appeared in Alice's courtroom many times.

"That was the unforeseen circumstance I was trying to tell you about. The defendant is still at Rikers. He's in solitary confinement. Early this morning he attacked another inmate with a plexiglass shank. Almost took out his eye."

The gallery explodes. Alice shoots them a warning glance. Everyone knows that she runs a tight courtroom. She won't abide lateness, laziness, or anyone trying to subvert the system or interfere with the process, whether it's a defendant or a lawyer.

After the courtroom quiets down, she again addresses Forster. "You say the defendant's in isolation? Not the prison hospital?"

"No, Your Honor."

"Was he wounded in this attack?"

"Not as far as I know."

Alice turns to Laszlow. "Did your client waive his right to appear at his own trial?"

"No, Your Honor."

"Then I demand that the defendant be produced. Today."

Now both prosecutor and defense attorney are looking at her as if she'd lost her mind. Forster finds her voice first. "But Your Honor, that will take hours."

"I'm well aware of that fact."

"But—" She's scrambling, which is unusual. At trial, she's never at a loss. "The man he attacked could lose his eyesight. What if the defendant tries something like that again?"

"Not in my courtroom."

"Then I request for him to be cuffed and shackled."

"Not in my courtroom," Alice repeats. "You know as well as I do that seeing a defendant in chains is too prejudicial for the jury." She turns to Tom. "We need Mr. Young sitting at the defense table this afternoon. Order a special bus if you have to.

"Your request is denied," Alice tells Laszlow. "We're adjourned until two-fifteen."

She brings down the gavel.

TWO

Back in her chambers, Alice disrobes and checks her phone. Less than forty minutes have passed since the last time she looked, right before court started. Since then, three new texts have come in, each one more frantic than the last.

She lets out a sigh and hits a number on speed dial. When Larry answers, Alice tells him that if Charles is refusing to bathe, he shouldn't force the issue. She'll give him his bath when she gets home. A bath in the morning isn't essential, although Charles frequently sweats through his pajamas overnight, especially when he's in the throes of nightmares that Alice can't even begin to imagine. But she can't keep running home every time there's a new fire to put out.

Twice in the past few weeks, she's had to adjourn early. Once in the middle of a hearing about search warrants after Charles threw a tantrum and wouldn't stop crying. The second time during a bail application in front of two extremely irate lawyers. Charles was refusing to eat, which was far more worrisome than his unwillingness to take a bath.

Something's got to give. Things can't go on this way.

"Judge?"

She looks up from her phone.

Her court attorney is standing in the doorway.

Alice feels vaguely guilty, like a child who has been caught out. "What's up?"

"I'm going out for coffee. Can I get you anything?"

Alice gives the question her usual measured thought, debating whether she should go home after all, which is bound to be stressful. Or she could take advantage of some much-needed downtime in the privacy of her chambers before the craziness begins.

"I'd love an iced cappuccino," she hears herself say. "Thanks, Shavonne."

"Sure." The younger woman makes no move to leave, concern wrinkling her dark features. "Is everything okay?"

Did she really think that her court attorney wouldn't notice? When the two of them aren't in court, where Shavonne always sits to the right of the bench, she's at her desk in her tiny anteroom in front of chambers, guarding Alice's private sanctuary. She'd have to be deaf, dumb, and blind to not know that something's going on. Which makes Alice question how many of her other colleagues are wondering the same thing.

Shavonne's waiting for her answer.

No! Alice feels like shouting. *Everything is not okay.*

If what's happening in her life is the new normal, she has no idea how she's going to cope.

What she really wants is a cigarette.

She's tempted to ask Shavonne, who's a pack-a-day smoker with no intention of giving up the habit. Unlike Alice, who quit four years ago and is feeling the craving more and more lately and would like nothing better than to share a smoke and exchange confidences the way she used to do as a girl with her best friend.

But as much as she'd like to, this is one secret that she can never divulge. Sometimes it feels as if most of her life has been about keeping secrets. Even if in this instance she has a very good reason, it doesn't make her feel less guilty.

"Everything's fine," she says now, the lie leaving a bitter taste in her mouth. She watches Shavonne turn and walk away, the look on her face letting Alice know that she doesn't believe her for a second.

Shavonne has been with her almost three years, longer than any of Alice's other court attorneys. But their days together are numbered. Sometime soon, a white-shoe firm is going to snap her up, the lure of a fatter paycheck a temptation most young lawyers can't resist or afford to pass up.

Alice will be sorry to see her go, something she'll have to chalk up as yet another loss in her life. Soon she's going to have to accept the fact that someone else she loves is in the process of leaving her too.

She questions now whether taking on a major trial was a wise decision. She, who makes decisions on the bench every day of the week. And the biggest one is hanging over her like a Damoclean sword.

She'd hoped that the trial would be a distraction from her increasingly chaotic personal life. An escape, if she were being brutally honest. But maybe she should be doing just the opposite—spending more time at home. Charles always seems better when she's there.

Maybe after this trial is over. She has four weeks' vacation owed to her that she hasn't used. All she has to do is ask another judge to take over her calendar after Labor Day.

And beyond that? She doesn't know. If things at home go from bad to worse, she could always arrange for an extended leave of absence. Short of stepping down from the bench altogether, which would mean forfeiting her pension that she isn't eligible to collect until she turns seventy.

More decisions.

Alice feels another powerful craving for a cigarette.

She's still fighting the urge three hours later when she gets the call.

The defendant is in the courthouse.

THREE

A hush falls over the courtroom as a door to the right of the bench opens.

The defendant stands there, flanked on either side by the two corrections officers who escorted him from the pens. From here Luiz Ramos, the court officer standing guard nearest the door, takes up the slack. Escorted by Luiz, who's been with Alice for years, the defendant walks into the courtroom.

Hobbles in would be more accurate, constrained as he is by the cuffs and shackles binding his wrists and ankles. The chains seem incongruous against the off-the-rack blue suit that looks a size too small for him. Even from the bench, Alice can see that he's *built*, his linebacker shoulders straining through the material of his suit jacket.

With a salt-and-pepper mustache and a beard that matches his thick head of wavy gray hair that's partially held back in a ponytail, he looks like an aging biker. That's a surprise. It's rare that an older defendant passes through her courtroom. Criminals who stand trial are usually in their teens or early twenties, a time in their lives when they possess the least amount of impulse control.

William Henry Young appears to be completely in control. Alice isn't the only one who can feel all that coiled energy beneath his submissive posture. Katharine Forster looks nervous as he's liberated from his chains, despite the six officers—four males and two females—strategically positioned throughout the courtroom, the maximum number due to the violent nature of the crime. All armed and ready to act should the defendant attempt a repeat of what he did at Rikers.

As if sensing the judge's eyes on him, Young raises his head. The smile transforms his face, making him appear almost human.

They rarely look like the monsters they are.

He's looking at the floor again as the last of the shackles are removed, making Alice wonder if she imagined the smile. Or maybe he's just trying to score points with her. Not that he'll get away with anything in her courtroom, not with two of the six court officers seated a few feet behind the defense table.

The male officer has been in Alice's courtroom once or twice before. She doesn't recognize the woman seated next to him, but officers typically rotate between courtrooms. The female officer is almost as tall as her male counterpart, with a gaze that's watchful and alert. If the need arises, she looks more than capable of restraining the defendant.

After Young takes his seat at the table, Luiz resumes his position by the door.

The corrections officers will return when it's time for the defendant to be taken back to the pens. From there, another set of officers will escort him to the Manhattan Detention Complex, aka the Tombs.

An underground jail excavated during the era of the infamous Five Points, the Tombs' official address is 125 White Street. Mazes of tunnels run beneath the stairways, and a bridge on the twelfth floor connects the building to the North Tower of 100 Centre Street so defendants can be transported to the courthouse without ever seeing daylight.

No elevator stops there. For civilians, that is. Only officers with keys can access the elevators that run down to the Tombs.

It's the temporary prison of choice for defendants deemed too violent to be taken back to Rikers every night. Less likelihood of escape. Or attacking a fellow inmate. No doubt this defendant will spend the rest of the trial there.

As the first group of prospective jurors file in, Alice glances at the defense table. Young is rubbing his wrists where the chains dug into his skin. He barely acknowledges his attorney. Mitchell Laszlow sits rigid next to his client, no doubt wishing he were anywhere but here.

You and me both.

Once the jurors are seated, Alice introduces herself and gives her speech welcoming them to her courtroom. Then she tells them how jury selection, also known as voir dire, is part of our system of law. She motions to Tom, who has risen and has his hand on a large drum in the center of his desk. Inside the drum is a wheel containing the names of all potential jurors. Tom spins the wheel. When it stops, he calls out the names and directs each juror to a specific seat in the jury box. Once they have their first panel of sixteen—twelve jurors and four alternates—Alice introduces the lawyers. She nods to the prosecutor, who's always first up. Katharine Forster picks up her legal pad as she gets to her feet.

They're off and running.

—⁂—

Juror #3—a retired Navy SEAL—just raised his hand. When Forster acknowledges him, he asks, "Isn't a fetus a life as well?"

Forster responds by instructing Juror #3 and the other members of the jury pool on the Reproductive Health Act that repealed the state fetal homicide law and doesn't recognize unborn babies as potential murder victims. Killing a fetus isn't a charge in the indictment against the defendant.

Juror #3 tells Forster that his conscience wouldn't allow him to follow the law because he thinks the law is a crime itself and a travesty of justice for unborn children everywhere.

He's dismissed for cause.

Alice glances at the defendant again as Forster moves on to the next juror.

He's doodling on the yellow legal pad on the table in front of him, as if he has no interest in the proceedings. As if it isn't his freedom being weighed in the balance.

Juror #6, a single mother, calls the defendant the worst kind of predator because his victim is dead and can't tell the world how he murdered her and her unborn child. In her mind, he took two lives; she doesn't care what the law says. She, too, is excused.

Two other jurors—#5 and #8, a middle school librarian and a mattress salesman—are dismissed because they can't accept a law that offends their religious beliefs.

Forster moves on to a woman in the back row. Juror #11.

She's a waitress at a wine bar in lower Manhattan. She tells Forster she isn't sure she can be objective because she's responsible for taking a life.

Once again, the courtroom erupts. Alice is as surprised by her response as everyone else. On their questionnaires, prospective jurors are asked if they have ever been a victim of a violent crime. Or convicted of one.

They aren't asked if they've committed a crime.

Looking as if she's about to burst into tears, the woman goes on to say that she killed her child in cold blood. "While he was still growing inside me. And the law makes my crime legal. So I can never be punished for what I did."

"Do you think you should be punished?" Alice hears herself asking.

The woman nods. A hush comes over the courtroom as she shares the story of finding herself pregnant at seventeen with no money or family. "I didn't think I had a choice. But I did. You always have a choice."

Alice thinks about choices as she gazes around the courtroom. There isn't a female here who hasn't been confronted with a life-altering decision at some point. Who can't understand this young woman's anguish.

Young has stopped doodling. He puts down the crayon, the only implement violent defendants are allowed to use in court, a pen or pencil considered too dangerous.

He looks at the juror.

There's something in the way he's watching her.

The woman stares back at him like someone transfixed.

As if sensing her distress, his mouth curls up in a parody of his earlier smile. One without a trace of empathy. A smile devoid of all human emotion.

The woman shrinks back in her seat.

After she's excused, Alice watches the prospective juror hurry out of the courtroom as if she can't get away quickly enough. The courtroom is so quiet you can hear the proverbial pin drop.

At the defense table, Young's head is down. The crayon once again in his hand.

He has gone back to his doodling.

FOUR

Her heart pounds as she runs.

The punishing pace feels good. She pushes herself to go faster, waiting for the moment when the physical overtakes the mental, obliterating everything else. When her body goes on autopilot and her mind becomes a blank, a sign that the endorphins are starting to kick in.

But the runner's high has been eluding her for weeks. And tonight, for the first time, she lost her temper with Charles.

When she arrived home from court, he was still in his pajamas. After she finally got him into the tub, he refused to let her wash him. He kept flailing his arms, which sent water splashing all over her and the floor. Alice became enraged and told him that if he didn't behave, he wouldn't get any supper. He started to cry and she was immediately guilt-stricken over her harsh words. Eventually, between the two of them, she and Larry got him bathed, fed, and settled down for the night.

By then, it was after seven. With the days growing shorter, Alice knew she had only a small window before daylight ended. She was usually back from her run by that time, safely tucked away inside before night fell. After weighing the pros and cons, the need for a stress-relieving outlet won out over her dread of the dark that had begun in childhood.

Now she regrets her decision. She's completed only one loop around the running track, and most of the light has been leached from the sky. Darkness is coming on fast, mitigated only by the silver ribbon of moonlight casting a ghostly glow over the reservoir.

The breeze has picked up, rustling the leaves of the trees she passes. The endless chirp of crickets that she rarely hears from inside her house, with the windows closed and the AC going full blast, drowning out everything else until their monotonous drone is the only thing she hears.

She runs faster. If she could only outrun her thoughts. As she speeds past the midway point where Central Park divides the east and west sides of the city, she notices a group of double-crested cormorants in the middle of the water. They're floating on a broken-off section of the white pedestal that holds the reservoir's century-old fountain. Alice looks over her shoulder at them as she runs, struck by the sight of so many of the aquatic birds crowded together.

Until they start pushing each other off.

Survival of the fittest.

Don't they know it's only a matter of time? That either way, they're doomed?

She's appalled at the morbid turn her thoughts have been taking lately. Especially after tonight's episode. She knows she has to make a decision, and it's weighing on her.

She blinks, her vision clouding over with the mist that seems to have appeared out of nowhere. It creates a film over the light from the century-old lampposts along the track that are visible where overgrown vegetation hasn't obscured them. Fog has begun to creep in, a harbinger of tomorrow's predicted heat wave. That will make the third this month.

The moon has disappeared behind a cloud. It's pitch-black now, not a single star in the sky. She feels the night settling over her like a shroud. The reservoir no longer shimmers with colorful reflections of the trees along the running track. It has become an opaque sheet, giving off a foul odor as the water laps against the pilings. The air feels heavier, with curling fingers of low-lying fog that makes it impossible to see two feet ahead. She slows down and slides her phone out of her pocket. Shines it over the ground as she runs.

Less than a quarter mile to go. Crushed gravel flies up from the track as she runs, the rising humidity making it hard to breathe. Her chest heaves with the effort. She pushes herself to go faster.

The sounds of night are deafening now, the crickets an unceasing buzz in her head. She can hear the wind whistling through the treetops.

A sharp stitch in her side forces her to stop. She doubles over, tries to catch her breath. When she can breathe without pain, she grits her teeth and starts running again.

Footsteps pound behind her.

Her heart leaps into her throat.

The runner hurtles past, his hooded figure barely visible. Adrenaline surges through her. She sprints ahead, tells herself this isn't a contest. The only one she's competing against is herself.

She can't see the runner anymore. He's been swallowed up in the mist.

She hears footsteps again.

When she looks over her shoulder, she can't see anything. The track is covered in fog.

The footsteps are getting louder.

Now they're right behind her.

She veers off the track, loses her balance, and stumbles against the low metal fencing half-hidden in the dense vegetation. She drops her phone and wastes precious seconds searching for it on her hands and knees in the sharp, pebbled gravel. When she finds the phone, next to the gnarled trunk of a massive tree, she jumps to her feet and races through an opening in the fence that curves down to the bridle path.

Then she's running again, out toward the 90th Street entrance. Hurtling past picnic tables, benches, and a water fountain as she races out of the park. Running against the stoplight across the deserted Fifth Avenue up to 91st Street. Sprinting past the Cooper-Hewitt Museum and Spence School before crossing Madison. She leaves behind the white marble columns of the Brick Church on the corner of Park and 91st as she continues east—another landmark she has passed hundreds of times before. She keeps running and doesn't stop until she reaches her town house halfway down the block, where she takes the steps two at a time.

FIVE

A lice closes her eyes and lets the water beat down on her.

What the hell happened out there?

One minute she was running along the track, lost in her thoughts. The next, she was terrified out of her wits. Spooked by the sight of the hooded jogger coming up behind her, as if he'd materialized out of thin air. The fact is, he was trying to pass her, and the fog made it difficult to see. End of story.

It has to be all the stress she's under. She can't remember the last time she had an uninterrupted night's sleep. Empirical evidence has shown that when people are sleep-deprived, they can become depressed. Lose the ability to make rational decisions. Even hallucinate.

Did she imagine that second set of footsteps?

She stands under the spray for several minutes more. She still feels unsettled when she steps out of the shower. As she towels off, she catches sight of herself in the medicine cabinet mirror. Her hair is a wild halo around her face. Even with the steam filling the bathroom, she can see how pale she looks. And there are hollows in her cheeks and circles under her eyes.

No wonder her court attorney's worried about her.

Her reflection frowns at her as she opens the cabinet, where several small vials line the bottom shelf.

She started taking prescription meds two years ago when Charles was first diagnosed. A few months ago, she finally weaned herself off them.

She closes the medicine cabinet in disgust.

She can't go down that rabbit hole again.

—m—

In bed, she tosses and turns, unable to find a comfortable position. Even with the dim light coming from the closet, she feels the night pressing down on her.

She was always afraid of the dark, for as long as she could remember. Terrified of what waited for her in the whispering, slithering blackness that seemed to take on the shape of her fear and threatened to swallow her whole if she relaxed her vigilance and closed her eyes.

After she awoke from a nightmare, only light could ease her panic and banish the monsters in the shadows.

The nameless terror hiding under the bed.

The unseen evil lurking in the closet.

But it wasn't until her mother came into her room and got into bed with her that the fear finally abated. When her mother died, when she was ten, she lost her champion. It had always been the two of them against the world. After the funeral, Alice went to live with her father, who'd left when she was a baby. Her new home was in a village three hundred miles north of New York. It might as well have been three thousand.

Decades older than her mother, her father was a cold, distant man. He couldn't comfort Alice in the night, and she was ashamed to let him see her fear. She'd lie alone in the dark, eyes open wide, heart thundering in her ears.

—m—

She must have drifted off.

When she opens her eyes, she isn't sure what awakened her.

Then she hears it.

The sound of the front door opening.

Footsteps on the stairs.

Her last thought as she slips back into uneasy sleep is that there aren't enough lights and locked doors to keep out the monsters.

SIX

*S*he *runs blindly, stumbling over rocks and tree roots. Low-hanging branches stab her face. The wind wails through the treetops, the chain saw chirp of crickets a continuous drone in her ears. Overhead, a sudden flapping of wings cracks through the night like thunder.*

When she looks up, she sees a flock of cormorants flying past.

Footsteps pound behind her.

She runs faster.

Alice bolts up in bed, her heart in her throat.

For a moment, she has no idea where she is. She looks around, still trapped in the terrifying purgatory between sleep and wakefulness.

She forces herself to take slow, deep breaths. She was just having a bad dream. As the tightness in her chest finally eases, the darkness begins to lift. The trees disappear, replaced by the familiar objects of her bedroom.

The cherrywood armoire with the curved doors, tall and regal against the wall that she had repainted in serene ochre earth tones this past December. The handsome Victorian bench at the foot of the bed she bought at auction several years ago following a frenzied bidding. The divan that sits a few feet from the French doors leading to the terrace. With the cheerful pattern of yellow and white English daisies against a soothing background of hunter green that matches the rectangular pillows against the backrest, it never fails to lift her spirits. Especially now, with motes of light dancing across the upholstery from the rays of sun sneaking in through the bottoms of the blinds.

Alice frowns. Her bedroom faces south. She doesn't get the early morning light, especially in the dying days of August when the sun doesn't rise before six. She looks at the clock on her nightstand, is stunned to see that it's after ten-thirty. In almost twelve years on the bench, she has never slept past five A.M., not even after a restless night.

In the bathroom, she splashes cold water on her face. As her reflection stares back at her, she sees herself running again. She shakes her head, and her vision clears. After brushing her teeth, she sheds the T-shirt she always sleeps in and throws on a pair of sweats.

Outside her bedroom, the house feels preternaturally silent. The door at the far end of the hall is closed. She has a vague memory of waking in the night, hearing her daughter on the stairs. God only knows what time that was. In the past, she could never fall asleep until she knew that Alexis was home, safe and sound. But lately, she's been drifting off at all hours, only to startle awake like she did this morning from a nightmare that still has its claws in her.

She stops in front of Charles's room. His bedroom door is open.

He isn't inside.

Panic chokes her. As she races down the stairs, she tells herself she's being irrational.

He isn't in the living room.

Or the study.

He isn't in the courtyard out back, where he used to love spending summer afternoons nurturing his flowers and plants.

It's a beautiful sunny morning. Maybe he was taken out for a walk.

Except that the chain is still on the front door.

Where *is* he?

Alice looks around, half expecting him to leap out from behind the coatrack in the hall where he'd hidden in an attempt to frighten her. Her heart rate spikes. Despite the brilliant sunlight pouring in through the bay window, she again feels the darkness closing in. Her hands shake, fingers itching to hold a cigarette.

She cocks her head at a sound. Follows the soft murmur of voices into the dining room, where Charles is seated in his customary place at the head of the table.

Alice stops in her tracks. She can't remember the last time she saw him sitting here.

"He's been waiting for you. Right, Charles?"

Her husband doesn't respond to the aide seated on his left. A pleasant, well-mannered young man from the South, Larry has been with them for the past five months. As she walks to the table, Alice instinctively smooths down her hair. She still hasn't gotten used to having strangers in her home. She doubts she ever will.

"He didn't want breakfast in his room this morning," Larry says as Alice sits on Charles's other side. "He insisted on coming down here."

At that moment, the grandfather clock in the hall tolls the hour. Eleven. That was the time they always used to have brunch on the weekends.

Charles hasn't said a word. Which isn't unusual. He sometimes goes for days without speaking. Then Alice realizes that he isn't wearing his usual robe and pajamas. He's dressed in a suit and the tie she bought him a few Christmases ago. The knot is off-center. In spite of herself, Alice smiles. Even when he was himself, Charles never could knot his tie properly.

"He thinks he's going to court."

Alice's smile fades. He hasn't had this particular delusion in months. "Good morning, sweetheart." She forces out the three words she greets him with every day. Leaning in, she kisses his cheek. It's smooth and cold.

Charles gives a polite nod, his face unreadable.

Alice turns to Larry. "I can take it from here. Why don't you tidy up Charles's room? Then you can take off for the day."

His shift is almost over. Alice deliberately carved out the midnight to noon hours to avoid Charles having to get used to a new face too close to his nine P.M. bedtime, which used to agitate him.

"Sure thing," Larry says. He understands. She wants some alone time with her husband.

After Larry leaves, Alice touches Charles's arm. She has less than an hour before the noon to midnight aide arrives. "Are you ready for brunch?"

Charles looks at her, then nods.

"How about bacon and eggs? Sunny-side up, the way you like them."

He nods again, his face growing more animated.

Fifteen minutes later, Alice returns with a tray containing a glass of orange juice and a steaming plate of bacon and eggs.

"Where's my coffee?" Charles asks, a querulous note in his voice.

Coffee was always his favorite part of the meal. He never left the table before he'd had at least two cups. Alice stopped giving it to him months ago, after he ended up pouring the scalding liquid all over himself.

"Later," she tells him. "After you've eaten your brunch."

Later, he won't remember that he asked for it.

She sits down next to him.

"Hey."

Alexis is walking into the dining room, no doubt awakened by the aroma of frying bacon.

As she approaches the table, Alice frowns at the sight of what has become her daughter's standard-issue attire lately: Gray sweats and baggy sweatshirt even though it's still the dead of summer. Today her sweatshirt is white, with the name "KillJoy" in black letters. Below that is a pyre of burning bodies.

She sits on Charles's other side, in the chair Larry recently vacated. Alice is shocked to see dark smudges under her eyes that mirror her own. In her daughter's case, that's likely a result of her late-night hours.

Is she losing weight? Alice can't see her figure beneath the shapeless clothes. "Let me make you some breakfast."

"I'm fine," Alexis says. "Don't bother."

"It's no bother." Alice is already out of her chair.

"I'm not hungry."

"You have to eat. Are you feeling all right? Maybe you're coming down with something." Alice leans over, touches a hand to her daughter's forehead.

Alexis swats her away. "I'm not sick! I'm just not hungry. So leave me alone, okay?"

Alice is stunned into speechlessness at the hostility in her voice. The cold fury in her eyes.

Charles is also staring at Alexis.

"Eat your breakfast, Charles," Alice says, trying to tamp down her own anger at her daughter. "Your eggs are getting cold."

He looks at her, then down at his plate.

"You'd better get a move on. You don't want to be late for court."

They're the magic words. Charles looks at his bare right wrist. "I didn't realize the time. I have a full docket today." He frowns as he returns his attention to his plate. The furrow in his brow deepens. After a moment, he reaches for the bacon.

"Use your fork," Alice tells him. "You don't want to get your hands dirty."

He nods. Looks at the fork next to his plate. His gaze shifts to his knife. Then to his spoon.

"Your fork is to the left of your plate."

He picks up the fork. Impales a slice of bacon on it. His hand holding the fork is shaking.

He doesn't know what to do next.

Alexis leans forward. Charles doesn't resist as she takes the fork from his hand and starts feeding him. After a few bites, he pushes her hand away. She ignores him.

Charles starts flailing his arms. Alexis is still trying to feed him. She bites down on her lower lip, tears welling in her eyes. Alice tries to remember that this has been hard on all of them, but especially her daughter. Finally admitting defeat, Alexis puts down the fork. That's when Charles whacks her across the side of the face.

Alexis lets out a yell. Her hand flies to her cheek as tears spill down her face. Then she shoves back her chair and runs from the room.

"Alexis!" Alice is up like a shot. She's halfway up the stairs when she hears her daughter's bedroom door slamming shut.

The sound echoes through the house.

Alice stands on the steps, overwhelmed by despair. She feels as if everything is slipping away, and she's powerless to stop it.

When she feels sufficiently in control of her emotions to return to the dining room, Charles is on his feet, staring at his arm as if he can't believe it belongs to him.

"Alice."

She's so stunned to hear him say her name that for a moment, she can't speak.

"What's happening to me?" He's crying now.

Alice goes to him and takes him in her arms. He murmurs her name over and over, like a mantra. As she strokes his hair, her tears mingle with his. She knows that the man she married is in there somewhere.

The worst part is that he knows it too.

When they're both cried out, she gently lifts his head and looks into the eyes of the man she fell in love with twenty years ago.

His hazel eyes as clear as she has ever seen them.

His doctors have warned that she shouldn't be encouraged by this. That these moments are few and far between and will occur with less and less frequency as time passes. That patients often seem to be getting better right before they take a turn for the worse.

But a part of Alice still refuses to accept that. And when he looks at her like his old self, it's hard to believe that he can ever be anything else.

"Are you all right?" Now it's Charles who's stroking her hair.

Alice gazes into the eyes that are once again ablaze with the fierce intelligence that made him such a formidable jurist, and it's as if the last two years have been miraculously erased.

He cups a hand under her chin. "Talk to me, Alice."

She'd like to do that, talk things out the way they used to do. But she isn't sure what's happening herself. And how can she tell him that he's the primary cause of her anxiety?

She studies his face. Have those worry lines always been there? The creases around his eyes that seem to have deepened into permanent grooves? The gray at his temples that she always found so distinguished is now completely white, like the rest of his hair. The sagging, parchment-pale skin that makes him look much older than his sixty-three years.

"I'm fine. Everything's fine." Repeating the same lie she told her court attorney. The difference is that she and Charles never kept secrets from each other.

He looks at her as if he sees right through her. They've always been attuned to each other that way. Sometimes Alice thinks of the disease as a tumor pressing on the part of his brain that controls emotion and intuition, making him even more sensitive and aware.

"You know you can tell me anything, don't you?"

His voice is low, hypnotic. With his thumb and index finger, he traces circles around her face. Frowns as he notices the shadows under her eyes. His arms tighten around her. Now Alice is the one holding fast to him, this man who has always been her anchor and her refuge. She wants him to comfort her, to ease her fears and doubts as he has so many times in the past.

Tell her that everything will be all right.

But something is shifting in his face, like a shadow creeping across the sun. She feels it happening before he even lets her go.

No! Alice wants to scream. *Don't leave me. Not yet.*

But he's already disappearing.

It starts in his shoulders. They sag as if all the air had gone out of him. His arms go slack; his hands dangle uselessly at his sides. He stares down at his legs as if he'd forgotten how to walk.

Then he raises his head.

It's as if a light has switched off.

There's no recognition in that dull stare.

He takes one tentative step, then another, like a toddler finding his feet for the first time.

Again Alice wants to scream, to shake the life back into him.

She does none of those things. Instead, she watches as he turns and walks back to the table. He sits down, unfolds his napkin and tucks it into his shirt collar. Then he picks up the fork and starts eating the cold eggs and congealed bacon. After he's finished, he pushes away his plate.

When he sees her, he gives a polite nod.

He's gone again.

SEVEN

I t was Charles who had encouraged her to go for the open seat on the Manhattan Supreme Court bench after seven years as a prosecutor. Like many judges, Alice started out as an assistant district attorney, but soon distinguished herself in a string of high-profile convictions that helped her rise quickly through the ranks of the Manhattan DA's office.

And Charles was there for her every step of the way. Giving her advice. Exerting his influence.

That was what people said. That he was helping his wife land a plum job. One that came with power and a lifetime pension. The truth was, Charles was a jurist who passionately followed the spirit of the law. He loved and respected the legal system and would never do anything to put it in jeopardy.

When Alice met him, he'd been a widower for three years. He had no children.

He'd just turned forty-three. She was twenty-seven, fresh out of law school. Behind her other classmates because she didn't graduate from high school until she was twenty.

Tall and handsome, Charles Evans McKerrity had been on the bench for eight years. He had a reputation for being fair and impartial. He was respected and well-liked and the rumor went that she married him to get ahead.

It couldn't have been further from the truth.

She married him because he was kind and gentle.

Gradually, the whispers stopped. She took his advice and went for the open seat. It was Charles who allayed her doubts about her ability to be fair and impartial.

Becoming a lawyer was her way of leveling the playing field. Seeking justice for those who had no voices. Putting away the rapists and murderers before they could brutalize other defenseless women.

Every time she convicted a defendant, it was a win for their victims.

Who else was going to fight for them?

—⁓—

Alice is outside her daughter's bedroom, pleading to let her in.

She shouts to make herself heard above the din.

"Go away," Alexis shouts back.

"Please, Allie. I just want to talk."

After an eternity, Alexis opens the door.

Alice follows her inside, the music piercing her eardrums. While Alexis goes over to the stereo, she looks around.

The room is a shambles. Clothes are strewn across the unmade bed; magazines litter the floor. Every inch of wall space is covered with posters.

This isn't the room of a woman on the cusp of turning twenty-nine, who graduated from college seven years ago.

It's a teenager's room, full of adolescent angst.

Alice stifles the urge to say something. Her daughter will just see it as a lecture. And what good would it do? It will only drive them further apart.

Alexis has turned to face her, the music now dissonant background noise. She's still wearing the KillJoy sweatshirt. Her arms are crossed over her chest. It's her defensive stance. She's done it since she was a child. But today, in the oversized sweatshirt, it makes her look even more vulnerable.

A small welt has risen on her left cheekbone, where Charles hit her.

It's Alice's fault. All of this is her fault.

"I'm so sorry."

"Sorry doesn't cut it, Mom."

Her voice is so hard and cold.

"Alexis—"

"I'm so sick of you acting like everything's okay. Like we're a normal family."

"We *are* a family."

"No, we're not. We were never a family."

"Alexis, please." Alice can't let her see how her words cut through her. "He didn't mean it. He can't help himself."

"I don't want to hear it."

"How do you know what I'm going to say?"

"Because you've said it so many times! What a wonderful person he is. How good he's been to me."

"But it's true. You know he'd do anything for you. "

"I don't care how wonderful he is! I don't care if he was the greatest judge in the world! It doesn't change anything!"

"Lower your voice."

"You just don't get it, do you? You are such a wimp. You're so pathetic."

"Alexis!"

In response, her daughter storms over to her closet. Beneath her sweats, her feet are bare, toenails painted with the same black polish as her fingernails. "Can't anyone have any privacy in this house?" she mutters.

Alice crosses the cluttered room, resisting the urge to pick up after her. Her daughter ignores her, flings open the closet door.

"Alexis," Alice repeats. "You will look at me when I'm speaking to you." Alexis reluctantly turns around, her face mutinous. Again, Alice is reminded of how immature she is for her age. "I will not tolerate this behavior. As long you're living under this roof, you will be respectful and act like you are part of this family. Do you understand?"

"Maybe I'll just have to move out."

"Is that a threat? And what will you use for money? Are you planning to get a job?"

Alexis hasn't worked since she quit her hostessing job at an Upper East Side restaurant over the winter. Alice had wanted bigger things for her only child. After Alexis graduated from college, she'd had lengthy conversations with her about going to law school. Not that she'd ever insist that her daughter follow in her footsteps. But Alexis had no interest. And for the past few months, she'd been floundering.

Alexis glares at her mother. This wasn't the way Alice planned their long-overdue conversation to play out. But now she can see the unhappiness beneath her daughter's bravado and all she wants is to make it better, to chase away all the bad things. The sunlight slanting in through the blinds accentuates Alexis's pallor. She looks gaunt, her weight loss concealed under baggy sweatpants.

How could Alice have failed to realize how her child was suffering? Her anger disappears as swiftly as it came. "I have an idea," she says, her voice softening. "It looks like it's going to be a beautiful day. I'll treat you to lunch." Where she'll try to get her daughter to confide in her. Away from this house. Away from Charles.

"I have plans," Alexis says in the clipped tone she's been using lately in the rare times she deigns to talk to her mother.

"What plans? Where are you going?" Alice regrets it the moment the words are out of her mouth. Peppering her daughter with questions is only going to alienate her more and make her think she's trying to control her life.

Alexis stomps over to the laptop on her desk and hits some keys. Music blares from the twin speakers Alice bought for her last birthday. She tells Alexis they can have lunch another time. Alexis ignores her. Admitting defeat, Alice leaves the room, the music pounding in her head.

—⁂—

The late-afternoon sun is still a fireball in the sky as Alice slides a cigarette from the pack she bought this morning after a furious debate with herself. The growing need for her old crutch overriding the fact that it had taken months to kick the habit the first time.

Half the pack's already gone.

She lights up, takes a long, deep drag and waits for the nicotine to work its magic.

She started smoking at thirteen, sneaking cigarettes with her best friend Connie after school. By the time she was sixteen, it had become a pack-a-day habit. She stopped only once before she quit—she had thought for good—four years ago. That was during the nine months she carried her daughter.

Her mind is still on Alexis.

Twenty minutes after she left Alexis's bedroom, Alice heard the front door slam. From her bedroom window, she watched her daughter race down the steps of their town house as if she couldn't get away fast enough.

She was wearing a different pair of sweats. On the back of her shapeless black sweatshirt was a skull and crossbones in white. Underneath that, a knife dripping blood.

For the first time, Alice wonders if she's taking drugs. That could account for her erratic behavior. One minute she's seething with hostility, the next she's patiently trying to feed Charles.

As she slides out another cigarette, Alice thinks about how hard she has tried to be a good parent. To be a positive influence on her child, even in those hellish early years. She spent all that time since trying to make up for that. Ready to sacrifice everything to give Alexis a normal life.

When did things change? When did Alexis start seeing her mother as the enemy? How did Alice allow it to reach the point that she knows next to nothing about her life? What she does and where she goes. Who her friends are. If she has a boyfriend.

She has no idea who her daughter is anymore.

She blames herself. If she hadn't been so consumed with Charles these last two years, she might have realized what was happening with Alexis. She's to blame for that too. Because of her need to protect her daughter in a way she hadn't been able to protect herself, she overcompensated.

Believing that if she kept her safe from the outside world, she could save her from the demons within.

EIGHT

F or the third time since she took the bench, Alice looks at the scarred
clock on the wall.

Jury selection was concluded yesterday. Opening statements are
scheduled to begin this morning.

At the prosecution table, Katharine Forster is talking to the attorney
who's her second chair. She taps her foot impatiently, looks at her watch.

There's no one at the defense table. Both lawyer and defendant are
conspicuously absent. "Tom," Alice calls out for the second time to the
court clerk, who's doing paperwork at his desk against the far wall. "Please
try Mr. Laszlow's office again. Then call Corrections and find out what's
delaying the defendant."

Tom's punching in numbers on his phone when the doors at the rear
of the courtroom open.

Mitchell Laszlow rushes in, his suit jacket flapping open.

A moment later, the door to the right of the bench opens.

The defendant stands there. After the two correction officers who
escorted him from the pens leave, Luiz brings him into the courtroom.
The ankle chain makes a hollow scraping sound as it drags across the
scarred wood floor.

"Your Honor?"

Mitchell Laszlow is on his feet. His tension is palpable, despite the presence of the male and female officers who are in their usual seats behind the defense table.

It occurs to Alice that she might have made an error in judgment in ruling against Young remaining shackled in the courtroom. She could reverse herself, but the prejudicial nature of a jury seeing a defendant in chains—the reason she ruled against it—could be grounds for an appeal if he were convicted.

After Luiz unshackles Young and returns to his post by the door to the pens, Alice addresses Laszlow. "Good morning, Counselor. Do you want to tell this court why you've kept us waiting for almost half an hour?"

"I apologize, Your Honor. But before you bring in the jury, I want to make an application."

"For what?"

"Relief."

It takes a minute for his words to sink in. "Are you asking to be relieved from the case?"

"Yes, Your Honor. I feel I can no longer represent my client."

As the decibel level in the courtroom rises, Alice bangs the gavel.

She does not need this now.

Over the past week, she's been feeling more anxious and on edge. Plagued by the same dream of running through the woods, footsteps pounding behind her. But when she looks over her shoulder, no one is there. As if that weren't unsettling enough, Charles has started crying in his sleep. Long, anguished howls that continue deep into the night. Her daughter barely speaks to her, making Alice feel like a trespasser in her own home.

And she's smoking like a fiend.

When the gallery finally quiets down, Alice addresses the defendant, who as usual is doodling on his yellow pad.

"Mr. Young? Is it your wish to have your lawyer removed?"

He puts down the crayon. "Yes, it is. Your Honor."

Is he mocking her? His voice is a surprise. It's soft and low, with a lilting rumble that seems to emanate from somewhere deep inside him.

"Do you want to tell this court why?"

"I can't be defended by someone who told me he doesn't believe in my innocence, can I?"

Alice has to think carefully before responding. She could ask Laszlow if what the defendant says is true, which would be skirting dangerously close to violating attorney-client confidentiality. On the other hand, the defendant in effect waived a portion of the privilege by stating what his lawyer said to him during an attorney-client conversation.

"Mr. Laszlow. Can you be more specific as to why you feel you can't represent the defendant?"

Laszlow doesn't answer right away. The courtroom's gone quiet. Everyone's waiting to see if a lawyer would admit he wants off a case because of a defendant's guilt.

That would be even rarer than a defendant who's innocent.

"There's been an irreparable breakdown of communication between my client and me," he finally says. "As a result, I don't believe I could do an effective job of defending him."

It's the pat response that reveals nothing. Alice could hold Laszlow's hands to the fire, order a hearing. But what would that accomplish? If she denied his request and Young were convicted, another lawyer could argue that Young's Sixth Amendment right was violated on the grounds of ineffective assistance of counsel, to which Laszlow himself just opened the door. It could be grounds for overturning a conviction.

"You've now had two attorneys removed," she says to the defendant, who's looking pleased with himself. "I'm giving you fair warning. Three strikes and you're out. Mr. Laszlow will remain your attorney until I notify Legal Aid to assign you new counsel."

"I don't need another lawyer, Your Honor. I plan to defend myself."

The gallery explodes again. Alice has to bang the gavel several times.

"You've already caused unnecessary delays by changing attorneys," she tells him after the noise has died down. "I won't allow you to waste more time or turn these proceedings into a three-ring circus."

"I'm only asking for what I'm entitled to under the Constitution of the United States. It's my God-given right."

"God has nothing to do with it. What makes you believe you can represent yourself?"

In response, he holds up the yellow legal pad. Even from here, she can see that what she mistook for senseless doodlings are notes.

Pages and pages of notes.

"I've been reading up on the law," he says. And proceeds to rattle off a list of questions for potential jurors, which shows he was paying attention during voir dire.

Alice isn't impressed. At best, his questions show only the most rudimentary knowledge of the law.

All she has to do is ask a few key questions regarding the rules of evidence and she could easily show that he fails to meet the threshold of competence. But a few years back there was an overturning of a State Supreme Court ruling by the Court of Appeals, holding that if a defendant is deemed competent to stand trial in the first place, and has knowingly and voluntarily waived his right to counsel, then he's competent to defend himself.

Therefore, precedent exists for allowing him to appear pro se.

Most defendants who choose this path end up convicted.

"In the interest of moving things along and to keep defendant's right to a speedy trial from being further violated, I'm granting defendant's pro se motion. Mr. Laszlow, you'll turn over all discovery to the defendant. Opening statements will begin Wednesday morning at ten." Alice picks up the gavel.

The voice of the defendant stops her.

"Your Honor."

What now?

"Now that I'm representing myself, I want to make a motion."

"For what?"

Young turns to look at the male and female officers. "I find it extremely disconcerting to have these officers looking over my shoulder. How am I supposed to defend myself with them watching every move I make? I'm fighting for my freedom here."

"Sorry to disappoint you. You may have chosen to represent yourself, but you're still a defendant on trial for a heinous crime. You also attacked and wounded a fellow inmate at Rikers. I have the safety of my courtroom to consider. Your motion is denied. And we're adjourned."

After Alice gets to her feet, Luiz leaves his post by the door and walks to the defense table.

Young is still looking at her as he's chained up again.

NINE

"The defendant will rise."

William Henry Young gets to his feet.

He's trimmed his mustache and beard.

His hair is shorter.

And he's wearing a new suit.

Alice can barely contain her anger. "How dare you make a mockery of this courtroom. If you think your latest exploit will get you a mistrial, you're mistaken." She indicates the newspapers spread out on the bench. "Do you know what these are? Articles written after you gave an interview in the Tombs."

"I've been unjustly accused," Young says. "I'm an innocent man being railroaded for a crime I didn't commit. The world has a right to know the truth."

"Save your speeches for the jury." Alice looks out over the courtroom. "I'm issuing a gag order. As of ten o' clock this morning, Ms. Forster and Mr. Young are barred from speaking to the media."

Alice can't help but feel a sense of vindication at the scowling faces of the members of the press seated in the first and second rows of the gallery. Two years ago, these same reporters camped out across the street from her town house so they'd be the first to get the scoop on why one of Manhattan's most prominent judges retired early.

The story she'd given out was that Charles had a heart condition. If the true nature of his illness ever became public, it could throw his last years on the bench into question. Convictions could be overturned; verdicts set aside.

When she left for court this morning, her husband was in bed, banging his fists on his breakfast tray and sending food flying everywhere. A world away from the esteemed jurist who'd handed down some of Manhattan Supreme's most brilliantly crafted opinions.

"You can't stop me from speaking my mind." Young's voice has gone shrill with outrage. "It's my First Amendment right."

Alice whirls on him. "Wrong. The First Amendment doesn't apply here. You're acting as your own lawyer in my courtroom now. You follow my rules. And that means no more press conferences from prison. If you violate my ruling, you'll be removed and forced to conduct your trial from your prison cell. Do you understand? Speak up, Mr. Young. The court reporter can't hear you."

"Yes."

"Yes, Your Honor."

"Yes, Your Honor," he repeats.

Even from here, she can see his anger.

It only feeds her own. Alice turns to the officer seated in the empty jury box and tells him to bring in the jury.

—⁕—

". . . The evidence will show that the defendant stalked the victim for a week leading up to the murder. He always sat at the same table at the dance club, where he had the best view of the victim. The evidence will show that he tried to get Angel Diallo into his car. When she rejected him, he became enraged.

"Now the defendant wanted revenge. When Angel left the club on December thirteenth of last year, the defendant followed her in his car. But on this particular night, Angel deviated from her normal routine. She got into a cab, the same as she did every night after work. But instead of having the driver drop her off at her apartment, she got out at a local bodega. It was a fateful decision. One that cost her her life.

"After she left the bodega, Angel started walking home. Her apartment building was three blocks from the bodega. To get there, she had to pass an abandoned lot, which was almost halfway between the bodega and her building, both on the south side of the street. As she approached the lot, the way she had dozens of times before, she had no inkling that the defendant was lying in wait."

Forster looks at Young. "The defendant was in that abandoned lot because he knew the victim had to walk past there on her way home. Because he knew where she lived." She turns back to the jury. "It was almost two-thirty in the morning. It was dark out. And cold. No one was on the street. Tragically for Angel Diallo, it was the perfect storm.

"The defendant was obsessed with her. But he never had the chance to get her alone. Until that last night. One change in routine, and Angel Diallo's fate was sealed. If she'd just asked the cabdriver to wait, she might still be alive. But she was watching her pennies. She figured instead of keeping the meter running and racking up a bigger fare while she shopped, she could walk the three blocks."

Forster starts pacing in front of the jury. "Angel Diallo never made it home. As she passed that abandoned lot, the defendant grabbed her and overpowered her. And there, in that dark, abandoned lot full of decomposing garbage and decaying pieces of junk, he savagely raped, tortured, and beat her and her unborn child to death."

"Objection!" Young's on his feet. "I'm not charged with killing her unborn child."

45

Once again, Alice underestimated him.

"Sustained. The jury will disregard Ms. Forster's last statement."

Forster doesn't look happy. She studies her notes to buy time to move on from her first big loss, knowing that eliminating mention of the victim's unborn child will diminish the emotional impact on the jury.

"When she was found the next day, Angel Diallo's keys were still in her bag. Her mail was untouched in her mailbox. She never made it home to the studio apartment she could barely afford. All she had in that cramped space was a bed, some used furniture, and a mobile suspended over a hand-me-down crib."

Forster pauses, hoping the jury will envision a baby in that crib.

"When the victim left that bodega, she had no inkling it would be her last night on earth. She was a hardworking mother-to-be who'd lost her job as a kindergarten teacher because of city cutbacks. Unable to find another job, she ended up falling through the cracks. She was desperate because she knew she'd soon have two mouths to feed. The dance club was a last resort, a temporary stopgap until she could get back on her feet. But the defendant didn't care about any of that."

Forster shakes her head as if she can't believe what she's saying. "After the defendant raped and beat her, he left Angel Diallo to die like an animal in the high weeds of that abandoned lot. If someone had found her in time, there's a chance she might have survived. But in that cold, desolate place in the middle of the night, there was no one to hear her feeble cries for help. She just lay there, the life leaking out of her as she bled to death.

"The man who committed this horrific crime is sitting there." Forster points at Young, whose head is down as he scribbles on his legal pad. "Make no mistake. This was a premeditated crime. The defendant brutally murdered a young woman. Don't let Angel Diallo's life count for nothing. Her killer must be punished for what he did. And when you hear all the evidence, I'm confident that you will find William Henry Young guilty of first-degree murder."

Alice studies the jurors as Forster returns to the prosecution table. They're looking at the defendant, their faces a mixture of shock, revulsion, and fascination. But if there's one thing she's learned in her twenty years in the criminal justice system, it's that you never know what a jury will do.

They're always the wild card.

She turns to Young. "Are you ready to deliver your opening?"

He looks up, as if surprised to find himself here. "Yes, Your Honor. If the court will bear with me a second. I want to make sure I get down everything Madam Prosecutor said so I can defend myself. I need to make sure these folks hear the truth." He smiles at the jury.

"Your Honor!" Forster's back on her feet.

Alice waves them up to the bench for a sidebar out of earshot of the jury.

Under normal conditions, she'd step down and stand in a semicircle with opposing counsel in a display of equity to show that she isn't judging the attorneys. But thus far, this trial is anything but normal.

The moment Young stands, the male and female officers seated behind him are on their feet. When he exits the well, they follow and station themselves at either end of the bench. As he approaches, two roving officers at the rear of the courtroom move into position; one in each far corner, near the double doors.

Rovers travel from courtroom to courtroom, armed with weapons and walkie talkies, ready to notify the riot squad at moment's notice. There is typically one rover in a Part at any given time. In the case of *The People v. William Henry Young*, the Department of Corrections doubled the security.

"Your Honor. The defendant is deliberately trying to inflame the jury."

"Mr. Young." Alice draws her robe closer around her and sits up straighter so that she's looking down at him from the bench. "You are to make no commentary in my court. You will speak to the jury and respond only to questions I ask you."

"Yes, Your Honor." But there's a defiant look in his blue eyes as he drags out the syllables in a way that's starting to grate on her.

"Step back."

Forster hurries away from the bench as if she can't wait to put distance between herself and Young, who ambles back to the defense table followed by the male and female officers. As they return to their chairs behind him, Young looks at the female officer.

When he picks up his yellow pad, he's smiling again.

TEN

"Good morning, ladies and gentlemen. My name's Bill. Bill Young. And like everyone, I've got a story. The only difference between the one you heard and the one I'm going to tell you is that mine is the truth. Madam Prosecutor can't tell you what happened. She wasn't there. One thing we agree on, though. Angel Diallo's murderer should be punished. That murderer just isn't me."

He shakes his head. "Madam Prosecutor thinks there's a lot of evidence against me. But there's things she's not telling you. Like the name of that dance club. It's called Private Eyes. She didn't tell you that after the club closes, the parking lot out back becomes a hotbed of activity. I think you know what kind of activity I'm talking about."

He flips a page on his yellow pad. "Sex for cash. That's what was going on in that parking lot. I don't want to be the one to soil Angel Diallo's reputation, may she rest in peace. Let's just say she wasn't lily white when it came to what those other girls were doing. But paying for sex in a parking lot in the middle of the night? That wasn't what I wanted. Madam Prosecutor lied to you when she said I tried to get Angel Diallo into my car.

"Don't get me wrong. I'm not faulting her for doing what she had to do to survive. She needed money. I can relate to that. Like I'm sure you all can. I'm truly sorry about what happened to her. But she took her life in her hands every time she got into a stranger's car."

Something flickers behind Alice's lids.

Bright lights.

Blinding her.

She blinks, and the image recedes.

". . . Maybe one of them raped and killed her. The other thing Madam Prosecutor didn't tell you is they have no evidence proving I was in that abandoned lot. Because I wasn't there."

He takes a few steps closer to the jury box.

"I did not rape, torture, or kill Angel Diallo. But I sure hope they find the monster who did. Do you know what it's like to be accused of something you didn't do? I pray it never happens to any of you. I've got my faults, sure. Let he who is free of sin cast the first stone. That lets out most of us, right?"

He chuckles. Then his expression turns serious again. "I know the truth in my heart and I believe that when this trial is over, you'll know it, too. In the meantime, maybe you can join me in sending out a prayer to Angel Diallo's family. Wherever they are." He looks pointedly at the row behind the prosecution table, where the family of the victim usually sits.

There's no one there.

All eyes are now on the empty row. Everyone no doubt thinking what he just set them up to believe: The victim was a prostitute. A world away from the tragic mother-to-be Katharine Forster portrayed.

"I know that in the end you want the same thing I do. To see justice served. For Angel Diallo. And for me. I would never hurt her. I would never hurt any woman. And that's the God's honest truth. Thank you for listening."

As he talks, his gaze sweeps up and down the two rows, making eye contact with the men and women on the jury.

One juror at a time.

ELEVEN

"**Y**our Honor."

Young flips a page on his legal pad, holding it close to his face so the two officers seated behind him can't see what's written there. "I want to make a motion."

Annoyance rips through Alice. "What is it this time?"

"I want to exclude those shameful crime scene photos."

Alice shakes her head. But much as she'd like to, she can't stop him from making the motion. She leans forward on the bench, the sound of reporters tapping away on their tablets the only sound in the courtroom. "You are aware, are you not, that the prior judge ruled them admissible?"

"He had no right to do that. How am I supposed to defend myself against these godless allegations with the jury already prejudiced against me?"

"When you return to your cell, you should read Judge Ryan's pretrial ruling where he found that the probative value outweighed any possible prejudice."

"I only want to see justice done, Your Honor. Same as you. Like I told the jury, I didn't do those terrible things."

His voice rings with impassioned fervor, as if he actually believes his own words.

Alice sees his face staring up at her from the metro section of the *Times*, the day after he gave his press conference from the Tombs. Before he cut his hair and trimmed his mustache and beard. Looking less like a biker and more like an impassioned evangelist, fire blazing from his blue eyes. His responses to reporters' questions full of quotes from the Scriptures about how truth was his salvation and would set him free.

Is it possible he's not just evil, but insane?

Yet not so crazy that he doesn't know how to turn on the charm to try to persuade a jury.

Or is that just another side of his insanity?

"If you've been reading up on the law, as you said, you'd know that the only way I can rule on your motion is if you make an offer of proof citing new evidence. What is your evidence?"

"I'm innocent."

"That's for a jury to decide." Alice starts to lower the gavel.

"Have you seen the photos, Your Honor?"

She has, and wishes she hadn't. "Are you challenging me?"

He puts out his hands, palms up, as if in supplication. "Put yourself in my place. Someone has to be blamed for what happened to that poor woman."

Whether wittingly or not, he has hit on a trial truism. This was what the State was banking on when Katharine Forster made a pretrial motion to rule the crime scene photos admissible, which is always a fight between the prosecution and defense: instead of the facts, the jury would vote with their emotions.

Alice remembers Young looking at the jurors yesterday during his opening.

There are seven women on the jury.

So that's the reason for the motion. There's a method to his madness.

He's afraid he'll lose those women.

"I'm not asking you as a judge, Your Honor. I'm asking you as a woman. If you were on the jury, would you decide I was guilty just so you could punish someone?"

Alice can't speak. How dare he try to turn this around and make it about her! But even as anger chokes her, light once again floods her vision.

Headlights slicing through the dark.

Lighting up the trees.

Gradually, she becomes aware of her surroundings.

The courtroom has gone silent as the grave, everyone waiting to see who'll win the latest battle of wills between the judge and the defendant.

When she can find her voice again, Alice tells Young he's out of order and denies his motion.

She has to shout to make herself heard above the buzzing in her ears.

It's coming from the pocket of her robe.

TWELVE

Alice watches the water rushing in, then slowly lowers her body into the tub. She leans back and closes her eyes, trying to relax.

And failing.

She keeps seeing her husband when she walked into the house half an hour after after receiving the latest text.

Charles was standing in the front hall, yelling at the top of his lungs and insisting that he'd been abducted. Although the East 91st Street town house had been his boyhood residence that he later shared with his first wife and, for the past eighteen years, with Alice and her daughter, he kept repeating that it wasn't his home. As usual, Alexis had locked herself in her room with the music blaring, oblivious to everything going on around her.

It was only when Alice brought him the handsome leather-bound legal volumes from his study that Charles finally calmed down. But he still eyed his wife and his daytime aide Edith with suspicion. He punished them by refusing to eat for hours.

Alice knows what she has to do. Knows that it means facing the truth she hasn't wanted to accept, especially after that brief moment of lucidity a few weeks back that now feels like half a lifetime ago.

The disease is accelerating.

But putting Charles in a care facility is a step she can't yet bring herself to take. She'd rather try one of the recently approved new drugs on the market. She'll feel better knowing that she has exhausted all the possibilities, even though her husband's doctors have warned that the new meds are controversial and there can be serious side effects. She doesn't need them to tell her that she's just putting off the inevitable. A part of her still refusing to accept the grim reality.

The water's gone cold.

She's shivering as she gets out of the tub. As she towels off, she can't shake off a sense of impending doom despite her rational mind telling her that it's depression. The feelings of powerlessness are getting worse. It's as if she were losing control of her life.

In the hall, she tries to tamp down her anxiety as she checks on Charles. He's asleep, thank God. In a chair next to his bed, Larry is reading. He nods at her, and she continues down the hall.

She startles at a sound.

Just the house settling.

She's about to go into her bedroom when she thinks of something. She can't remember if she locked up downstairs. Over the past few weeks, she has never gone to bed before making sure that the house is locked up tighter than a drum. Now she can add forgetfulness to her list of mental lapses. Cinching the belt of her terry robe around her waist, she creeps down the stairs.

The front door is locked. She heaves out a relieved breath, then goes into the kitchen. Sure enough, the back door is unlatched. Chastising herself again for her distracted state, she snaps the latch in place, then walks through the dining room to the French doors that open out to the courtyard.

On impulse, she steps outside. A breeze rustles the flowers and plants that Alice and Charles's aides have snipped and watered ever since her husband stopped being able to complete those simple tasks. Alice tries to keep her mind from drifting, focusing instead on the soothing sensation of the cool air wafting over her.

After a few minutes, she goes back inside. She relocks the French doors, then continues on to the other side of the house. In the living room, she's passing the large bay window that overlooks 91st Street when she stops.

There's someone out there.

Across the street, standing next to a tree.

He's looking up at her window.

Her hand flies to her mouth. She stifles a scream as she steps back.

Did he see her?

Heart racing, she pulls the heavy burgundy curtain across the glass. Then bunches a small section of material in her fists and peers out.

He's still standing there.

He just lit a cigarette. She can see the tip glowing in the dark. She has no idea how long he's been there. A hood covers his head. All she can see are the whites of his eyes. She flashes to the jogger who ran up behind her on the running track. The memory is still vivid, even though she hasn't been back to Central Park since that night.

Is it him? Even with the streetlamps casting a soft glow, it's impossible to tell. With his dark clothes, he blends in with the night. Maybe he's just out for a smoke. If he lives in the neighborhood, that could explain why he was running around the reservoir. She can't even be sure if the person who passed her in the fog was a man or a woman.

He—or she—grinds out the cigarette underneath his shoe. Starts walking. But he doesn't go into any of the town houses on the south side of the street. He heads east on 91st Street. When he reaches Lexington Avenue, he turns the corner and vanishes from sight.

If he was ever there.

THIRTEEN

T he front door squeaks as it swings open.

Alexis McKerrity holds her breath as she enters the house.

So far, so good.

She rebolts the door, the sound of the three locks snapping back echoing through the silent house.

Alexis remembers the day her mother had the third lock installed, the week after that horrible scene with Charles at the breakfast table. It's so crazy. In all the years they've lived here, they never even double-locked the door. It's not like anyone's going to break in. Carnegie Hill is one of the safest 'hoods on the Upper East Side.

What's up with that?

She slides the chain into place and heads for the stairs. Halfway up, she stops.

Charles is crying in his sleep.

That really freaks her out. And he's doing it more and more lately. Can't her mother see that he's getting worse?

She just heard it again.

It isn't Charles.

It's her mom.

Should she go to her? Make sure she's okay?

What if she's still asleep? But if she's having a nightmare, maybe it's better if she wakes her up. The way her mom used to do when Alexis was a little girl and had bad dreams.

She listens, but everything's quiet now. She keeps climbing. When she reaches the landing, she looks down the hall.

Her old night-light is shining out from under her mother's door.

What's up with *that*?

Alexis shakes her head as she goes into her bedroom. Across the room, her computer sits on her desk like a silent sentinel. Almost against her will, she goes over and sits down in front of the black screen.

She hits the space bar and her password box appears. She presses six keys—the month, day, and year of Damien's birthday—and the screen returns to the page she was looking at earlier tonight.

She stares at the blank comment box.

She pretty much knows what she's going to write. Has known for days.

So what's her problem?

Maybe she doesn't want to find out.

It's not like she made any effort. All these years, knowing her mother was lying to her face. As if she was too young or too stupid to tell a lie from the truth.

Or maybe she doesn't want to believe it could be the truth.

Because then she'd have to accept what her mother told her.

That she's the product of a one-night stand with a boy her mother met at a dance in a town called Renegade Falls.

She told Alexis she didn't know his name.

Really, Mom?

Her mother knew his name, all right. She just didn't want to tell her because she was afraid Alexis might try to find him.

Like she's doing right now.

It's *so* probably a waste of time. And it makes her feel the tiniest bit disloyal, like she's going behind her mother's back.

All she's doing is checking out her old school. Alexis knows her mom went to Lowood High. But she moved away when she was in the eleventh grade. She never graduated. She said it was because her father got a job in another town. Alexis always thought they moved because she was pregnant. Back then, in that tiny village, it would've been like some kind of scandal. Grandpa was pretty strict. And old-fashioned. Probably thought he was protecting her mom's honor, or something. Alexis never knew her mother's mother. Her grandmother's death was the reason her mom left the city to go live with Grandpa Nathan in Lowood.

She still misses her grandfather.

Her mother ended up finishing high school in Jonasville, the town she and her grandfather moved to from Lowood. Her mom graduated when Alexis was three.

When Alexis asked why she didn't graduate until she was twenty, her mother just smiled that smile that was mysterious and sad at the same time and said it was because Alexis kept her busy. That it wasn't easy being a teenage single mom.

Alexis knew there was something she was leaving out.

That was *so* Mom, telling her some things.

Not telling her others.

The difference now is that Alexis won't accept the lies anymore.

She already ran the numbers. She's going to be twenty-nine next month. September 8. Her mother was sixteen when she was born. Which means she was still in high school when she was carrying her. The high school in the town where she used to live.

That's why Alexis is on Lowood High's Facebook page, getting ready to post a comment on their timeline. Her mother went to school in Lowood for five years. There's a good chance the boy she slept with lived there too.

Her father.

A fact of life Alexis still can't wrap her mind around even after all these years.

How she's going to find him is another story. It's not like she can walk up to some stranger and say, *Excuse me, did you have sex with my mother almost thirty years ago?*

Maybe he won't even remember. Alexis doesn't know if she could handle that.

A beep sounds.

She looks around for her phone. It beeps again as she fishes it out of her bag.

It's a text from Damien.

don't 4get
show tomorrow night
10

Did he honestly think she'd forget? Has she ever missed one? Alexis texts back:

c ya

She's about to send it; stops. Even though she just saw him less than an hour ago, she adds:

miss u

He doesn't text back.

She's hit with a sudden attack of butterflies.

Damien doesn't know yet.

Maybe she'll tell him tomorrow.

One thing she knows for sure: *She's* not going to be a single mom.

She wonders if it was meant to be. She doesn't believe in fate. But still. They've been together almost six months. She loves Damien, she really does. And he loves her, she knows he does. He'll make a great daddy.

Daddy.

Alexis rolls the word around in her mouth to see how it feels. Damien's going to be as thrilled as she is, even if he and his acoustic guitar are joined at the hip.

Everything's going to work out. She doesn't even have morning sickness. Not yet, anyway.

She wasn't thrilled at the beginning. She was stunned. Then scared. That's what she got for being a guinea pig and trying that new birth control patch that had just come on the market. It was a lot cheaper than the Pill. And it wasn't like she was raking in the cash. And soon she's going to run out of the money she saved from hostessing.

Seven years out of college, and she's still living at home.

All that's going to change soon.

Charles is crying now. She can hear him through her closed door. At least he isn't screaming like he was earlier tonight before her mother got home from court and tried putting her usual Band-Aid on everything.

Alexis thinks about the morning he hit her when she was trying to feed him his breakfast. What if the next time he hurt her? Or hurt her mom?

It's not like she doesn't care about him. But her mother's got to start living in reality.

And there's something else.

Charles isn't her father.

She needs to know who that is.

Needs to know what kinds of traits she'll be passing on to her son or daughter.

She can just picture her mother's face when she tells her.

Or maybe she won't.

Her mother's not the only one in this family who can keep secrets.

Alexis walks back to her desk and sits in front of the computer. She thinks a minute, then starts typing.

It's a little weird signing off with that name. It's the one she recently created so she'd have a separate Facebook page. You're not supposed to have multiple accounts, but so far she hasn't been busted. She can always delete the bogus page once she finds out what she needs to know.

She rereads the message. Even if her mother decides to check out Lowood High's Facebook page, there's no way she'll know it's her. And if she tries to log on to either of her Facebook pages, both accounts are password protected. She also took the added precaution of changing the privacy settings so only friends can see her posts.

She reads the message one last time. Then hits *Enter* before she can change her mind.

FOURTEEN

"**C**an I bum a cigarette?"

Alice cringes at the words that haven't left her mouth in decades. But she's desperate. In the past day and a half, she has smoked her way through two packs. It's gotten so bad that she can't even wait to get home and go to the store for her fix.

"Sure, Judge."

At her desk in the tiny anteroom outside Alice's chambers, Shavonne smiles. She doesn't seem surprised. Did Alice really think she could hide the habit from her court attorney?

Shavonne reaches into her handbag, which is as elegant and attractive as its owner. "Marlboro Lights okay?" Alice nods. Lucky Strike has always been her brand of choice, but right now she'll take anything. Her hand trembles as she accepts the cigarette, which she's sure doesn't go unnoticed by the younger woman.

"Join me?"

One of Shavonne's beautifully sculpted black eyebrows arches upward. In nearly three years working together, Alice has rarely invited her into chambers for anything other than court business.

But she doesn't want to be alone.

She's too afraid.

Nights are the worst, despite the fact that she's sedated by the sleeping pills she started taking the night she saw—or thinks she saw—the figure standing across the street. That was when she finally gave up the ghost and found a prescription that hadn't expired after a frantic search through the medicine cabinet. Followed by a pit stop in her daughter's room to dig out Alexis's old night-light from the back of her closet.

She hasn't been able to sleep without the light since.

Now, as Alice watches her court attorney rise from her desk with her usual self-possession, she tries to shake off her irrational fears. She reminds herself that she's a mature, accomplished woman who has come a long way from the frightened child she once was.

Shavonne follows her into her chambers with the conspiratorial air of doing something illicit. Like everywhere else in the city, smoking is forbidden in the courthouse. But no one can tell a judge what to do in the privacy of her chambers.

After she closes the door, Alice indicates for her to sit next to her on the chocolate leather sofa—another first. As she lights up from Shavonne's lit cigarette, she's hit by a sudden feeling of déjà vu. She sees herself at fifteen, lighting up with her best friend behind the Lowood High bleachers after a game, waiting for the track star Connie was dating that year.

Alice feels a sharp ache of regret. She misses Connie. She never had another best friend after moving away in the middle of the winter semester of her junior year. By then, she had other things to worry about. Like what she was going to do about the life that had started growing inside her.

Next to her, Shavonne smokes in silence, waiting to take her cue from her employer. With an effort, Alice forces her mind back to the present. The last thing she wants is to go down that particular rabbit hole.

She takes a deep drag and turns to the younger woman. "Have you thought about your future?"

Shavonne looks at her in surprise.

"It's okay. I know you have to leave me sometime." Alice smiles, the nicotine finally starting to calm her nerves. She watches her court attorney lean forward and reach for the ashtray on the octagonal walnut table, marveling how she manages to make even the simple act of putting out a cigarette graceful.

Shavonne sits back against the pillows. "I know it sounds so *Perry Mason*, but all I ever wanted was to defend the innocent."

Alice has heard those words from idealistic young attorneys many times before. Her own tortuous path to law school was based on exactly the opposite.

"I can't believe how naïve I was." Shavonne shakes her head. "I know now that most defendants are guilty. But this trial really clinched it for me. I know we're supposed to be objective and not draw our own conclusions. Maybe it's because the victim was pregnant. I mean, I'm pro-choice and all that, but the defendant didn't give Angel Diallo a choice when he murdered her and her unborn child, did he?"

"No," Alice says after a moment, letting out her breath on a slow exhale. "He didn't."

"So now I'm thinking about applying to the DA's office."

"And I'll give you a glowing letter of recommendation."

"Thank you, Judge. I appreciate that."

Shavonne gets to her feet, as if afraid she might have overstayed her welcome.

Alice feels a familiar panic settle in her chest at the thought of being left alone. "I'll walk out with you."

The minute she says the words, she's instantly ashamed of her childish fears and for showing weakness in front of her court attorney. She tries to cover her mortification by busying herself retrieving her handbag and jacket from the closet. She picks up the tiny key from one of the two disks in the scales-of-justice sculpture that sits on top of her desk, then turns for a last-minute check before switching off the lights.

Her gaze sweeps over her familiar chambers. At the shelves filled with legal volumes, many of them gifts from Charles, built into the mahogany-paneled wall that bookends the large picture window. The standing lamp with the leaf-and-vine bronze finish and cream drum shade next to the high-backed maroon armchair that sits on the multihued Oriental rug, where she used to spend quiet time reading.

But she isn't seeing the place that has always been her refuge from the brutality of the courtroom. Her escape from the endless procession of violence and tragedy that she sees on a daily basis. In fact, lately her onetime sanctuary has been feeling more and more like the four walls of a prison.

Maybe it is time for a break.

As they leave through the door that leads to the outer hallway, deserted now with hers the only courtroom in session, Alice renews her resolve to ask a colleague to cover for her right after Labor Day. After she unlocks the elevator, she and Shavonne ride down together in silence. When the doors open on the ground floor, the security guard stationed at the judges' entrance greets Alice warmly.

"Looks like rain," Henry says as he holds open the door for the two women.

Outside, a breeze has started to kick up.

When Alice glances at the sky, she can see the dark clouds gathering.

FIFTEEN

The train slows as it approaches Astor Place.

"This is my stop."

As Shavonne unwinds her long, lissome body from the seat, it takes every ounce of willpower for Alice to stop herself from begging the younger woman not to leave her.

The fear is completely irrational, of course, but that doesn't quell the anxiety that has been steadily building ever since they left the courthouse. Even the usual cacophony of city sounds made her want to jump out of her skin, from the blast of a car horn to the wail of a siren. And under it all—the moaning of the wind as the skies grew increasingly more ominous.

Then, in the Canal Street station, while Shavonne added cash to her MetroCard, Alice couldn't shake the feeling of eyes on her. When she looked around, all she saw was the usual commuters, with no one paying her the slightest attention. Wondering how she could feel isolated among so many people, she still felt uneasy on the platform waiting for the No. 6 local, rather than the No. 4 or 5 express she typically takes, so that she could keep her court attorney company.

Or so she told herself.

Now, as Alice watches Shavonne leave the train and disappear into the crowd thronging the Astor Place platform, anxiety blooms into full-bore panic. By the time the train pulls into the 14th Street–Union Square station, her heart is racing and she has broken out in a sweat. Afraid that she's going to start hyperventilating, she stays in her seat and forces herself to breathe slowly out and in before following the other passengers through the open doors.

Once out on the platform, people brush by her in their haste to make it into the train before the doors close again. Alice feels lightheaded and unsteady on her feet. Once she trusts herself to put one foot in front of the other, she crosses to the other side of the platform.

When the No. 5 pulls into the station, the train is packed. She debates between fighting her way in—which could set off another panic attack—and getting home faster versus waiting for the next train. Her decision is made for her when she suddenly feels herself stumbling forward through the train's open doors. She turns around, but can't see anything beyond the throng of people crowding into the car.

—⚹—

When the doors open at 86th Street, she's the first one off the train. She still has no idea if someone deliberately pushed her, or if she should add paranoia to the growing list of mental aberrations. The skies are black with storm clouds as she emerges from the subway at the northeast corner of 86th and Lexington. Not yet dusk, and it feels as if night has fallen. The streets have emptied out in anticipation of the approaching storm.

She can't shake the feeling of being watched. She feels exposed out here, looks for a taxi even though her house is only a few blocks away. When she spies one, she frantically tries to wave down the cab. It passes her, its light off. A passenger is in the back seat.

In defeat, she starts walking. Turns at a sound.

Light floods her vision.

She freezes.

When she comes back to herself, she sees a driver with his head out the window. He's cursing at her.

She looks around. She's standing in the middle of the street. She stumbles back onto the curb, watches the car speed down Lexington.

Thunder echoes in the distance as she continues north on Lexington, shaken by what just happened. Had she been crossing against the light? Behind her lids, she still sees headlights slicing through the dark. Blinding her as the car comes toward her.

As she walks, she tries to shake off an intensifying feeling of dread. She's almost at 90th Street when the first drops of rain start to fall. She walks faster. A flash of lightning electrifies the trees. She breaks into a run. Collides with someone in a shiny raincoat. And hood.

Alice screams and staggers back, her voice carried away on the rising wind. Then she's running again, looking over her shoulder as the rain comes down harder. Craters of water are forming on street corners. She almost slides out of the brown pump on her right foot. The rain pummels her from all sides as she turns left on 91st, toward Park.

She reaches her town house just as a deafening clap of thunder splits the air. Another blinding flash lights up the trees as she tries to slide her key into the lock. The key slips from her fingers and drops into the urn of flowers in front of the left double door. She digs frantically through the sodden earth. When she finally retrieves the key, the rain has become a drenching downpour. As she turns the doorknob, she can still hear the wind shrieking behind her.

Once inside, she sags against the doorframe, oblivious to the water puddling on the tiled floor. Summoning the energy to move again, she locks the door, the sound of each bolt snapping into place echoing through the silent house like a pistol shot.

She creeps through the rooms like a silent wraith, methodically locking doors and bolting windows. When she walks into the living room, a noise sends her heart into her throat.

It's coming from the bay window.

Terror roots her to the spot even as the rational part of her mind tells her that there's a logical explanation. When she finally gets her feet to move, she approaches the window with dread.

She parts the curtains. Lets out a relieved breath.

It was just a tree branch knocking against the glass.

As she stares into the blackness of the rain-swept night, more trees fill her vision.

Crowding out the sky.

Trees everywhere.

As far as the eye can see.

And nowhere to hide.

SIXTEEN

Constance Moore keeps one eye on the cash register and the other on the new girl as she wipes down the counter.

It's after nine in the morning and the temperature's still in the fifties, a rarity for mid-August. But it's been cool and damp ever since that tropical storm passed through a few days ago. Not that she's complaining. A week or so back, they suffered through ten straight days of ninety degrees. She can just imagine what this month's electric bill's going to look like. Her blood pressure's going up just thinking about it.

At the register, Sean Conklin is telling the couple paying their bill that they don't take American Express. Not since they upped their fees. Connie wasn't going to pass it on to her customers by raising her prices again. She justified it last year because of the cost-of-living increase, but the truth is most of her regulars are locals who lost their jobs in last year's economic downturn.

Sean's looking her way now, a frantic look on his acne-pitted face. He's a junior at Lowood High. With the place short-staffed, Sean seemed like a good choice for the summer. He does an okay job when he's not texting his girlfriend on his phone.

Connie palms the perspiration off her forehead and comes over, politely explaining the situation to the man and woman standing at the register. She can tell from their clothes that they're tourists. Acting put out, the man reluctantly slides another card from his wallet. As Sean puts it through the archaic credit card machine that desperately needs to be replaced, Connie looks around the diner.

After clearing the table in the back, the new girl pockets the tip like it's the last few dollars on earth.

When she first showed up in answer to the ad, a thin wisp of a girl with wild hair who looked as if she hadn't had a decent meal in months, she told Connie she wouldn't sign any forms. And she had to be paid in cash. Her pale face a curious mix of defiance and fear. But Connie needed someone to take over Jolene's seven-to-four shift after Jolene got knocked up again, and the only candidates were either too young or too old. Connie would have done it herself—she has before—but she was already manning the counter with Wanda Loper out on disability after slipping on a patch of black ice over the winter.

No one figures Mia for staying past the end of summer. Connie hopes that won't be the case. She's quiet and efficient and does her job. Doesn't talk back or give her sass. And so far, she hasn't broken anything.

Right now she's wiping down the table in the back with a single-mindedness of purpose that reminds Connie of herself when she was married to her second husband. After he finished eating she'd clean up, making sure she didn't leave so much as a crumb. Not a speck.

The bell over the door tinkles.

Walter Church walks in, stopping in the doorway to exchange pleasantries with customers.

A smile creases Connie's face. You could set your clock by Walt, that's how regular he is.

He takes off his tall black sheriff's hat as he walks into the diner. "Hey, Con." At the counter, he puts his hat on an empty stool and lowers his long frame onto the adjoining one. "What's on tap this morning?"

It's a game they always play. Connie recites the daily specials and Walt listens thoughtfully, forefinger on his chin, as if he's not going to order the same eggs over easy, well-done bacon, and dry wheat toast he's been eating for years.

"Where's Lamont?" he asks.

"Sherry went into labor late last night. I gave him the day off."

"So now you're the short-order cook, too?" Church shakes his head. "Ever think it might be time to think about slowing down? You know we're not getting any younger."

Connie shakes her head. Forty-six hardly makes her a senior citizen. Her hormones sure haven't shown any signs of slowing down. She has her latest lover to thank for that.

"Speak for yourself," she says as she pours his coffee. As if this isn't a conversation they've been having for years. "You telling me you're ready to be put out to pasture?"

He's been sheriff for more than thirty years. Ever since the longtime sheriff died of a sudden heart attack and twenty-three-year-old deputy sheriff Walter Church took over the reins.

It was his youth and eagerness to prove himself that caused him to make a bad judgment call.

Or so Connie's been telling herself for the past three decades.

"I've given it some thought," Church says as he pours a dollop of cream into his mug.

"Sure you have. Election's coming up end of next year. Ever think somebody might beat you?"

"Not a chance."

He's right. No one has run against him in a long time. No one has the money. The recession hit everyone hard. The Lowood Village PD lost some men too. With the crime rate falling more and more every year, Church could end up being the last man standing.

"How's the new girl working out?"

Connie glances across the diner as she lays four slices of bacon on the hot griddle. They immediately start to sizzle. "Mia keeps to herself."

Church watches as she starts cleaning another table. "Doubt it's her real name. And that red hair came straight out of a bottle. She isn't staying anywhere in town, that I can tell you. Whatever she's running from, it's got to be pretty bad."

"Maybe she took a room over in Cannonville. Or Renegade Falls." Lowood's sister towns, separated only by deep woods. "Doesn't want anyone to know."

"I don't blame her. Probably afraid he'll come after her. These guys don't stop. I always wondered if Donegan would turn up after you married Moore."

"Not likely," Connie says, turning the bacon. "Not after you ran him out of town. You must have put the scare of Jesus into him."

"You got that right. That bastard ever shows his sorry face here, I'll lock him up and throw away the key. He lays a finger on you again, he'll answer to me, swear to God."

Connie believes him. It's also his way of letting her know that even if he can't change the past, he'll do right by her now.

"Speaking of Moore, I hear there's a warrant out on him in Pennsylvania."

No surprise there.

Something Connie knows well. She shakes her head as she cracks two eggs on the griddle. You'd think she would've learned her lesson after Husband Number Two. But no, a few weeks after the Omaha salesman breezed into town, she was shacking up with him. A couple months after that, she married Josiah Moore. Half a year later, she made him her business partner.

Until he took off with a nineteen-year-old waitress.

And most of Connie's money.

It's taken her two years to get back on her feet. When it comes to husbands, she's zero for three.

"It wasn't your fault, Con. Don't beat yourself up over it."

"I'm not," she lies, dropping two pieces of wheat bread into the toaster. She can feel Walt's eyes on her as she turns the eggs. Still feels his gaze as she slides eggs and bacon onto a plate and pulls out the toast.

"Smells good," he says when she places it in front of him.

"More coffee?"

"Sure." His eyes are still on her as she pours.

After all these years, he's still got a thing for her.

She watches him as he tucks his napkin into the collar of his white starched shirt and digs into his eggs.

"Delicious," he pronounces as he looks up from his plate. "You haven't lost your touch. Join me?"

Connie shakes her head. Thinking about her exes killed her appetite.

"You look tired, Con. Why don't you take a break? Breakfast crowd's thinning out. You got some time before lunch."

"Maybe I will."

He looks at her as if he isn't sure he believes her. Then he nods and returns to his breakfast. Connie studies him again as she cleans the griddle. After his wife died, all it would have taken was a little encouragement on her part and she could have been Mrs. Walter Church.

In spite of what happened back then, there's no denying that he's a good man.

Just not good enough to make her forget.

Or forgive.

After she finishes, she heads to her office at the back of the diner. She should use the break to go over the books. Instead, she unlocks the bottom drawer of her desk and pulls out a joint. Mindful of Church out front, she opens the back door.

It's windy out here, an unwelcome reminder of the long winter to come. Hopefully they won't get hit with any major snowstorms this year. She can't afford to lose more help or, worse, have to close the diner like she did during last March's surprise blizzard.

She puts on a jacket and steps outside, trying to ignore the cold. After lighting up, she takes a deep drag and waits for the mellowness to wash over her.

After a few more tokes, she goes back inside. Puts the half-smoked joint back in the drawer and locks it. She'll finish it tonight with Monte. The thought of him always brings a smile to her face. He may be almost half her age, but he's great in the sack.

Connie looks up at a *ping* from her computer. She sits down and hits the space bar. The hibernating screen comes back to life.

In her inbox is an email from her co-chair on the committee for the Lowood High fundraiser. Connie doesn't know how she got roped into this, but it's for a good cause. And it's going to be a big deal. They're charging $200 a head, with food provided by the Lowood Diner of course. That should put money back into the village's coffers.

Connie shoots back an email, then sits back and puts her feet up on the desk. But she's restless. The pot didn't take the edge off, the way it usually does. She lowers her feet to the floor and clicks on the Lowood High Facebook page that's still open at the bottom of the screen. She tells herself she's just checking for today's posts about the upcoming event.

Instead, she scrolls halfway down the page to earlier posts. The one about Alice is still there. Posted at 11:26 Monday night.

Talk about a blast from the past.

It's not like she hasn't thought about Alice over the years. She was her best friend, for chrissakes. From the chilly September morning the assistant principal brought Alice Dunn into Connie's fifth-grade class at Lowood Elementary. Alice wore a red hooded jacket and barely spoke a word. Connie found out later that her mother had recently died.

She remembers the hot July afternoon they carved their initials into that pine tree in the woods.

Best friends forever.

Until the third weekend in December. Alice had just turned sixteen. When she showed up in the wee hours of Saturday morning, Connie was shocked. Alice was supposed to be spending the weekend at Connie's house. But she wasn't there when Connie got back from the party late Friday night. She figured Alice had gone home, despite the fact that it was a long walk back in the freezing cold and dark that Alice was so afraid of.

And now here she was. Connie was still pretty wasted from partying most of the night. But not too wasted to miss that something really bad had happened.

That was when guilt sank its teeth into her.

She should never have let Alice leave the party alone.

That Saturday morning was the last time she saw her.

Alice never came back to school. Two months later, Nathan Dunn sold the hardware store that had been in his family for generations and they moved away.

Alice didn't even call to say goodbye. Could she blame her?

Connie wrote to her anyway, telling her how sorry she was and could she ever forgive her? Her letters were forwarded on, but they all came back unopened.

And now here was someone dredging everything up again.

She rereads the post.

Hi! I'm trying to get in touch with someone who went to Lowood High. Her name was Alice Dunn. If anyone remembers her, I'd love to hear from you. You can friend me on Facebook.
Thanks!
Natalie Damien

Alice didn't finish her junior year at Lowood High. She never graduated.

So who's Natalie Damien, and why is she—or he—posting a message on their timeline?

On impulse, Connie goes to Natalie Damien's Facebook page.

Her heart squeezes when she sees the photo at the top left-hand corner of the page.

She looks so much like Alice.

She has to be her daughter.

Connie never knew Alice had a child. But after so many years, there's probably a lot she doesn't know. Just like there are things Alice will never know about her.

Connie had a daughter too. Even if she never made it out of her womb.

After the first miscarriage, she and Luke kept trying. He wasn't really father material. Hell, he was barely husband material. As wild as the day she married him, right out of high school. By the time Luke died a couple years later—so drunk he crashed his Harley into the concrete divider on the highway—she'd lost three babies. Some malformation in her womb that stopped her from bringing a child to term.

Connie blinks back tears. It's not like her to dwell on what's dead and buried. But she can't stop staring at Natalie Damien's photo.

The resemblance really is uncanny. It's like she's looking at Alice.

Maybe Alice didn't write back because her father confiscated her letters. After all, she came to Connie's house that Saturday morning. Through the years, Connie tried to take comfort in that.

She moves the cursor to the top of the page to click off the site. Something at the top right-hand corner catches her eye. Natalie Damien's birthday.

She was born on September 8th, 1990.

Connie feels something cold creep across her skin.

There were rumors Alice was pregnant when she left Lowood. Connie put it down to the usual gossip. If Alice were having a baby, wouldn't she have known?

But Alice was keeping a lot of secrets that last year.

Connie looks at the date again to make sure she didn't read it wrong.

If her daughter was born in September, it means Alice likely conceived her in December.

When she was still living in Lowood.

An icy finger snakes down her spine.

Is that why Natalie Damien is trying to reconnect with her mother's past?

As if it were yesterday, Connie hears the hail of pebbles against her bedroom window. Feels the freezing December air rush in as she throws open the sash. Looks down to see Alice shivering outside. Mud and twigs on her clothing, which meant she'd been in the woods, the place that scared her the most.

That just doubled down the guilt.

Connie had made it her mission to cure her best friend of her fears. Alice saw danger lurking in every tree. In the sounds of the woodland animals. In the tall tales told by the town kids who hid among the headstones and swore Old Lowood Cemetery was haunted by the ghosts of the Revolutionary and Civil War soldiers buried there.

But it wasn't a centuries-old ghost who assaulted Alice.

She wouldn't let Connie call the police or take her to the hospital. She swore her to secrecy, made her promise she wouldn't tell another living soul.

But she never told her who did it.

Maybe she didn't know his name. He was just a stranger passing through.

But Connie always wondered if he was someone Alice knew and she was afraid of reprisal.

Nine months after she was assaulted, Alice gave birth. In another town many miles from Lowood.

Connie should have forced her to tell her the truth. Should have taken her to the police herself.

Then they might have caught whoever assaulted her. Stopped him before he could hurt anyone else. If it had been the same man, Walter Church wouldn't have gone looking for other suspects.

Other people to blame.

Alice might have stayed in Lowood.

Had her child here.

Once again, Connie's eye is drawn to Natalie Damien's photo.

Under the photo are the words: "To see what she shares with friends, send her a friend request."

She can't believe she's even thinking about that.

She'd just be opening up a whole other can of worms.

Better to let sleeping dogs lie.

SEVENTEEN

The days pass in a blur of witnesses.

On the bench, Alice sips bitter espresso from the cardboard container her court attorney brings her every morning now without being asked—a not-so-subtle hint?—and makes an effort to stay *present*.

Which is getting harder and harder to do.

Yesterday she missed key moments while an important witness was on the stand—a dancer at the club where the victim had worked. The witness testified to seeing the defendant parked in front of the club on the night Angel Diallo was killed, then seeing him follow the victim's cab. She was the one who gave the police the first three letters of the license plate that led them to Young.

The day before that, Alice nodded off while Young cross-examined the hostess who'd testified to always seating him at the same table, the one with a direct view of the section of the stage where Angel Diallo performed her nightly pole dance. Forster had to repeat her objection twice.

And this morning, Alice had to ask the court reporter to read back several questions after Forster objected to Young harassing the homicide lieutenant who'd arrested him, accusing him of trying to coerce a confession. Which Young never gave.

People are starting to notice.

The night of the storm, she doubled her dose of sleeping pills. Soon after, another panic attack left her hyperventilating on the sidewalk two blocks from her house, prompting a passerby to offer to take her to an emergency room, and she was forced to call her internist for a new script. While the antianxiety meds are supposedly more effective than the ones she began taking two years ago, they still make her sluggish and slow, despite the fact that she's punishing her body with three times her normal caffeine intake.

Ironically, as she's been sinking deeper into darkness and depression, her husband seems to be improving.

Ever since Alice pressured his doctors to start Charles on a new drug regimen, he has been less agitated. Although he hasn't shown signs of returning lucidity, she no longer hears him crying in the night. Not that she would, given the pills that leave her dead to the world, cocooned in a dreamless sleep from which she awakens in a panic that doesn't ease until she pops one of her morning meds.

"Your Honor?"

She blinks. Did she miss something again?

Katharine Forster is on her feet. "The People call Dr. Hannah Liu."

Alice takes another sip of espresso and makes a renewed effort to focus.

After her witness is sworn in, Forster establishes her credentials as the chief forensic pathologist of the Manhattan medical examiner's office. Then Forster turns to the bench. "With the court's permission, the People would like to set up our PowerPoint presentation."

"Proceed." The word bounces around in Alice's head as Forster and her second-seat attorney set up a projection screen in front of the jury box.

"Your Honor, at this time we'd like to show the witness a series of photographs, which have been previously marked as People's Exhibits A through E."

Forster's second chair presses keys on his laptop and an image appears on the screen. It's long shot of Angel Diallo. She's half-naked, lying on her back on the ground.

The attorney hits another key, bringing the body into closeup.

"Dr. Liu, please tell us the cause of death."

"The victim died from blunt-force trauma to her head and body." Liu looks at the jury. "She suffered massive injuries to her internal organs."

"What else did you find when you examined the victim?"

"We found evidence of extensive vaginal bruising and tearing consistent with a violent sexual assault."

"Did you find any DNA aside from the victim's?"

"Yes. There were traces of salivary DNA on the victim's left breast."

On the screen, a second image has replaced the first. It's a close-up of the top half of Angel Diallo's torso, her left breast clearly visible through her shredded clothing.

"Did you find anything else on the victim's left breast?"

"A significant amount of blood."

The image enlarges to zoom in on the bloody breast.

"What caused the victim to bleed so profusely?"

"Wounds so deep they lacerated her nipple."

"What caused those wounds?"

"Human adult teeth."

The courtroom erupts.

Alice's hand finds the gavel.

Forster waits for the noise to die down. "Did you take physical evidence from the defendant?"

"Yes. After he was arrested, a dental impression was taken of his front upper and lower teeth and gums. The results showed that the defendant's teeth were consistent with the bite-mark pattern found on the victim's left nipple."

The courtroom reacts again. Alice bangs the gavel.

"Did the mutilation of the victim's left nipple occur before or after she was killed?"

"Her wounds occurred premortem." Dr. Liu turns to the jury. "If they'd been made after she died and her heart had stopped pumping, only gravity would allow the blood to escape. Because the blood vessels typically contract after they're severed, there would have been very little bleeding."

"So the victim was alive while her nipple was being bitten?"

"Yes."

"Dr. Liu, you testified that cause of death was blunt-force trauma. What forensic evidence, if any, did you find at the scene?"

"We found blood DNA belonging to the victim."

"Only the victim?"

"Yes."

"Is that typical?"

"Yes. In a brutal killing like this, where the victim was left in a pool of blood, even if she and the killer were both bleeding it would be virtually impossible to separate out his blood from hers."

Forster turns over an index card. "Dr. Liu, how difficult is it to beat someone to death with your fists?"

"Extremely difficult. And rare."

"Can you tell us why?"

"Bone density is the same in the hands and head, so when force is applied to break one, chances are the other breaks at the same time. In my experience, blunt-force attacks are usually carried out with a weapon that gives the killer the advantage of density or inertia."

"So beating someone to death with your fists is rare, but not physically impossible?"

"No, not physically impossible."

"After he was arrested, did you examine the defendant's hands?"

"Yes. I found split skin on his knuckles and microfractures on his fingers. These cuts and abrasions are consistent with someone who had used his fists."

"Are you aware that in his statement the defendant said he sustained those injuries in the apartment building where he is employed, repairing a boiler that had burst?"

"In my opinion, injuries sustained repairing a boiler would have been different."

"Different in what way?"

"The most obvious injuries would be burn marks on the skin of the hands, especially the palms. And blisters. When I examined the defendant, I saw no evidence of the kind of injuries you'd expect to see from handling a boiler."

Another photo appears on the screen.

It's a close-up of Angel Diallo's face, her features brutalized almost beyond recognition.

"Is what we're looking at the result of the victim being beaten to death?" Forster asks.

"Yes."

"Would you characterize this rare kind of beating as one delivered with extreme force?"

"Yes."

"Dr. Liu, in your expert opinion, does the brutal nature of this murder match the sexual assault that tore the victim's vaginal wall and the bite-mark attack that resulted in the mutilation of her left nipple?"

"Yes."

"Thank you. Nothing further."

The minute Forster returns to the prosecution table, Young picks up his legal pad and crosses the courtroom, shadowed by the female and male officers.

"How are you today?"

Hannah Liu doesn't answer, her obsidian eyes fixed on him as he stops a few feet from the witness stand.

"Do you believe in God?"

Alice sustains Forster's objection.

The defendant flips a page on his pad. "You told these folks that none of my DNA was found inside Angel Diallo. So you didn't find any of my seed?"

"Your what?"

"My seed. You know, the thing that creates babies. Like the one Angel Diallo was carrying in her womb when somebody beat her to death. Because I'm not the one who impregnated her, isn't that the truth?"

Hannah Liu looks baffled by the question. "No one said you were the father of the victim's child."

"Do you know who the father is?"

"Objection."

"For all we know, he's the one who committed this crime."

"Move to strike!"

"Ms. Forster's objection is sustained, and the jury is ordered to disregard the defendant's last comment." Alice turns on Young, her brain fog finally starting to clear. "Try that again, and I'll hold you in contempt."

He stares at her, a muscle jumping in his jaw.

She can see the rage under that veneer of false charm.

Rage that could rape and torture a defenseless woman and beat her and her unborn child to death.

Young shifts his gaze, so that he's facing the jury. "Angel Diallo wasn't married, was she?"

"No."

He looks at the jurors. "Does anyone know how many johns she slept with while she had another man's child growing inside her? What about her pimp? Did you folks know that ninety-nine percent of all prostitutes are murdered by their pimps?"

"Your Honor!" Forster's on her feet. "I object to this whole line of questioning! There's no evidence to show that anyone other than the defendant committed this crime."

"Sustained. I warned you, Mr. Young."

"But did the police investigate any other suspect? No! They decided it was me even though they had no evidence and knew what was going on in that parking lot. The father of Angel Diallo's baby could have been any of those johns who paid for sex with her. He got jealous because she was sleeping with all those other men so he followed her to that abandoned lot!"

Forster's objections are drowned out by Young. Alice bangs the gavel to no avail.

"Or maybe he wasn't the baby's father. And when he found out she was just taunting him and it was all a lie, he punished her by raping and killing her!"

The gavel still in her hand, Alice leaps to her feet.

"Chambers!"

EIGHTEEN

Alice has to shout to make herself heard above the pandemonium. When she orders Young to return to his seat and remain there until he's escorted out of the courtroom, he grins at the jury.

Letting them know who won this round.

That only fuels her fury. She can barely get out the words as she orders the jurors to be sent back to the jury room.

At the defense table, Young watches the female officer return to her seat behind him. She doesn't react. Alice remembers her the first day of voir dire, looking as if she couldn't wait for the chance to restrain the defendant. Even through the haze of her anger, Alice is aware of the delicious irony of Young being controlled by a female.

An armed female.

Alice starts to order her and the male officer to escort him out. Then she has second thoughts. She doesn't like the way Young has been looking at the female officer throughout the trial.

No matter how capable, she's still a woman. How can she expose her to him?

"Luiz," Alice calls out to her longtime court officer. "Please take the defendant to the holding cell."

All eyes are on Young as Luiz takes him out of the courtroom. After they've gone, Alice motions to Forster and the court reporter to follow her. They leave the courtroom through the door behind the bench and walk down the narrow hallway. As they pass the holding cell, Alice instructs Luiz to bring the defendant into her chambers.

When Young walks through the doorway, the atmosphere seems to shift.

He's bigger than he appeared in the courtroom.

He looms over her chambers, dwarfing everyone else.

Alice can see the tension in Katharine Forster. Remembering that the defendant almost blinded another inmate with a shank, it occurs to her that she might have made a calculated error by letting a violent criminal into her chambers. If he weren't representing himself, he wouldn't be allowed in here at all. She regrets now that she didn't assign a second officer to escort him into her chambers for additional security.

Young watches her with a knowing look in his blue eyes, as if aware of what she's thinking.

Anger reignites, so swift and hard it steals her breath.

Reminding her that she's the one with the power.

"Mr. Young, I have granted you a great deal of latitude. But you continue to defy my rulings. No matter how hard you try, I will never grant a mistrial. If you act out of order one more time, I will assign another attorney to conduct your defense."

"I don't want another attorney."

"The decision isn't yours to make. I will also remove you from my courtroom and you will be tried in absentia. Do you understand?"

"Yes, Your Honor." Young's smile belies the rage emanating from him, like a palpable energy force in the room. Alice isn't the only one who feels it. Across her desk, where only a few feet separate Forster from the defendant, the prosecutor has gone pale. On Young's other side, Luiz's right hand starts moving toward his gun belt.

Young's smile widens, as if sensing their fear and trying to figure out a way to exploit it, like the predator that he is.

When she can find her voice again, Alice orders everyone back into the courtroom. Young is still smiling as Luiz escorts him out, Katharine Forster several steps ahead, as if she couldn't get away fast enough.

After they're gone, Alice closes the door and reaches into the pocket of her robe. Taking a cigarette from the nearly empty pack, she goes over to the picture window that overlooks the judges' entrance at the rear of the building. Angry with herself for letting a defendant get to her, she starts lighting up. Stops in mid-motion.

He's standing outside the building. His back is to her. He's facing the street. As if he knows she's watching, he slowly turns around. He's dressed all in black, a hood covering his head. His features further obscured by a pair of dark sunglasses.

He's getting bolder. Stalking her in broad daylight.

Her phone buzzes. She slides it out of her pocket. It's Shavonne, asking if everything's okay. The court's waiting on the judge.

Alice is tempted to ask Shavonne to come into her chambers to be a witness.

A witness to what? There's no law against standing on the street. And what if he pulls a vanishing act again? Then she'll really look like she's out of her mind and start the courthouse rumor mill churning more than it undoubtedly is already.

When Alice returns to the window, he's still there.

NINETEEN

By the time she left the courthouse after adjourning early, he was gone.

Of course he was.

The difference is that she's wise to him now. He thinks he can manipulate her, make her believe that she's going crazy.

He's about to have a rude awakening.

He has no idea who he's dealing with.

She picks up the revolver in her lap, studying it from every angle. The gun's lighter than she remembers. But then, she hasn't held the weapon in her hands for years.

The first thing she did when she arrived home was to check on Charles, who was in bed, Edith reading to him. He didn't look up as she stood in the doorway.

After changing into sweats, Alice went back downstairs.

The box was in his study, where it had been gathering dust in the bottom drawer of his desk.

He bought the gun for her eight years ago, when the defendant on trial—a member of a New York City gang—threatened her in open court. He insisted she learn to protect herself and took her to a shooting range on the city's West Side, where she mastered the basics.

"Just in case," Charles said.

Just in case never arrived. Despite sentencing many defendants to the maximum allowable under the law, Alice never had occasion to fire the weapon at a living person.

Now, as she cocks the hammer and aims the gun, she envisions herself pulling the trigger.

This time, she'll be ready.

—◆—

She must have dozed off.

When she opens her eyes, her back feels stiff and she has a crick in her neck from falling asleep in the chair. She yawns. Must have been the second sleeping pill, although she doesn't recall actually taking it. She'd planned to wean herself off the meds, starting with reducing the two pills to a single one. She needs to be alert, to stay vigilant.

As if to give the lie to her intentions, she yawns again. Looks across the room. Her bed looks so inviting. And she's tired. Bone-tired. She feels as if she could sleep forever.

—◆—

A noise awakens her. She sits up, heart hammering in her chest as she stares into the darkness. The sheets are in a tangle at her feet.

She doesn't remember getting into bed.

Downstairs, the grandfather clock chimes again. Just past midnight.

She moves aside her pillow and lets out a relieved breath. Although she doesn't remember placing the gun there, either.

She startles at another sound.

Someone's moving around downstairs.

Now that she thinks about it, didn't she hear a door opening? Before the clock chimed?

It wasn't the front door.

She struggles to make sense of the muddle in her mind.

Why would Alexis use the back door?

Maybe she hoped her mother wouldn't hear her and find out how late she came home.

Except that tonight she's home earlier than usual.

Now Alice can hear her in the kitchen. No doubt having a late-night snack. God only knows when she last ate. Her daughter hasn't joined her for a meal in months.

Things can't go on like this. Alexis has to learn that she can't continue coming and going as she pleases without a thought for anyone else. Not while she's living under her roof. Alice tries to summon self-righteous anger, but she's lost the thread of her thoughts.

Her head is growing heavier. It's a battle to keep her eyes open.

She eases her body down and pulls up the blanket, luxuriating in the soft, crisp feel of the cotton sheets. The world drifts further away. She barely registers the creak on the tread of the fifth step that they never got around to fixing.

Footsteps approaching the landing is the last thing she remembers.

TWENTY

A lexis takes the buds out of her ears.

For the first time, the music isn't making her feel better. And it would be just her luck to end up going deaf.

She goes over to her closet and flings out hangers, then stares with disgust at the clothes strewn across her bed.

There's nothing even remotely right for her to wear anymore. She'll never fit into anything. The spandex dress on top of the pile is so tight it's like a second skin. She'll be lucky if she can get it over her thighs and belly.

Damien's sure to notice. He likes his women rail thin. That's a joke. In the next few months, she's only going to get fatter.

This whole pregnancy thing is getting to be a drag.

Just a week ago she thought she'd ace through it, no problem. Then, the other night at the club, the nausea hit her. Luckily, Damien was busy auditioning the replacement drummer so he didn't see her taking off for the ladies' like a shot, afraid she'd puke up her dinner before she got there.

As if being fat and throwing up all the time wasn't horrible enough, now her face is breaking out like it did when she was a teenager.

How's she supposed to look hot with all this stuff going on in her body?

She goes motionless.

This can't be happening.

It's not supposed to start until week fourteen at the earliest. She's only into her thirteenth week, even if it feels like she's been pregnant forever.

Maybe she was wrong. Maybe it's just gas or hunger pangs, like the articles said.

It just happened again.

It wasn't gas or hunger pangs.

The baby moved.

Alexis presses her hands against her belly.

This is totally amazing. She's never felt anything like it.

Damien should be here, sharing this historic moment with her.

But how can he, when he doesn't know yet?

It's not like she doesn't want to tell him.

But every time she's planned to, she's wimped out.

And he's so distracted lately, with KillJoy finally getting its name out there. So distracted he didn't notice she stopped ordering her usual margaritas. She didn't have to read about that to know it's bad for the baby. And then there's the sex. Asking him to do it from behind because she read that it's safer that way when you're pregnant. Damien just thinks it's a turn-on.

That's not the only reason he's distracted.

It's the new back-up singer.

The *rail-thin* new back-up singer.

Her name's Apple.

What the hell kind of name is *Apple*?

The conniving bitch is always there, wedging herself on the banquette between them at the bar after the show, showing off her skinny little body with those big tits that are as fake as her name.

But the worst thing is the way Alexis sometimes catches Damien looking at Apple.

The way he used to look at *her*.

She can't put it off anymore. She has to tell him.

Butterflies start fluttering in her belly. But this time she knows it isn't the baby.

What if Damien doesn't react the way she hopes?

What will she do then? She can't hide her pregnancy forever. Soon she's going to start showing, and her mother's going to start asking questions. That won't happen if she moves in with Damien.

But first she's got to tell him.

Maybe the timing's not right. Tomorrow night, the producer from that new record label is coming to the club. If he signs the band, KillJoy will be in the big time. Damien'll be doing gigs all over. Not exactly the best life for a new father. Or for her if she stays with the band as lead singer. Which is going to be a problem.

There's a bigger problem.

What if Damien doesn't want to be married?

What if he tells her to get rid of it?

Her hands go to her belly again. Now the baby's totally quiet. As if it knows.

"Don't worry," Alexis whispers. "I'll never let anyone hurt you."

Damien wouldn't do that, would he? It's not like she hasn't thought about this. She thinks about it all the time. The truth is, she's afraid he'll see her and the baby as albatrosses around his neck who'll get in the way of his career.

And there's something else.

How can she tell him he's going to be a father when she doesn't know who her own father is?

Her eyes stray to her computer. To the photo in the top left-hand corner of her Natalie Damien Facebook page. Every time she sees it, she curses herself for her stupidity. All that trouble to create a bogus account, and there's her face, big as life. And her birthday, too, in the top right-hand corner. She's not even sure how it happened. Maybe she clicked on something she shouldn't have. Or Facebook is smarter than she thinks and knows it's a bogus page.

So much for double-protecting her password and changing her privacy settings. All her mother has to do is click on the page and she'll know it's her.

She deletes the photo. Her face disappears, leaving an empty silhouette. Then she hides her birthday, so only she can view the date.

That makes her feel better, even though her heart's still racing. She has to calm down. It's bad for the baby. And her mother would probably never go on Lowood High's Facebook page in the first place. It's not like she ever talks about going to school there. She probably doesn't even know about the upcoming fundraiser.

Alexis takes some deep breaths, slowly in and out through her diaphragm the way the articles said she should.

Then she rereads the message she already knows by heart.

> *Dear Natalie Damien,*
>
> *I'm responding to your recent post on Lowood High's Facebook page. I don't know if Alice ever told you about me, but I knew her many years ago when she lived in Lowood. If you want to write to me, I can be reached at constancemooew20@gmail.com.*
>
> *Very truly yours,*
> *Constance Moore*

Her new Facebook "friend." On Google, Alexis found out that her name was Constance Wilcox when she graduated from Lowood High in June of 1990.

Moore is the current owner of the Lowood Diner, has been married three times, and still uses her third husband's last name. There was a related article in the *Lowood Banner*. In 2003, she took out a restraining order against Wade Donegan, her second husband. A week later, she was attacked in her home. Her assailant broke her arm and cracked three ribs. Nothing was ever proven, and no arrests were ever made.

She doesn't have children, at least none that Alexis could find.

So far, Moore is the only one who responded to her post.

That was over a week ago. Alexis still hasn't emailed her.

She doesn't know if Moore will be able to tell her anything. Her mother never mentioned her. For all Alexis knows, she and her mom were just acquaintances.

But something tells her they were more than that. Or why would Moore take the trouble to write back?

Maybe she's better off not knowing. Maybe there's a reason her mother didn't tell her.

Maybe her father isn't someone she'd want to know.

She wishes she had someone to talk to. She doesn't have any close girl-friends. She doesn't really have any girlfriends at all. Damien's her best bud. Her mom used to be. But after Charles got sick, everything changed. It's not just that he gets all her mother's attention. Or the fights with her that seem to be getting worse.

Her mom has changed too. Especially lately.

Not only is she smoking like a chimney, but Alexis is pretty sure she's taking pills. And when she came upstairs tonight, her old night-light was again shining out from under her mother's door.

She hasn't heard her mom crying in the night for a while. Probably too drugged out. Maybe she should check on her.

Alexis unlocks her door and goes into the hall.

Outside her mother's bedroom, she stops.

She could be asleep.

Or passed out. What if she overdosed?

She presses her ear to the door. Doesn't hear anything.

She jiggles the knob.

It's unlocked.

TWENTY-ONE

The door is opening.

"What are you doing?"

Alexis is standing in the doorway. Her hands are in front of her face, as if warding off a blow.

Alice looks at her in confusion. Then down at her own hand.

She's holding a gun.

"Mom, will you please put it down? You're freaking me out."

Her daughter's words—and the terror on her face—finally get through to Alice. As she places the weapon on her nightstand, everything comes rushing back.

Seeing the figure outside the window in chambers.

Coming home and retrieving the gun from Charles's study.

Sitting in the chair across the room, loaded revolver in her lap. Ready to shoot on sight.

How can she tell her daughter any of that?

Her eyes on the gun, Alexis comes into the room. "What's going on? Did you think someone was in the house?"

Still Alice doesn't answer, ashamed of her unfounded fears that seem foolish now with the reality of her daughter here.

"No one can get in, Mom. All the windows and doors are locked. It's just us. You, me, Charles, and Larry."

"Is Charles all right?" She can't remember if she looked in on him tonight. Alice starts to get out of bed.

"It's okay. That's what Larry's here for. But I checked on Charles when I got home. He's sleeping. Like you should be."

Alice obediently lies back down as her daughter resettles the blanket around her. "You were just having a bad dream."

The familiar words send Alice back to her childhood, to memories of her mother who would stay with her until the terror receded. Even as a part of her is thinking: *No, this is wrong. I'm the one who should be comforting my daughter.*

"Try to get some rest, Mom."

After Alexis leaves, Alice feels a familiar panic. Even the steady glow of the night-light fails to reassure her.

Trembling all over, she sits up and takes the gun from the nightstand. Puts it back under her pillow. Then she lies slowly back down. She pulls the blanket up to her chin and stares at the ceiling.

Is this the way it began with Charles?

Is she starting to lose touch with reality?

TWENTY-TWO

Alice keeps her hands clasped tightly in her lap to stop them from shaking.

She didn't take her antianxiety pill this morning. She has to stay alert, must keep her wits about her. That's what her rational voice, the voice she can still hear, is telling her.

She can't afford a repeat of what happened less than eight hours ago. So pumped full of drugs that she pointed a loaded weapon at her own child.

Last night was a wake-up call.

In the wee hours of this morning, as the first light of dawn cast out the deep shadows of night, she flushed all the pills down the toilet.

Craving a cigarette, a habit she's determined to kick again, Alice takes a deep breath and forces herself to focus.

On the stand, Norman Rush, DDS, JD, is describing his specialty.

". . . I analyze wounds made by human teeth to help identify criminal suspects."

"So forensic odontology is a recognized field of criminal forensics?" Katharine Forster asks.

"Not only is it recognized, it predates DNA by more than twenty years."

"Really?" Forster feigns surprise. As if her expert witness's testimony hadn't been carefully rehearsed ahead of time.

"Oh, yes." Behind his horn-rimmed glasses, Rush blinks. "In fact, it was through odontology that the remains of Josef Mengele were identified in Argentina by comparing his teeth to postmortem photos."

He turns to the jury. "Then there was the 1979 trial of Ted Bundy. It was the first case in Florida's legal history that relied solely on bite-mark testimony. There were no fingerprints or physical evidence linking Bundy to any of the thirty-six victims he confessed to murdering. All they had was a bite mark Bundy left on one of his victim's left buttock. A detailed analysis revealed a match to the dental impressions of Bundy's teeth."

Forster picks up something from the table. "Dr. Rush, do you recognize this?"

"Yes. That's a dental impression I made of the defendant's front upper and lower teeth and gums."

After Forster identifies the mold as People's Exhibit M, her second chair hits keys on his laptop and an image appears on the projection screen. It's the angled close-up of Angel Diallo's left breast, blown up to three times its size. The semi-circle of what appears to be bite marks on the nipple stand out in stark relief against all the blood.

Forster approaches the witness stand and hands her witness a pointer. "Dr. Rush, please tell us the nature of these wounds."

Rush steps down. "The wounds are bite marks that represent a combination of a contusion, a hemorrhage, and avulsion, which results in the removal of skin." He touches the pointer to the screen. "You can see where part of the victim's nipple was bitten off."

After Rush returns to the stand, Forster continues. "Did you analyze the defendant's dentition?"

"Yes. I made a plaster cast of the defendant's teeth and created a compound overlay through digitally enhanced photography. These scanned images were compared with the bite marks."

"What was the result of your findings?"

"By using these methods to create exemplars of the defendant's unique mandibular anterior dental pattern, I concluded that the bite marks were consistent with the defendant's dentition."

"So in your expert opinion, the multiple bite-mark wounds on the victim were made by the defendant, William Henry Young?"

"Yes."

"One more question. Dr. Rush, is there special significance to the biter attacking the victim's breast?"

"Yes. Mutilating the female breast indicates a high index of heterosexual aggression. Because this attack is done slowly, with the perpetrator taking his time, it's considered extremely sadistic."

"Thank you."

After Forster is seated at the prosecution table, Young looks up at the bench. "Beg pardon, Your Honor, but I've been trying to make sense of what the doc said. I don't know about the jury, but it went completely over my head."

"Objection!"

Before Alice can rule, Young speaks again. "My apologies, Your Honor." He gets to his feet, and the two officers behind him follow suit. Young gives a fleeting glance to the male officer, ignoring the female officer as if she were no longer worthy of his attention. Her face is impassive as she and the other officer shadow Young to the prosecution table.

"Excuse me, Madam Prosecutor." Young picks up the mold of his teeth Forster just put down and walks to the witness stand, followed by the male and female officers.

"Mornin', Doc." Young sets down the teeth mold in front of Rush. "I think everyone here knows this is an impression you took of my teeth. You said—hold on a second—" He flips through his legal pad "—here it is. You said my 'unique mandibular anterior dental pattern' made you conclude that the bite marks were consistent with my dentition. So what's unique about my teeth, Doc?"

"Everyone's teeth are unique."

"I don't care about everyone's teeth. I want to know what's unique about mine."

"My examination revealed that you hadn't been to a dentist in years."

"That isn't a crime, last time I checked." Young glances at the jury. "Can anyone blame me for not wanting to go to the dentist?"

A few jurors smile. Alice notices Young's gaze lingering on the woman in the fifth seat from the right in the first row.

"Actually, that's what makes your teeth unique," Rush says. "Each person's grid is unique, and if they have dental disorders or poorly formed teeth, it makes them easier to identify because they create their own exclusive pattern." He picks up the mold. "In your case, my examination revealed advanced gum disease as well as some degeneration in the teeth in your upper jaw. The rotational value of your upper right lateral incisor—in your case a malformed or abused incisor—revealed a pattern consistent with several of the bite marks found on the victim."

"Consistent with? Not a match?"

Rush hesitates. On the bench, Alice leans forward. This goes to the heart of the state's case. Given the absence of fingerprints or any physical evidence such as semen or DNA, the odontologist's response could mean the difference between conviction and acquittal.

Again Alice's eyes are drawn to Juror #5, who is still riveted on the defendant.

"Bite-mark analysis doesn't operate under the same rules as DNA," Rush finally says, putting down the mold. "As I testified earlier—"

"You bet it doesn't. Did you know that between 1985 and 1998, ten wrongful conviction cases were brought because of erroneous bite-mark evidence?"

Alice overrules Forster's objection. Young's question was within the scope of cross-examination. "The witness will answer."

"That's only a fraction of the cases where the evidence was ultimately upheld." Rush shoots Young a dark look as he continues. "As I testified earlier, bite-mark analysis uses pattern analysis, which can often succeed where DNA fails."

"Sorry for sounding thick, but what does that mean?"

"It means bite-mark analysis reveals a pattern that can be accurately attributed to a suspect."

"But you just said—let me just find it here—you said, 'A detailed analysis revealed a match to the dental impressions of Mr. Bundy's teeth.' So matches do exist in your science. Or were you lying to us?"

"Certainly not. In bite-mark analysis, what we call a match is a reasonable medical certainty, which is the highest degree of certainty that the suspect made the bite mark. In Ted Bundy's case, he had a chip on his upper left front incisor which matched the bite-mark pattern on his victim."

"A chip, huh? Guess Mr. Bundy didn't like going to the dentist, either. You didn't find a chip on any of my incisors, did you?"

"No."

Young paces in front of the witness stand. "So my teeth aren't as unique as Mr. Bundy's?"

"I never said that."

Young stops pacing. "You said they found a bite mark on only one of Bundy's victims?"

"As far as we know, yes."

"What about all the others? How many women did Bundy rape and kill? You never told us the total number of victims."

"No one knows the exact number."

Young's gaze flicks to the left. He has gone completely still.

Only his eyes move.

He's looking at the blow-up of Angel Diallo's left breast.

Now he's staring up at the bench. His blue eyes bore into Alice's.

Her breath catches.

He wants her to know.

Angel Diallo wasn't his first.

"Your Honor, I object to this whole line of questioning. Ted Bundy is not relevant to this case."

Young turns away.

Alice feels as if she'd been released from a spell. She starts to sustain Forster's objection when she spies someone in the last row of the gallery.

She tells herself that it's her mind once again playing tricks.

Seeing someone who isn't there.

Like the figure outside her window?

She blinks.

Alexis is still there.

Someone else has noticed her.

Still holding the mold of his teeth, the defendant stares at her daughter as if he were sizing up his prey.

His next victim.

TWENTY-THREE

He's on top of her.

His hands around her neck.

The screams dying in her throat as his fingers squeeze her windpipe.

The only thing not moving are his eyes.

They're unblinking, like the ancient yellow eyes of the owl perched on the highest branch of that tree.

She feels eyes everywhere.

Watching them.

His head drops lower.

His eyes aren't old.

Or yellow.

TWENTY-FOUR

"**A**ll rise. The Honorable Alice D. McKerrity presiding."

Alice waves everyone back into their seats as she walks into the courtroom.

Behind the prosecution table, Katharine Forster is conferring with her second chair as if this were just another day in court.

As if the judge who just seated herself on the bench hadn't lost her mind.

Alice turns toward the defense table with dread, terrified that she'll see him as he was in her nightmare. Blue eyes flashing out of the darkness as the weight of his body presses her harder into the cold, hard earth . . .

No one is seated at the table.

"Where is the defendant?" No one looks at her askance. She must be keeping up a fairly convincing semblance of normality.

"I'll call Corrections," Tom says from his desk against the far wall.

In a way, it makes a terrible kind of sense.

As she has on and off for the past several weeks, Alice sees herself running through the woods. It's the same dream that began three decades ago and recurred for years.

A dream that wasn't a dream at all.

It was a memory her brain could no longer hold. The memory she buried in the deepest recesses of her psyche.

Not that she ever forgot. Not for a single day in all these years.

She thought she'd moved on. Endured the most horrific ordeal that a woman can face, and survived. She became a mother. Graduated from high school. Then college and, finally, law school.

But maybe you can never truly move on from something like that.

He was never caught.

Never punished.

Young said it himself. When he made a motion to suppress the crime scene photos.

"If you were on the jury, would you decide I was guilty just so you could punish someone?"

Was he right? The need to punish so strong that she projected his features onto the face of the monster who raped her in the woods thirty years ago?

But why now?

The door to the right of the bench opens.

William Henry Young stands there.

Alice reminds herself that this is the same defendant who has been in her courtroom every day for weeks. If there were something familiar about him, wouldn't she have noticed?

Last night's dream was just that.

A dream.

Not a memory.

Yet another by-product of her stressful home life.

After the two corrections officers who escorted Young from the pens leave, Luiz accompanies the defendant into the courtroom. His ankle chain makes a familiar scraping sound as it drags across the wood floor.

Alice's heart races as Luiz unlocks the shackles.

She tells herself that it's a symptom of drug withdrawal. Having gone cold turkey.

Luiz resumes his position by the door, and the male and female officers take their seats behind the defendant.

At the defense table, Young's head is down as he writes on the yellow legal pad.

Under her robe, Alice has begun to sweat.

The still-rational part of her wondering if she is in her right mind after all, and her rapist has been here all this time. Not outside her window. In her courtroom. The one place where she still felt in control.

But how would she know if she were in her right mind? Believing herself capable of rational thought could be just another delusion.

Isn't the hallmark of insanity believing that you're sane?

"Your Honor, the state rests."

Katharine Forster's voice brings her back. Alice heaves in a breath. Then she turns back to the defendant.

Light floods her vision.

Slicing through the dark.

Electrifying the trees.

Her vision blurs and she sees him, an indistinct silhouette blending in with the night.

Then it's gone, and the defendant is once again seated at the table, gray head bent over his legal pad.

The courtroom's growing restless. Alice runs her tongue over dry lips. "Is the defense ready to present its case?"

Young looks up, his expression radiating innocence. It's the same false mask he has worn throughout the trial. Concealing the face of the killer who compared himself to Ted Bundy. Who wanted her to know that he'd raped and murdered before.

His eyes change. A faint smile touches his mouth. He knows what she's thinking. "I'm ready."

Is it her imagination, or has his voice dropped? His tone personal, almost intimate. As if they were the only two people in the courtroom.

"Who is your first witness?" She can barely get out the words.

"Just me, myself, and I." He lets out a chuckle that sets her teeth on edge. She clamps down to stop their chattering.

Young picks up his legal pad. Now that he's no longer looking at her, she can breathe again. Today he's wearing a suit that brings out the blue of his eyes.

He smiles at the jury as he ambles out of the well, the male and female officers right behind him.

Out of the darkness comes a flash of white.

He's still baring his teeth as he walks to the witness stand.

She sees him in the courtroom yesterday, holding the mold of his teeth as he homed in on the person seated in the last row of the gallery.

Her daughter who, at almost twenty-nine, is nearly the image of Alice at sixteen.

Her heart pounds, this time with rage.

The result of a mind that has lost its moorings?

Or memories fighting to be heard?

His right hand in the air, Young swears to tell the truth, the whole truth, and nothing but the truth.

But Alice isn't listening to his lies.

She's hearing something else.

A sound just below the whistle of the wind.

The purr of an engine.

He takes his seat on the witness stand.

As he talks, Alice stares at the back of his head.

He's physically closer than he has been during the entire trial.

Close enough to see the strands of white-blond hair mixed in with the gray.

A smell drifts up to the bench.

Something rancid. Like meat that has been left out too long.

Something bestial.

It's coming from him. From the freshly laundered white shirt beneath the blue suit.

She watches his jaw move.

He's still talking.

". . . never followed Angel Diallo home from that dance club."

". . . never stalked her."

". . . would never hurt a woman or force her to do anything against her will."

She turns.

Headlights blind her.

She puts up a hand to shield her eyes.

The car cruises slowly down the street.

Pulls up next to her.

The passenger window rolls down.

And she sees him.

TWENTY-FIVE

She called a recess.

Shaking so hard she could barely bring down the gavel. Shavonne shooting her a worried glance as she left the bench.

She lights up her third cigarette as she paces her chambers, still not sure what just happened.

All she knew was she had to get out of there. Had to get away from the defendant. Away from the stench that filled her nostrils, making it impossible to breathe. Saturating her heart and lungs, as if her entire body were being infected with the stink of his evil.

She still smells him.

But everything else is fading,

The face she saw is now hazy. Blurry around the edges, like a photo out of focus. Features disintegrating into an indistinct mass.

Shades of light and dark.

Puzzle pieces that don't add up to a recognizable whole.

Once again, she sees the passenger window rolling down.

The shadowy form behind the wheel.

She couldn't have seen his face. She never saw him clearly that frigid December night.

She didn't have to.

She knew who he was.

TWENTY-SIX

Her heart races as he stares at her.
  She looks away, down at her hands.
  When she looks up again, he's still staring.
Even in the dim light, she can see his blond hair.
The blue of his eyes.
She's never seen eyes that blue.
Or hair that blond. Like white gold.
Time stops. It's as if they were the only two people on earth.
She doesn't move. Barely breathes.
He turns away. Retreats back into the shadows.
It feels as if she'd been released from a spell.
At the same time she's bereft, as if she'd lost something precious.
His head swivels in her direction again.
She lets out a shaky breath.
Now his lips are moving.
She can see him only in profile now.
He's talking to someone.
The girl next to him. She just flagged down the bartender.
He smiles. The flash of his teeth in the smoky dimness of the bar dazzles her.
He throws back his head. Laughs.

She imagines the sound his laugh would make.

A sexy rumble deep in his throat.

He's still laughing at something she said.

Jealousy rips through her.

He isn't looking at her anymore. Now he's talking to the bartender.

The girl sidles closer to him.

Jealousy digs its claws in deeper.

Now the girl's flirting. She can tell from her body language. From the way the girl cocks her head at him.

She picks up her empty glass. Puts it down again. In another minute, she's getting up and walking right up to him. She doesn't care if the bartender figures out that she isn't twenty-one. That the IDs her best friend got for them are fakes.

She doesn't move. Still the same scaredy-cat she was when she moved here five years ago.

He zips up his black leather jacket.

He's leaving.

She watches him walk down the length of the bar and into the shadows until he blends in with the darkness.

She has no idea who he is or where he's from. He looked older, which explains why she hasn't seen him hanging around at school. Maybe he isn't from Lowood. He lives in Cannonville. Or Renegade Falls.

Or he isn't from around here at all. A stranger passing through.

Which means she'll probably never see him again.

But she can't stop thinking about him. As the days pass, he's all she thinks about. The hazy memory of his blond hair and blue eyes fading more every day.

Only the obsession remaining.

Then one unusually warm night in early December, as she walks home from church after choir practice, she hears the purr of an engine. She turns, sees the headlights of a car. Coming down the street. Slowing as it approaches, then continuing past her.

She's sure she saw a blond head behind the wheel.

She looks for the car but doesn't see it again.

Until the night of the party.

She was sorry she went. It was a mistake.

She should have known better.

That night a few weeks back was a mistake too, something that should never have happened.

She had to get out of there. Had to clear her head. It didn't help that she'd drunk too much of the spiked punch and her head felt like it was about to burst open.

After she leaves the house of the Lowood High senior hosting the party, she starts walking. She's sorry now that she agreed to wear the high heels Connie loaned her for the party. She doesn't realize how far she's gone until she hears something. She turns, but the car is already disappearing around the corner.

Then all is silent again. Not a single other car on the road. She has no way of knowing if it was the same car she saw the night she walked home from church. But what were the chances that he was in Lowood tonight and would know the exact moment she left the party?

Unless this is all part of the game they started playing that first night at the bar.

She smiles to herself as she starts walking again, even though it's freezing and her fingers and toes in the open heels are numb. What happened before she left the party forgotten in her mounting excitement.

A few minutes later, she again hears the purr of an engine. When she turns, headlights blind her.

She puts up a hand to shield her eyes.

And to let him know that she knows.

The car cruises slowly down the street.

Pulls up next to her.

The passenger window rolls down.

She can't see inside because he's dimmed the lights.

But it's him.

The car's still running.

As if in a trance, she takes a step. Then another. As she walks off the curb, her left heel catches on something and she stumbles. She ignores the voice saying that this is a sign, warning her to not get into a stranger's car.

Except that she'd been fantasizing about him for weeks, so he wasn't a stranger.

The passenger door opens.

Inside the car, it's warm and toasty. She can feel her fingers and toes again. She looks at him, but he doesn't turn his head. She stares at his profile, trying to see the face she saw across the smoke-filled bar. But it's pitch-dark because he's turned off the lights.

A sound startles her.

It's the door locks clicking into place. The sound echoes in her head, unnaturally loud in the silence.

He still hasn't looked her way.

She feels another stab of fear. Brushes it away. This was what she wanted, and she wasn't going to miss her chance. She'd already spent the last three weeks burning up with regret.

Telling herself if only she'd waited.

If only she'd saved herself for him.

He shifts gears.

Starts driving.

They turn down a street.

There are no streetlamps here.

She can see the silhouettes of trees up ahead.

They're headed toward the woods.

Her heart hammers against her ribs, but she tells herself he's just driving to a place where they can be alone.

Where no one will see them.

Another part of her wondering why he didn't pull over on one of the dark streets they passed.

It wasn't like anyone else was outside on a night like this.

He keeps driving.

She tells herself to stop being a wimp, like Connie's always telling her she is. Then she pictures Connie that night in the bar, flirting with him when she was supposed to be getting them fresh drinks. She thinks about how secretive her best friend has become, how lately she hasn't seen Connie with Luke, her high school boyfriend.

The car doesn't feel warm and toasty anymore. It's hotter than hell. It's hard to keep her eyes open. She feels his presence next to her. Jealousy eating away at her again as she wonders if Connie's sleeping with him. Which would just make everything more complicated than it already is. Guilt consuming her as her mind replays that other night, three weeks before seeing a stranger in a bar changed her life.

She forces the memory of that other night from her mind.

She isn't going to let one mistake spoil this moment.

Tonight isn't about anyone else.

Tonight is only about him and her.

Because she's the one he chose.

He turns off the main road.

Onto the path leading into the woods.

She sees headstones rising out of the dark.

They're getting close to Old Lowood Cemetery.

And the soldiers' burial ground.

He switches off the engine.

Turns to her.

His teeth a sudden flash of white in the darkness.

It isn't the way he smiled at her across the bar. It seems like a thing apart from his eyes. The blue eyes that now look so cold.

And empty.

He leans toward her.

So close she can smell him. Under the cologne he's wearing.

Bile rises up in her throat.

He reaches for her. He's still smiling.

She tries to unlock the passenger door. His hand closes over hers.

Her elbow shoots out. His grip loosens. She reaches again for the lock. It snaps open. She pushes open the door. He grabs her arm. She wriggles out of his grasp. Bolts from the car.

And runs.

TWENTY-SEVEN

The cigarette has burned down to ash.

Alice barely feels it singe her fingers.

She sees herself running in those heels, her terror of the woods eclipsed by her terror of him.

Night sounds filling her ears.

The drone of crickets.

The shrieks of owls.

The thunderous flapping of bat wings.

She knows what comes next.

She has seen this particular film playing out for decades.

Filtered through the distorted lens of false memory.

In that version of events, she doesn't get into his car.

The lie she repeated to herself to rewrite history.

A fiction devised so that she could live with the guilt.

The shame.

It wasn't as if she didn't know the truth.

Or that she forgot.

She just chose to not remember.

There's a difference.

She adjourned for the day.

Stated on the record that an emergency had come up that needed her immediate attention. An excuse some might have viewed with skepticism, if not considered an outright lie, after she'd already called for a recess earlier.

But no one questions a judge's actions.

In her courtroom, she reigns supreme.

The irony of that isn't lost on her.

When Alice arrived home, Charles was taking a nap.

Down the hall, Alexis's door was closed, as usual. There was no loud music blaring from her room. Her door wasn't locked, and when Alice looked in on her, she was struck by how different her daughter's face looked in sleep.

Innocent and peaceful, an expression Alice hadn't seen in a long time.

Was she really in her courtroom yesterday?

Wondering once again where Alexis went at night and what kept her out so late that she was still asleep at almost one in the afternoon.

—m—

Alice is in front of her personal computer; the reason she left the courthouse. She didn't want to use the laptop in her chambers, which records every online search.

Then some might have wondered why Alice needed to read the discovery materials in *The People v. William Henry Young* this late in the trial, with the case going to the jury as soon as closing statements have been completed. The truth is, she'd given only a cursory glance at the paperwork after coming into the case late, with pretrial motions already having been ruled on by the previous judge.

What she gave greater attention to were the crime scene photos.

And the defendant's rap sheet.

There is no doubt in Alice's mind that William Henry Young raped and murdered Angel Diallo.

But is he the monster who raped her almost thirty years ago?

She has to know. Has to put an end to this madness.

That's why William Henry Young's rap sheet is on the screen. This is his first arrest and she recalls there being a sketchy personal history the first time she read it. Now she's checking to see if the rap sheet has been updated, as frequently happens.

What she's looking for is information.

First, she studies his face, which she didn't do with any degree of detail before.

The mug shot was taken seven months ago, on the date of his arrest. January 15, 2019.

In the grainy photo, he still has the mustache. But his hair is shorter. Not the ponytail she saw on the first day of jury selection, the morning he walked into her courtroom. His beard is shorter too.

She skips down to the physical details, which of course haven't changed.

Hair Color: Gray.

Eye Color: Blue.

Facts already in evidence.

There's nothing dispositive. Nothing telling her that it's him, that she wasn't substituting the features of the defendant onto the shadowy face of her rapist.

Her mind's eye dyeing Young's gray hair blond.

Even if his hair was blond at one time, what of it?

He's not the only man in the world with blond hair and blue eyes.

That doesn't mean it's him.

Further details confirm what she has also read before. The defendant is of average height and weight.

She sees him in her chambers again. The way he seemed to dwarf everyone else.

Towering over her.

Or was that her fear?

She reaches for the crumpled pack of cigarettes on her desk.

She lights up, then scrolls back up the page.

As she feared, the boxes next to *Date of Birth* and *Place of Birth* are still blank.

Not that unusual. More often this happens if the defendant is older. Rap sheets don't always go back that far, especially if this is his first arrest.

There's no official record of William Henry Young's birth. No certificate listing the names of his parents or the hospital where he was born.

Of course, where he was born doesn't mean that was the place where he grew up. He could have moved to the Lowood area at any time.

That information wouldn't be on his rap sheet.

She scrolls down to the box below his photo.

His current address.

Many rap sheets list multiple addresses, especially if the defendant has a prior record.

On Young's, only one address is listed.

Four-Eleven West Fourteenth Street, New York, New York.

She vaguely recalls homicide lieutenant Vincent Medavoy testifying on direct that he went to the apartment building where the defendant lived and worked to bring him in for questioning.

And there's something else. She tries to bring it back, but she was taking all those meds during that time and missed a lot of witness testimony.

Alice emails Shavonne. A few minutes later, the trial transcript is on the screen.

She scrolls through until she finds the page she's looking for. Young's cross-examination of Vincent Medavoy.

"Twenty-seven years without a single complaint against me. Now how am I supposed to earn an honest living?"

Alice leans back in her chair.

Twenty-seven years.

Which means that Young wasn't working for his building's superintendent thirty years ago.

Maybe he wasn't living in New York City at all.

Because he was living in North Country? Somewhere off the radar?

She thinks again how little she knew about the man she first saw in the bar that long-ago night.

She had no idea if he was single or married. If he had a family.

Next, Alice scrolls through the defendant's Criminal Justice Agency sheet.

There had been no one in court to vouch for Young at his arraignment, forty-eight hours after he was arrested. Long before she came into the case.

No next of kin is listed.

On the CJA sheet, the *Family Contact* box is blank.

It's as if his entire earlier life has been erased.

He has no history. No past.

But he had to have come from somewhere.

He had a mother.

And a father.

Alice sees him in court during his cross-examination of Hannah Liu, the chief forensic pathologist for the Manhattan medical examiner's office. His crazy ranting and raving moments before she called everyone into chambers.

She clicks on the transcript again. Scrolls through until she finds what she's looking for.

Question: "Do you know who the father is?"

And thirteen questions and responses below that:

"The father of Angel Diallo's baby could have been any of those johns who paid for sex with her. He got jealous because she was sleeping with all those other men so he followed her to that abandoned lot!"

And two below that:

"Or maybe he wasn't the baby's father. And when he found out she was just taunting him and it was all a lie, he punished her by raping and killing her!"

At the time, Alice thought this was just more smoke and mirrors intended to distract and confuse the jury.

But now she's remembering the rage.

Rage at not knowing who his own father was?

She clicks again on the rap sheet. Scrolls up to the heading *Identification Information* above his mug shot.

There's only one name. The name she saw when she clicked on his rap sheet.

No aliases.

Nothing to tell her that William Henry Young was someone else thirty years ago.

And even if he were, what difference would that make?

She never exchanged a single word with the man she saw in the bar that long-ago night. Never heard his voice.

Yet from the moment their eyes met across the smoke-filled room, she felt as if she knew him.

And he knew her.

In the deepest, most primal sense.

Even if she didn't know his name.

TWENTY-EIGHT

Connie watches the new girl wipe off the salt and pepper shakers with her usual meticulousness. She places them carefully back on the table, then picks up the ketchup bottle. She takes off the lid and wipes that, too. Connie can't remember anyone she hired ever doing that, especially since no one sat in that booth during breakfast. She never does that herself, and she prides herself on keeping a clean diner.

Mia looks her way, as if she knows she's being watched. Connie smiles. The other woman doesn't smile back, her face expressionless as always. She goes back to cleaning the table. Wiping it down as if her life depended on it.

Connie's heart goes out to her. Although Mia's been working here going on five weeks now, she still knows so little about her, including her last name. What she does know is that behind that mask is a world of pain. Afraid if she lets down her guard, she'll shatter into a thousand pieces.

Connie knows all about that, too. God knows, it took her long enough to stop seeing herself as a victim. To stop defining herself by what her second husband did to her.

What she let him do to her.

For months after Walt ran Wade out of town, she lived in fear he'd come back and finish what he started. Knowing that the next time he'd do a lot worse than break her arm and a couple of ribs.

What kind of monster is Mia running from?

Was she forced to flee a place that had always been her home?

Connie can't imagine what it would be like to have to leave and start over in a strange new place.

She has lived in Lowood all her life. Her parents and their parents lived and died here. Like her children might have, if she'd carried any to term. Got lucky when she took over the diner from the man for whom she'd been waitressing for over ten years. Even with the small inheritance from her parents—God rest their souls—and the money she'd managed to squirrel away, it was a stretch. She had to take out a mortgage. And work her butt off, even now. But in the end it was worth it. Having a place of her own, knowing she has a stake in this town. Monte thinks she should rename the diner *Connie's Eats.*

The thought of Monte makes her smile. He's one of the good things in her life right now.

She doesn't look too far ahead anymore. She tries to take it one day at a time. It's the only way to get through.

She'd like to tell these things to Mia. She wished she had someone to talk to back then.

Someone who understood.

Someone who'd been there herself.

Who could tell you that everything was going to be all right.

It wasn't your fault.

You didn't do anything to deserve this.

Mia finished cleaning and setting up the booth for lunch. Now she's just standing there, staring out the window.

Connie can imagine the thoughts running through her mind.

Sooner or later, she's going to have to let it out. She can't keep her emotions bottled up forever. Can't spend the rest of her life running. Always looking over her shoulder.

She just needs someone she can trust. Walt could help her if she'd let him. "Mia?"

She doesn't react. Connie calls her name again.

The other woman whirls around, eyes wide.

Jesus. That bastard must have really done a number on her.

"Want something to eat before the lunch crowd shows up? I can fix us something."

"No, thanks." Mia's face shutters again.

"How about a piece of apple pie? It just came in today. I'm dying to taste it. I think I can manage to steal a slice for each of us. Just don't tell anyone." Connie winks.

She doesn't respond, but Connie didn't miss the way the other woman's eyes lit up when she mentioned the pie.

Mia has a sweet tooth.

"I've got some fresh coffee brewing," she says as the bell over the diner tinkles and Sean walks in from his break. "Want some pie?" Her words fall on deaf ears. Her summer cashier is too busy texting on his phone. "Got a hot date later?"

That gets his attention. The tips of Sean's ears turn red. Even after almost three months, he doesn't know how to react to her good-natured ribbing. "I was just kidding," Connie says as she cuts two slices of apple pie. "How is Jen?"

He doesn't answer. He looks like a deer caught in the headlights.

"You grew up here, Sean. You know you can't keep secrets in Lowood." She pours two mugs of coffee as Sean pulls up a stool. Mia's still staring outside. Connie can feel the tension radiating from her, as if she were ready to bolt at the first sign of danger.

Mia hasn't moved from the window when Connie heads for her office in the back to steal a few minutes before the next round of craziness starts. Lately, lunch has been even busier than breakfast.

Not that she's complaining. She remembers a time when she had very few customers and wondered how she'd stay in business. It took a long time for the stigma to wear off. Not that it ever faded completely. Not in this town.

She goes over to her desk. Flips the switch and waits for the ancient computer to rumble to life.

When the screen flickers on, she goes to her inbox.

She has a new email.

It came in late last night. But she's been expecting it for days.

She stares at the sender address, then clicks on the email.

> *Dear Ms. Moore,*
>
> *Thank you for your message and for friending me on Facebook. I'm happy to hear you knew Alice Dunn, who is my mother. As you probably know, my mother's family is from Lowood. Her father owned a hardware store on Main Street. His name was Nathan Dunn. Maybe you knew him. I'm interested in finding out about my mom's life when she lived there. I know it was a long time ago, but I'm hoping you can fill in some of the blanks.*
>
> *You can email me back at this address or message me. I look forward to hearing from you.*
>
> *Sincerely,*
>
> *Alexis McKerrity (Natalie Damien)*

Connie sits back in her chair.

She really did it now. Opened up that can of worms.

She flashes again to the last time she saw Alice, outside her window that freezing Saturday morning.

Her first thought was that she'd been attacked by an animal. Until she got her undressed.

Only a human animal could have inflicted those wounds.

And there were other wounds. Red bruises and welts on her throat. It took Connie a minute to realize that the necklace Alice wore on a gold chain around her neck was gone. Alice never took off the necklace that contained three entwined hearts, not even in phys. ed. class. She told Connie it was a gift from her mother. It was all she had left of her.

The necklace must have gotten ripped off during the attack.

Connie closes her eyes, pictures the half-smoked joint in her drawer. Getting high this early in the day would be a record, even for her. And she'll need more than that to shake off the memories.

She opens her eyes and rereads Alexis McKerrity's email.

After she saw her profile on her Natalie Damien Facebook page last week, she Googled Alice again.

This time she was looking for something specific.

She found it in the wedding announcements in the archives of the *New York Times*.

Alice Dunn married the Honorable Charles McKerrity on June 10, 2001.

Eighteen years ago.

Alexis McKerrity would have been ten.

That has to be why she posted on Lowood High's Facebook page. Using an alias on the page because she doesn't want her mother to know what she's up to. Alice's daughter has probably known for years that Charles McKerrity isn't her biological father.

I'm hoping you can fill in some of the blanks.

If she's right about this, what Connie doesn't know is why now.

Does it matter?

If Alice didn't see fit to tell her daughter—and Connie can understand that—how can she?

How can she betray her old friend?

She lied when she said you couldn't keep secrets in Lowood.

She did.

She kept Alice's secret all these years.

Never breathed a word to another living soul. Swore on the oath they took as blood sisters that she'd never tell.

Not even when those girls went missing.

Three weeks after Alice moved away, seventeen-year-old Kimberley Evans disappeared after leaving a party in the neighboring town of Renegade Falls.

Two months after that, sixteen-year-old Cannonville resident Ela Comstock vanished while walking home from the United Methodist Church where a Tuesday evening bingo game had been in progress.

That was when people stopped believing that wild, troubled Kim Evans had run away.

It was after Comstock disappeared that the words *serial killer* started to be heard on everyone's lips. When young Sheriff Walter Church led posses and cadaver dogs through the deep woods separating the three towns.

If Connie was right and it was the same man, only Alice could come forward with the truth. Connie had badly needed her to do that. All she had to do was tell Church what happened to her.

Describe her assailant.

But Alice had left town without so much as a goodbye.

After Connie's letters came back unanswered, she looked Alice up in the Yellow Pages, but there was no telephone number corresponding with the address in the town she and her father had settled in. The operator told her the number had been kept private at the owner's request.

Alice had severed all ties with Lowood and her best friend.

Not that Connie could blame her. If it weren't for her, Alice wouldn't have been attacked in the first place.

Those girls might still be alive.

And Teddy wouldn't have been brought in for questioning.

Connie's been thinking about Teddy a lot lately, what with Alice's daughter dredging up the past. Not that she ever stopped thinking about him.

How could she?

That's what she can't forgive Walter Church for.

To be fair, there had been mounting pressure to bring someone to justice. But in Connie's mind, Church made a rush to judgment.

Everyone had grown up on the legends about the soldiers buried in Old Lowood Cemetery. The tales just grew taller after the search disturbed some of their graves.

Teddy tried to defend himself by saying he was protecting their final resting place.

Church saw it as the act of a killer trying to cover up his crimes.

For months afterward, kids swore they saw the ghosts of the long-dead soldiers, vowing eternal vengeance.

Connie tried telling Church. Telling anyone who'd listen.

Teddy would never hurt a woman.

Her pleas fell on deaf ears.

Everyone was too busy pointing fingers.

She knew what was really going on.

They needed a scapegoat.

They had no real evidence against him. One of the town's biddies saying she saw a car driven by someone matching his description near the woods the night Kim Evans vanished?

How anyone could see the devil in Teddy's beautiful blue eyes and blond hair that framed his face like a halo was beyond her comprehension.

The bodies of Kimberley Evans and Ela Comstock were never found.

No one was arrested.

But the damage was done.

Teddy left town.

Connie never saw him again.

Just like Alice.

And now here was Alice's daughter trying to dig up the missing pieces of her mother's past.

She could stop it now, before it goes any further. All she has to do is write back and say *I'm sorry. I can't help you. I knew your mother, but not that well.*

A small lie to protect the bigger one.

So why is she hesitating?

Because Alexis McKerrity is the last link to her old friend.

Even if Alice wants to keep the past dead and buried.

Connie feels the old hurt bubbling up.

Once again, she's hit by a wall of memories.

The hot summer night Alice tore her new dress on a tree branch climbing out her bedroom window.

The snowy January afternoon she and Alice got drunk on Connie's father's expensive Scotch.

Having crushes on the same sexy senior when they were in ninth grade.

Inviting Alice for a sleepover the weekend of junior prom so Alice wouldn't be the only eleventh grader without a date.

Pricking their thumbs with Alice's grandmother's old sewing needle when they were thirteen. Becoming sisters in the flesh, swearing that nothing and no one would ever come between them.

Best friends forever.

TWENTY-NINE

Katharine Forster is getting ready to deliver her closing.

Alice looks at the defendant, his gray head bent over his legal pad.

Again, she realizes how little she knew about the man who raped her that long-ago night. She has thought about nothing else for days.

Who was he really?

Someone she saw across a crowded bar.

A fantasy who existed only in her mind.

In the head of a naïve sixteen-year-old girl desperate to escape her stifling home life and the fear and loneliness that were her constant companions. Jealous of her best friend. Tired of playing it safe.

Looking to a total stranger for danger and excitement.

For the love and attention her father couldn't give her.

All eyes are on Forster as she approaches the jury box.

This is the last time she will speak to the women and men seated there.

Then it will be up to them. To vote acquittal or conviction.

But it will be Alice's decision to hand down the sentence.

To find for mitigating circumstances and give him the minimum.

Or to deliver the maximum—life without the possibility of parole—that will lock him away in darkness for the rest of his natural life.

". . . The defendant talked to you about the parking lot behind the dance club. He told you that after hours, the dancers were selling sexual favors there. When he told you he wasn't interested, he was lying. Sex was the only thing he thought about. Sex was the reason he was at the dance club where he was observed at the same table every night . . ."

The courtroom fades as images fast-forward behind Alice's eyes.

She's seated at a table in a bar.

Waiting for her best friend to return with fresh drinks. Thinking it's going to take forever, what with the huge crush of people at the bar. Wishing she'd never come. Wondering if the guilt would ever go away. The mess she'd made of things. So many conflicting emotions raging through her.

". . . The defendant was sitting there because he was watching the dancers. But he was watching one dancer in particular. It was why he chose that table. Where he could have the best view of the victim . . ."

Something makes her look up.

She sees him.

But now Alice remembers something else.

The feeling that she was being watched before their eyes met across the bar.

"The defendant told you he wasn't stalking the victim. But the evidence tells a different story . . ."

She's walking home from choir practice on an unusually warm early December night.

She hears the purr of an engine.

She turns around.

Headlights are coming toward her.

". . . the evidence shows that the defendant was stalking the victim in the week leading up to her murder . . ."

The car slows down, then picks up speed as it races past. But she knows it was his blond head behind the wheel.

It's all part of the game that began that night at the bar.

Or had it started before then?

". . . You have heard multiple witnesses testify to having observed the defendant stalking the victim. Trying on numerous occasions to get her into his car . . ."

Her mind races ahead to the night of the party.

Hearing the sound of an engine as she walks down the street.

She stops. Turns.

Sees a car disappearing around a corner.

She continues walking. A few minutes later, she hears it again. When she turns around, she's blinded by the glare of headlights.

How long had he been stalking her?

How long before his eyes found hers that night at the bar?

". . . The defendant was obsessed with the victim. He was determined to consummate that obsession. But not in the parking lot behind the bar. Not like every other john. He told you that himself in his opening. 'Paying for sex in a parking lot in the middle of the night? That wasn't what I wanted.' He was telling the truth. That wasn't what he wanted. What he wanted was to have her all to himself. That's why he tried to get her into his car. But Angel Diallo refused."

Alice sees herself stepping off the curb that freezing winter night, ignoring the warning voice in her head.

Unlike Angel Diallo, she got into his car.

A willing victim.

". . . It should have saved her life . . ."

It takes a moment for Forster's words to sink in.

The prosecutor's right.

The fact that Angel Diallo didn't get into William Henry Young's car should have saved her life, and the life of her unborn child.

Why didn't it?

". . . Instead, the defendant became so enraged that he savagely raped and beat the victim with his fists. Then left her to die in that abandoned lot. All because she wouldn't get into his car to have sex."

Alice feels the spiked punch sloshing around in her belly. The combination of the alcohol and heat blasting through the vents making her sleepy.

She hears the groan of gears shifting.

The car starts moving.

She opens her eyes.

They just turned off the main road.

Onto the path that leads into the woods.

In the distance, she sees the headstones of Old Lowood Cemetery . . .

Alice feels a prickling at the back of her neck.

The defendant's looking at her.

She's running through the woods, the wail of the wind drowned out by the thunder of her heart. Then she hears something even more terrifying: a car door slamming. The sound echoes in her ears. He's coming after her. The headstones loom closer as she runs faster, picturing all the dead soldiers buried here.

Feeling as if she were passing over their graves . . .

And her own.

Young's eyes are still on her.

"What about all the others? How many women did Bundy rape and kill? You never told us the total number of victims."

He's smiling.

He knows he's safe.

No one knows about his other victims.

That was why he needed Angel Diallo to get into his car.

He said it himself, during his opening.

"... *she took her life in her hands every time she got into a stranger's car.*"

That was the reason he targeted working girls.

Because they're the only ones who get into strange men's cars, no questions asked.

They have no idea that they're being driven to their graves.

Forster's wrong.

It wasn't about sex.

It was never about sex.

"... the defendant has tried to portray himself as the victim here. Don't let him bamboozle you. Make no mistake. There is only one victim here."

Forster's wrong about that too.

That's what Young was trying to tell Alice during his cross-examination of the bite-mark expert.

He wanted her to know that Angel Diallo wasn't his first.

Alice was.

THIRTY

The jury's out.

Alice paces her chambers.

She can't stop thinking about them.

The women William Henry Young raped and killed.

She slides another cigarette from the pack. Her hand shakes so hard it takes three attempts to light up. As the nicotine starts to calm her nerves, she tries to reason things through.

If she isn't imagining things and Young really has been at this for decades—and he didn't graduate from her to Angel Diallo without others in between—his victims have to be buried somewhere.

She sees herself in his car again that long-ago night, driving into the woods.

There are endless miles of forestland in New York State. Plenty of places to bury bodies.

Or maybe he isn't burying them. Maybe he's disposing of them in different places.

Dump sites. Landfills. Rivers. Wastelands. Does it matter?

If he's acquitted, his victims will never be found.

He'll go on abducting working girls from the city like Angel Diallo. Marginalized women no one will miss.

And no one can stop him.

Because there's no living proof.

No other survivors.

Except Alice.

But what exactly is she proof of?

She can't connect Young to any other victims.

Nor can she connect those victims to herself.

Or prove that William Henry Young is the man who raped her.

—⁂—

The jury is still deliberating.

As the days pass without a verdict, doubt creeps in, poisoning her mind.

She never saw her rapist's face.

Angel Diallo was assaulted and murdered eight months ago in an abandoned lot in Manhattan.

Alice was assaulted almost thirty years ago in the woods in a town more than three hundred miles away.

And there's something else.

Unlike Angel Diallo, Alice wasn't tortured.

In the end, what does she really have?

Conjecture and supposition.

Suspicions without foundation.

And nightmares.

Dreams that reveal as much about her as they do about him.

None of that has any place in the law.

The only thing that matters is facts. Evidence.

Not that that would make any difference now.

The statute of limitations on her rape expired a long time ago.

He can't be held accountable for what he did to her.

He can't be punished.

—◊—

There's a note from the jury.

Alice studies him as she enters the courtroom. He's on his feet with everyone else, staring at the floor.

He hasn't looked at her since Katharine Forster's closing.

If he even did.

Did she imagine that?

Imagine all those other times he looked at her?

—◊—

She's starting to unravel.

Not sleeping.

Barely eating.

One minute, she's sure it's him.

The next, she's certain that she's being paranoid.

She's afraid she can't trust her own senses.

Can no longer distinguish between what's real and what isn't.

—◊—

She's counting the days until the trial is over.

Only then can she move on. Move beyond this agonizing uncertainty that's destroying her fragile equilibrium. Making her doubt her sanity even more.

The truth is that she can never know for sure.

She has to make peace with that.

Or she really will lose her mind.

—m—

She wishes she could talk to Charles.

But she knows what he'd say.

She can hear him now. Telling her that even if she can't be sure to an absolute certainty—the legal benchmark that leaves no room for doubt—if there's even a one percent chance that it's him, she knows what she has to do.

It isn't too late. As long as the jury's out, the trial is still ongoing.

Alice knows what would happen if she recused herself.

There would be a mistrial. Young would be remanded into custody until a new trial began. With a new jury.

And a new judge.

She'd also have to give a reason for her recusal. Go on record.

Then the world would know her secret.

Including Alexis.

There's so much that her daughter doesn't know.

THIRTY-ONE

Alexis checks her mail again.

Constance Moore still hasn't written back.

Maybe she never got Alexis's email.

Or she knows something and doesn't want to tell her.

Then why did she respond to Alexis's Facebook post?

Maybe she got cold feet. Decided to stay loyal to Alexis's mom. Loyal about what? All she wanted was for Moore to fill in the blanks about her mother. Alexis never mentioned anything about her father.

Maybe the reason Moore is staying silent has nothing to do with him.

Then why is Alexis so sure it does?

Or she just wants it to be. Damien always says that if you want something badly enough, you can make it happen. He had to believe that. Or he'd never have survived that horrible foster home.

He never knew his father.

That's why it's so important for her to find *her* father.

She rubs a hand across her belly.

I'll never abandon you, Natalie or Nathan.

She hopes it's a boy. So he can have her grandfather's name.

She's going to keep her promise.

At least her mother didn't do that to her. Leave her in some creepy orphanage or foster home.

In her heart of hearts, she knows her mom did the best she could. What she can't forgive are the lies.

And why her mother lied in the first place.

He's got to be married. That's the answer that makes the most sense. Her mom got involved with some older guy who wasn't going to leave his wife and family.

She was so young when Alexis was born. Being an unwed teenage parent must have been really hard back then. Especially with Grandpa Nathan being so strict. It must have been hard for him, too, the reason he sold his family's hardware store in Lowood and moved to Jonasville, a town even farther north. Although he was never anything but sweet and loving to her.

She can only imagine how scared her mother must have felt, knowing she was responsible for this life growing inside her.

Alexis feels that way now. But she isn't sixteen. She has Damien. And her mom.

Except Damien doesn't know yet because every time she plans to tell him, the timing isn't right.

And she can't tell her mother because she's been acting so crazy lately. Alexis is still freaked out about the night she pointed the gun at her.

That's why she went to court last week. She was worried about her.

Big mistake. She still has nightmares about the defendant holding that mold of his teeth, staring at her. It was like something out of a horror film. He really creeped her out.

She doesn't know how her mom can stand being around scary guys like that every day. Maybe that's why she's been acting so weird.

Her phone beeps.

Alexis swipes it off her nightstand.

It's the alert she set to remind herself that the train leaves in an hour.

She already has a story for her mother.

If her mom even notices that she's gone.

THIRTY-TWO

Katharine Forster just informed Alice that she discussed the possibility of a plea with the defendant, who rejected the offer.

Not surprising. It's been over a week. Everyone knows that the longer a jury's out, the better the chances for acquittal.

Young must be confident that he's going to get off.

Alice thinks she knows who it is.

Juror #5.

Alice is sure she saw her looking at Young as if she believed he was innocent.

She must be the holdout.

It takes only one.

—m—

It's Friday, the eve of Labor Day weekend.

Shavonne just texted her.

There's another note.

As Alice puts on her robe, she already knows what the note will say.

They're unable to reach a verdict.

But the note isn't from the jury.

THIRTY-THREE

The defendant watches her as a court officer hands Alice his note.

She unfolds the single sheet of paper.

And sees five words that almost stop her heart.

I KNOW WHO YOU ARE.

She looks up.

He's still staring

She forces herself to read the rest of the note.

> *Meet me in your chambers.*
> *Alone.*

He's smiling now, a closed-mouthed grin that doesn't show his teeth.

If she had any lingering doubts, she knows now.

And if she doesn't take the bait?

What will he do then?

Tell her secret to the world?

That means he'd have to admit that he did it before. Maybe he knows he can't be charged with Alice's assault because the statute of limitations has expired.

All she'd have to do is deny it. Who would believe a rapist and killer over a respected judge? There's no evidence to back up his story. She never went to the police. Even her best friend Connie didn't know the details about that night.

Especially her.

But what if by some chance Young were believed?

There would be a mistrial, after all.

But this mistrial would be the result of judicial misconduct.

Double jeopardy would attach.

He'd walk out of her courtroom a free man.

Over her dead body.

The courtroom's growing restless.

He's still smiling.

She's going to wipe that death's-head grin off his face.

Alice tells the jury that she's excusing them for the holiday weekend. She instructs the court clerk to order extra security to the south side of the building to escort the jurors out.

After the jury is gone, Alice looks out over the courtroom.

She's thinking about karmic destiny.

In a voice that's strong and steady—the voice that's been silent for thirty years—she explains that the defendant has requested a conference to discuss a plea in light of the fact that the jury has not yet returned a verdict. The conference can't take place at One Hogan Place, the offices of the Manhattan DA. Young may be acting as his own attorney, but he's also the defendant and not permitted to leave the courthouse.

He's obviously looking for a deal and thinks he has something to bargain with.

Over her dead body.

THIRTY-FOUR

A little over an hour after she calls a recess, Alice is back in the courtroom.

She orders the defendant to rise.

As Young gets to his feet, the officers seated behind him—two males who have served in her Part before—follow suit. The male and female officers who were here during the trial are absent today, which isn't uncommon. Court officers often trade shifts, especially on the eve of a holiday weekend.

It doesn't make a whit of difference. The only thing that matters is that Alice's loyal officer Luiz is here.

She instructs Luiz to bring the defendant to the holding cell behind her courtroom. She'll let him know when to bring the defendant into chambers. Luiz doesn't cuff Young before he leads him out, just as he didn't when Alice called them into her chambers after shutting down Young's cross-examination of Dr. Liu. She ruled on the first day of voir dire that the defendant wasn't to be shackled in her courtroom. Before she ever laid eyes on William Henry Young.

Her chambers are an extension of her courtroom.

Everything is falling into place.

Alice tells Katharine Forster that she has a call to make and to wait in the courtroom. She'll let her know when she's ready for the conference.

The court reporter stands. Alice waves her back into her seat. "This isn't for the record."

Young gives an imperceptible nod.

He thinks she's caving into his demands.

She is.

The two of them will be alone in her chambers.

But only one will leave alive.

THIRTY-FIVE

Charles surveys the wreckage of the room.

This won't do. This won't do at all.

Everyone knows he likes things orderly. Everything in its place. Who's responsible for this mess?

Someone must be held accountable. Someone commits a crime. Someone has to be punished. That's the way the law works. The trick is to temper the law with mercy. That's the hallmark of a great jurist.

The law isn't justice. Whoever said it was? The law has nothing to do with justice. The law must prevail. Justice may not. That doesn't give you the right to take the law into your own hands.

Charles frowns. Something's buzzing around his head. He swats at the air. Now the buzzing has become a dull roar in his ears. He stamps his foot in frustration.

Why did he come in here?

Objection!

Charles looks around the courtroom in amazement. On what grounds is the defense attorney objecting? It was a properly framed question. That was one of the first things he learned in law school. The secret is always in how the question is framed.

If he could just remember what the question was.

In his most authoritative voice, he asks the court reporter to read it back.

But after it's read back, Charles shakes his head. The words make no sense.

He has no idea how to rule.

The seconds stretch into minutes. Panic tightens his chest. The entire courtroom is waiting. Then he hears it. The sound of computer keys. Thank god. On his right, his court attorney finishes typing on her laptop. Within seconds, the email comes soundlessly into the computer open in front of him on the bench. He reads the word in the subject line.

"Sustained." His voice rings out, clear as a bell.

The prosecutor resumes questioning the witness. The defense attorney makes another objection. It sounds like gobbledygook. How is he supposed to rule on this nonsensical jabberwocky? Behind his eyes he sees Alice having high tea with the Mad Hatter and the March Hare.

Alice?

Alice?

There it is again, that droning in his head.

It's my brain, Charles thinks in a fading moment of lucidity. It's dying.

All the more reason to figure out why he came in here. He knows it was important.

With renewed determination, he moves through the rubble, stopping at an overturned dresser drawer. Getting down on his hands and knees, he sorts through the clothing strewn all over the carpet. He picks up a nightgown and holds it against his face as he sniffs at the delicate material.

Images flood his brain.

She's lying in bed, the blanket pulled modestly up to her chin. He can't believe she's his, that he found someone after being lonely for so many years. He'd been secretly in love with her for months, since the first day he saw her, in his courtroom arguing a case. So brilliant and fearless in court, now cowering in their marital bed.

"Don't you know you have nothing to be afraid of?" he said as he moved closer to the bed. "I would never hurt you. Never." Feeling his own anger rising at the monster who did this to her. Smiling reassuringly as he reached for her, ready to show her that passion between a man and a woman could be tender and gentle. It was a promise he was determined to keep, because he loved her. And in spite of what had happened to her, she'd chosen to give him the gift of her love in return. Which made him the luckiest man in the world.

The memories are fading. Charles claws at the air to bring them back. But they're already disappearing, as ethereal as Alice's nightgown.

Tears blur his vision as his body starts to shut down. The body always goes first, reducing him to a trembling, babbling idiot. Now his thoughts are losing their moorings, bouncing around in his head and echoing back at him without direction or meaning. A familiar film descends over his mind, turning day into night. A not entirely unpeaceful state of being. As seductive as sleep, as permanent as death.

Charles struggles to stay conscious. He can't give in. Alice needs him.

He sniffs the air again. It's the perfume she always wears. Alice was here recently.

He knows that this, too, is important. But why? Why did he come in here?

Think, man!

But it's no good. Everything's fading.

Alice. He has to stay focused on Alice.

He looks around the room.

Where is Alice?

Why is Alice?

"Objection! Improper foundation."

"Overruled!"

What is he overruling? He's lost the thread of his thoughts.

He sees his mother at the kitchen table, sewing a button back on his white shorts. It popped off after he aced that serve. He won the match, *two, love.*

Wrong court!

Not a tennis court, then.

A kangaroo court?

His vision fills with kangaroos, hopping up and down.

Stop it! He shakes his head, but the images won't go away. He heaves himself to his feet and starts trudging through the mess. Halfway across the room, he stops. So does the person who's been watching him. Charles raises an arm. So does he. Charles forces himself to keep moving. He stops again when he gets to the bureau. An old man is staring back at him, his eyes full of fear and confusion. In a sudden fury, Charles slams his hand down on the dressing table, sending brushes and combs and bottles flying.

He sinks back down to the carpet in despair. Sobs wrack his body as he looks wildly around. His gaze fixes on the nightstand next to the bed. He tries to ignore the din in his head as he struggles to concentrate.

"Charles! There you are."

A stranger is standing in the doorway.

He's still talking as he comes into the room. Charles wishes he'd stop. The twanging of his voice is distracting him from his purpose.

"Why are you in here? Were you looking for something?"

That's it! With a cry of triumph, he scrambles to his feet, almost losing his balance in his haste.

He has to find it.

After all, he bought it for her. And now he's taking it back.

He's doing this for her own good. Alice hasn't been herself lately. He's worried about her.

Afraid she's going down the slippery slope.

Slope?

He sees himself skiing down the mountain, the sun reflecting off the snow blinding him.

Not a ski slope, you idiot!

Another image fills his brain.

He and Alice are at a gun range. Alice just hit the bullseye. She's becoming a good shot.

"Is it on Alice's bed? Tell me what it is and I can help you find it."

Charles looks at the pillow he's holding, then down at the empty sheets.

He was so sure it was there.

Don't most people keep them under their pillows?

Where is it?

Doesn't Alice know it's a dangerous weapon?

Someone could get killed.

He has to stop her.

"Where are you going? Charles?"

He pushes roughly past the stranger. He races down the stairs, the man in hot pursuit.

"Charles, come back here! You're not dressed!"

He covers his ears as he hurries through the front hall, the man's voice more white noise in his head.

But he keeps on talking. He clearly doesn't understand the gravamen of the situation.

At the front door, he stops. A chain lies across the top half. He wrinkles his forehead as he tries to figure out how to remove it. As he reaches for the chain, a hand touches his shoulder.

"Let go of me!"

But the man holds fast. Now he's gripping both his shoulders, pulling him back from the door. Charles struggles against him, almost losing his footing, shocked to glance down and discover he's barefoot.

The man's still holding him, babbling some nonsense about having breakfast. Doesn't he realize what's at stake? Charles wrenches himself away. Before the man can grab him again, he turns on him. As his arm shoots out, the man grabs his wrist.

"What have I told you about hitting people? You don't want to hurt anyone, do you? Remember how you cried for days after you hit your daughter?"

That stops him in his tracks.

What is he talking about?

He doesn't have a daughter.

Confusion clouds his brain. He sees himself getting into bed with Alice. Did they make a baby? Not on their honeymoon, even though she put on that pretty new nightgown just for him. She was too frightened. It was months before she let him touch her. He had to be so gentle with her. So patient.

He loves her so much. Does she know?

"Charles?"

He feels so tired. Is it time for bed?

"Come on. You haven't eaten yet today. I'll make you some eggs."

Charles doesn't resist as the man leads him away from the door. In the dining room, the man pulls out his chair for him. Then he hands him the newspaper. Charles nods as he takes it from him. He likes the feel of it in his hands. He likes the neat, orderly way the black symbols march across the white page. When he has finished counting them, he turns to the next page.

"Here you go."

Charles peers out from behind the paper. Delicious smells are permeating the air. His stomach grumbles as the man places a steaming plate in front of him.

"I have to get a move on. I have a full calendar today."

"There's plenty of time, Your Honor. Maybe before you get dressed, we could clean up Alice's room."

Charles looks up from his plate. He frowns.

Who is Alice?

THIRTY-SIX

Her court attorney never takes her eyes from her as Alice rises from the bench.

Shavonne starts to get to her feet as well, as if to stop her before she does something she'll regret.

It's too late.

Alice leaves the courtroom through the door behind the bench and goes into the hallway that leads to chambers.

As she passes the holding cell where Young is seated on a bench, Luiz standing guard over him, Alice feels a sense of déjà vu. It's the same tableau she saw the day she called everyone into chambers after Young acted out during his cross-examination of Dr. Liu.

The difference is that she didn't have a gun in the top drawer of her desk, where she placed it a short while earlier after making a pit stop at home.

She was glad Alexis was away. Spending a few nights with a friend, her note had said. Otherwise, her daughter might really think her mother had lost her mind.

It's very likely that she has.

When Alice checked on him, even Charles looked at her with a worried frown. As if he knew what she was about to do.

Her initial instinct had been to conceal the gun in her robe pocket. But walking into her courtroom with a loaded weapon for the brief time it would take to put her plan into action would have made her feel too much like a criminal. Even a deranged one. Not having it on her physical person will make her feel less guilty and be easier on her conscience when she tells the story of how the defendant overpowered her in her chambers. That was when she opened her desk drawer—where, as she'll explain, she kept a licensed firearm for years—and shot William Henry Young in self-defense.

After telling Luiz that the prosecutor will be along in a few minutes, Alice instructs him to bring the defendant into chambers. As she walks down the hall, she can hear them behind her. When she reaches the door, Alice tells Luiz to wait outside.

"I'm sorry, but you can't come any farther. You can't be a witness to what I have to say in camera."

Luiz's dark eyes narrow as a frown crosses his face. "But—" He gestures toward Young. "He's the defendant."

Alice was prepared for this. "And as you know he elected to represent himself. That's his right under the law." And the critical component of her plan.

Defendants aren't allowed in chambers.

But their attorneys are.

"Your Honor." Luiz is struggling to come up with an argument. "The defendant may be acting as his own lawyer, but he's still my responsibility."

In court, a judge's power is absolute. Everything that goes on there is under her control. Except for the physical bodies. They're under the jurisdiction of the Department of Corrections, which is responsible for transporting defendants between Rikers, the Tombs, and the courthouse. Once a defendant enters the courtroom, the correction officers cede their power to the court officers, who are employed by the New York City courts. Which is under the aegis of the NYPD.

Luiz's boss.

Luiz is also an officer in her courtroom. He has been with Alice a long time.

And everyone knows that the last thing you want is to get on the wrong side of a judge.

As Luiz weighs his options, his right hand rests on his holster.

Young's eyes track his every move.

Alice is abruptly aware of how close together they're standing. She could have ordered Young to be reshackled before they left the courtroom. Would have loved nothing better than to chain him up. But that wouldn't have fit in with her plan.

"You'll call if you need me?"

Luiz is capitulating. His future as an officer in her courtroom carried the day, as she hoped it would.

"Of course," Alice tells him. "And you'll be here, right outside."

Inside, the mahogany-paneled walls should muffle some of the noise.

Luiz nods. "Whatever you say, Your—"

He never finishes his sentence.

Young just stabbed him in the neck.

Now he's got his gun.

"You scream or try to run, you both die."

Young points the Glock at Alice. "Open the door."

"You'll never get away with it." Her teeth are chattering so hard, she can barely speak.

"Now."

Young follows them into the anteroom. As they pass the empty chair at her court attorney's desk, where Shavonne is her barrier to the rest of the world, Alice feels hysteria bubble up. Still unable to believe that this is actually happening. Until they reach the door to her chambers, and she feels the barrel of the Glock in the small of her back.

Once inside, Young closes the door. As Luiz tries to stanch the blood gushing from his throat, Young butts him in the head with the gun.

He falls.

"Take off his jacket."

Alice shakes her head, doesn't realize she's backing up until Young aims the Glock at her heart.

She drops to her knees.

Luiz isn't moving.

Young places the Glock against Alice's forehead.

"Do it!"

Her hands are shaking so badly she can barely get the buttons undone.

"Faster!"

When she's finished, Young switches gun hands to shrug off his suit jacket and puts on Luiz's dark-navy jacket, with the *NY State Courts* insignia on the sleeve. He unsnaps the handcuffs attached to Luiz's belt and slips them into one of the jacket pockets. Then he reaches into the upper left pocket and removes Luiz's sunglasses.

Alice looks down at her court officer, who still hasn't moved, his blood staining the carpet.

Rage rises up.

That was supposed to be Young's blood.

There's a knock at the door.

"Judge? Is everything okay?"

On the other side of the door, her court attorney's voice is muffled. Alice presses her knuckles against her mouth to keep from screaming. Shavonne is repeating the same question she asked as she stood in the doorway to Alice's chambers on the first day of voir dire.

Before William Henry Young walked into her courtroom.

No! Alice wants to shout, just as she wanted to shout that morning. *Everything is not okay!*

Young grabs her, shoves her to her feet. "Get her out of here," he whispers. "Don't try anything. If you open the door, everyone dies."

He places the Glock against the back of her head.

"Everything's fine." Alice raises her voice, knowing that no one will hear her but Shavonne. Forcing out the same lie she told her that morning, when Shavonne looked at her as if she didn't believe her.

Praying that she doesn't believe her now.

The Glock's pressing into her skull.

"Go back into the courtroom," Alice hears herself say, her voice unnaturally loud in her ears. "We'll be out in a few minutes."

In the silence that follows, she holds her breath.

"Okay, Judge. Text if you need me."

As she hears her court attorney's footsteps on the wood floor of the anteroom die away, Alice feels her own hope of rescue dying.

"Get the key to the elevator. Now!"

How does he know about that?

Then she realizes that this is her chance.

Biting down on her lower lip to keep calm, she goes to her desk. Her mind picturing her gun in the top drawer.

But how can she shoot him with the Glock against the back of her head?

"This what you're looking for?"

Young's holding the elevator key he just scooped up from the disk on top of her desk.

"Walk to the door." He indicates the door that leads to the outer hallway.

Despair fills her as she moves away from the desk.

Outside, the hallway is empty. It's the eve of Labor Day weekend. Hers is the only courtroom in session.

The Glock is against the small of her back as Young secures the stairwell, which can be locked from the outside in the event of a prisoner escaping.

"Unlock the elevator."

He planned everything, down to the last detail.

He had to have had help.

Alice unlocks the elevator. Young follows her into the car, her stomach bottoming out as they descend.

The door opens on the ground floor.

She almost faints with relief when she sees the officer at the door. It isn't Henry, the usual weekday officer, but that doesn't matter. She'd been afraid that when she diverted security to the south side of the building, this entrance would have been left unguarded.

All at her direction.

"Jury was dismissed early," Young tells the officer. "I'm escorting Judge McKerrity out of the building."

Alice stares at the officer, pleading with her eyes.

He looks at her, then at Young. Reaches for his weapon.

A shot rings out.

The officer falls.

Alice hears a loud crack, followed by the shattering of glass.

Young just shot out the security camera in the ceiling.

"Move!"

He pushes her past the officer's body.

Outside, a car is parked at the curb.

A woman is behind the wheel.

Young forces her into the back seat, then gets in next to her.

Alice looks over her shoulder.

There's no one on the street.

When she turns around, Young is smiling.

With a roar of the engine, the car speeds away from the curb.

PART II

PUNISHMENT

THIRTY-SEVEN

"**W**e're running low on gas."

Her voice is deep and husky; unfamiliar. In the courtroom, she never spoke. Alice remembers how she watched him, her eyes tracking his every move. Ready to act at the slightest provocation.

No one would have ever guessed they were having a relationship.

Planning his escape.

While she sat behind him in court every day.

Until this morning.

He got the idea when Alice called everyone into chambers after she shut down his cross-examination of Dr. Liu.

She was the one who told him everything he needed to know about how to escape from the courthouse.

He already had the weapon.

It wasn't the shank he used on another inmate that landed him in solitary confinement until Alice ordered him to be produced the first day of jury selection.

This was something more ingenious. And diabolical.

It started at the Rikers dental unit, where a mold of his teeth was made to be used at trial. After a badly decayed tooth was discovered, he was sent to Bellevue, where urgent procedures are performed on inmates with poor dental hygiene or who have gotten into fights with other inmates.

At Bellevue, his tooth was drilled and ground down with a sharp tool shaped like a dart that was attached to the end of a handheld instrument. After he finished, the dentist, a recent dental school graduate inexperienced with inmate patients, disengaged the tool and laid it on a swivel tray next to other tools he'd been using.

He inadvertently left the tray within Young's reach.

Young made his move when the correction officer standing guard outside was distracted by another officer and the dentist told Young to rinse his mouth, then turned his back to wash his hands. Young's handcuffs had been unshackled from his leg chains so he could reach for the cup. Which was what he did, right after he took the tool off the tray and put it in his mouth. He already had an explanation if it set off the metal detector when he was taken back to Rikers: The dentist had accidentally left it in his mouth.

The detector didn't go off.

That was because the tool didn't contain any metal. It was a diamond bur, a small cutting tool three millimeters in diameter commonly used by dentists for crowns. Young concealed the bur in his cell in a tiny hole at the bottom of the concrete wall that he'd watched a cockroach crawl out of.

The bur was in his mouth when he was brought into court this morning. It would have been hard to talk, but he didn't have to. His words were in the note he'd given the court officer to hand off to Alice.

Everything went according to plan until Alice instructed Luiz to wait outside, forcing Young to stab Luiz in the hall instead of her chambers, which was riskier. Even when Shavonne showed up, luck was still on his side.

Every ruling Alice made he managed to turn against her.

Refusing to let him be shackled in court.

Allowing him to go pro se, which gave him access to her chambers.

Now she's his prisoner. And her gun is still sitting in the top drawer of her desk.

As if he knows what she's thinking, he presses the Glock harder into Alice's side. "How much you got left in the tank, darlin'?"

"We're on reserve." In the rearview mirror, the court officer's eyes meet his. She seems tense. Uneasy.

Afraid?

"There's a station in the next town. Quarter mile at most. Should be enough to get us there."

Where?

Where is he taking her?

She has no idea how much time has passed since he abducted her from the courthouse. It feels as if they've been on the road forever, Young boasting about his brilliant escape as they drove along non-toll and service roads to avoid detection. How no one was ever going to catch up to them. Unlike the botched escape by two killers from Dannemora a few years ago.

As the hours go by, Alice's hope of rescue grows dimmer.

Thanks to her, they had a sizable head start while Katharine Forster waited in the courtroom to be given the green light to join them in chambers. Who knows how long it took before she grew suspicious about the call Alice told her she had to make? Or Shavonne realized that Alice was lying again. Or someone noticed that the camera in the ceiling on the first floor wasn't working.

And the security guard's body was found.

Alice prays that Luiz is alive.

Or that will be two deaths that can be laid at her door.

"I can't tell you how long I prayed. On my knees every night in that filthy, godforsaken cell. Only this time it wasn't the Lord answering my prayers. It was you. I couldn't have done it without you, sweetheart."

His voice rasps like sandpaper in her ear. He presses the Glock deeper into Alice's ribs. Her eyes water.

"How do you reckon I should show my appreciation?" he whispers. "Any ideas? I can think of a few." He moves closer. Her flesh crawls where his hot breath touches her skin.

In the mirror, the officer's watching them.

The fear Alice saw earlier replaced by something else.

Jealousy.

"Turn right here."

As they pull into the station, Young instructs her to drive to the full serve pump at the far end. "Pay in cash. Don't get out of the car."

The place isn't busy; too far off the beaten track. There are only two other cars, both at self-serve pumps. One driver—a man in a checked shirt and shorts—is pumping gas, his eye on the gallons racking up. The other—a woman in a green-and-white halter dress—is getting back into her SUV.

As they drive to the other end, Alice looks around for other signs of life. All she sees is a small, squat building with the garish multi-colored signs advertising different brands of beer, along with tickets for Powerball.

Through one of its long windows, Alice can see the man behind the cash register. He's on his phone. A woman in a flowered blouse and white pants emerges from a small, stand-alone structure next door. She glances briefly their way as she passes. She stops at the cream-colored sedan at the other end where the man in the checked shirt has finished pumping and is getting his receipt. Alice watches them get into the sedan. As they drive past, the woman turns around. But it's just to drag her seat belt over her shoulder.

Now they're the only car in the station. An attendant approaches. He's small and thin, with long dark hair pulled back in a ponytail. He doesn't look older than sixteen.

The officer rolls down her window.

"Cash or charge?" the attendant asks.

"Cash."

"Regular or premium?"

"Regular."

"Fill 'er up?"

She nods.

The attendant's gaze shifts to the back seat.

Young smiles at him.

The attendant doesn't smile back.

The Glock is in Young's pocket now. But Alice feels it digging into her ribs as the attendant's gaze shifts to her.

She holds her breath, praying he can read the message in her eyes.

Hope dies as he walks around to the passenger side. He twists off the cap and inserts one of the nozzles into the gas tank. After the tank is full and the gas cap on again, he walks back around to the driver's side.

"Forty bucks."

She hands him two twenties.

"Want your windshield cleaned?"

"No, thanks."

"Need a receipt?"

"No, thanks."

With a shrug of his narrow shoulders, the attendant walks away. Alice chokes down a sob of despair.

When they pull out of the station, a mist hangs over the road. What began as a hot, sunny morning has deteriorated into a gray, bleak afternoon.

As they drive, the mist grows thicker.

The decreasing visibility will cost them more time.

But the fog also provides cover.

The Lord answering his prayers?

"Pull over."

THIRTY-EIGHT

She sees it in the mirror.

The fear is back in the officer's eyes that Alice is sure mirrors her own.

Have they reached the endgame? After all this?

To be shot on the side of the road like animals?

Young laughs. "You should see your faces. Don't worry. It'll only take a few minutes. Can't ignore the call of nature." In a flash, he's out of the car and leaning into the driver's window. "While I relieve myself, be a good girl and keep an eye on the judge."

He winks at Alice, then turns and vanishes into the gloom.

For a second, neither of them moves.

"What was he whispering to you about?"

She's half-turned in her seat, her weapon pointed at Alice.

"Does it matter? He's going to kill us. We have to get out of here." When she doesn't answer, Alice presses her advantage, talking fast while keeping an eye out for Young. "We can drive away now, before he gets back."

The officer shakes her head. "I'm not going anywhere without Bill."

Alice stares at her in disbelief, even as her mind's eye conjures a blond-haired, blue-eyed stranger across a crowded bar.

Almost thirty years later, he can still cast a spell.

"Don't you understand?" Alice says, desperate to get through to her. "You served your purpose. We're going to end up like his other victims."

"What other victims?" The officer's eyes spark with suspicion. And jealousy. "I should have known. I could feel it in court. There's something going on between the two of you. You're just trying to get me out of the way so you can have him all for yourself."

"No! You've got it all—"

Alice's words are cut off by the officer's scream.

A face is plastered against the passenger side window.

In the darkening gloom, it's impossible to make out any features.

Alice sees his profile that long-ago night as they drove down dark, deserted streets.

The face disappears from the glass.

Seconds later, Young sticks his head in the driver's window. "Scare easily, don't you?" He plants a kiss on the officer's forehead, then opens the rear door and slides in next to Alice. "You girls have a nice chat while I was gone?"

In the mirror, the officer's eyes shoot daggers at Alice. "She tried to get me to leave you."

"You don't say?"

"Let's get rid of her. We don't need her anymore."

"Not yet."

"Why not?"

"Don't you read the good book? Patience is a virtue."

"But—"

"All in the Lord's good time. Enough chitchatting. Let's get this show on the road."

The car starts moving again. At a snail's pace because of the fog.

Now it's impossible to see out the window at all.

"Bill?"

"What?"

"We're still going to Mexico, aren't we?"

"Sure."

"What are you going to do with her?"

"I haven't decided yet. The judge and I go back a long way, don't we, darlin'?"

Alice couldn't answer if she wanted to. The Glock's digging into her side. She clenches her teeth against the pain.

"What does that mean? Are you sleeping with her?"

"I said that's enough chitchatting for now."

He eases up on the pressure, but now it hurts just to breathe.

"You'd never hurt me, would you?"

"I said enough! Stop whining and keep your eyes on the road."

Something moves in front of the car.

"Watch out!" Young shouts.

She cuts the wheel. The car swerves to the left, then brakes to a stop.

Alice's body pitches forward. Young grabs her before she hits the passenger headrest.

Outside the window, it stands frozen in the glare of the fog lights, eyes glowing with terror.

"You missed her. One of the Lord's stupider creatures. Serving no earthly use. Roll down the window."

Young raises his arm. The gunshot thunders through the car.

Through the open passenger window, Alice watches the deer fall. Hears a sickening thud as it hits the ground.

"Should have run when she had the chance."

Young's voice is tinged with regret. "Staring at me with those innocent doe eyes like she was waiting for me to save her. Only the Lord can do that. And I'm not sure even He can. Let's get the hell out of here."

She guns the engine. It sputters, then dies.

"Try it again. Again!"

On the fourth try, the engine ignites.

Young looks up. "Thank you, Lord. Forgive me for losing faith for a moment back there."

Alice's heart sinks as the car starts moving again.

Whoever he's giving thanks to isn't her God.

It isn't anyone's.

THIRTY-NINE

The sign rises out of the mist like a mirage.

WELCOME TO THE TOWN OF LOWOOD

POP. 3,500

A part of Alice is still in shock. The other part wondering why she didn't figure it out sooner.

North Country.

They're driving on Route 12, a twisting, two-lane highway that follows the Black River Valley and cuts through all the towns and villages. Even in the fog, she can see that it hasn't changed in all these years.

She also knows what lies on the other side of the highway.

Woods.

Miles and miles of woods.

The place she sees in her worst nightmares.

Young starts whistling.

Through his teeth.

"Bill?"

He doesn't answer.

"We are going to Mexico, right?"

He stops whistling. "Turn here."

He turns off the main road.

Onto the path leading into the woods.

As they drive in deeper, she sees them.

The headstones of Old Lowood Cemetery rising out of the dark.

"You can stop here, darlin'."

He switches off the engine.

Turns to her.

His teeth a sudden flash of white in the darkness.

It isn't the way he smiled at her across the bar. It seems like a thing apart from his eyes. The blue eyes that now look so cold.

And empty.

He leans toward her.

He's still smiling.

"Something wrong, Your Honor? You're not afraid of the woods, are you?"

"What are we doing here? Bill?"

"Just making a pit stop, darlin.'"

"But—what about—"

"I'll take care of the judge. Don't worry."

The officer looks at him in the mirror.

Her face changes.

She reaches for her weapon, but she's too late.

Young shoots her in the back of the head.

She slumps over the wheel.

The horn starts blaring.

It rouses Alice from her shock.

The officer just moved.

She's still alive.

As Young aims the Glock again, Alice realizes this is her chance.

Her hand is on the door handle as the second shot rings out.

She pushes open the door. Bolts from the car.

And runs.

FORTY

She's running blindly through the darkness.

Her high heels are long gone, sharp pebbles slashing her bare feet as she stumbles over rocks and tree roots. Low-hanging branches stab her face.

She runs faster, the wail of the wind drowned out by the thunder of her heart. A car door slams, the sound echoing in her ears. Now she's running between the headstones, where the soldiers are buried.

Running over their graves.

And hers.

Gunfire shatters the silence.

A bullet sails past her.

She keeps running.

Footsteps crash through the underbrush.

He's gaining on her.

She trips over a fallen branch.

He fires again as she regains her balance.

This one misses her by inches.

Just when she thinks she can't run anymore, she sees it. An enormous tree, its branches spread like broken umbrellas. She ducks behind it, willing herself to be invisible as she crouches behind the gnarled trunk, trying to blend in with the darkness.

In the sudden silence that falls, the sounds of the forest seem magnified.

The chainsawing chirp of crickets.

The growls and shrieks of owls.

A high-pitched screech, followed by a flapping of wings as a bat flees its perch.

Then all is quiet again, as if all the animals were holding their collective breath.

She's sure he can hear her breathing.

But she can't hear him.

He could be anywhere.

A sound echoes through the forest, distorted by the dense foliage.

A car door?

Has he given up?

So easily?

A bullet bounces off the headstone.

Behind it, Alice crouches lower.

Silence, again.

She peers out from behind the tree.

It's so dark, she can't see anything

She takes a tentative step. Then another.

Too late, she sees him. A silhouette in the blackness.

Just waiting to ambush her.

She starts running again.

She runs faster, rage propelling her forward.

He didn't succeed in killing her thirty years ago.

She's not going to die here. Now. In the woods.

She hears the sound of the safety releasing.

It shatters the stillness.

Something snaps around her right foot.

And she goes down.

FORTY-ONE

The pain is excruciating.

Alice struggles to free her foot. Something in her ankle pops; blood spurts out from the torn skin.

He's coming toward her. She can see his shadowy form moving through the dark. She screams, praying someone—maybe the hunter who laid the trap—is nearby.

He stops next to her. As he leans over, she once again sees him on that long-ago night.

Waiting next to the tree.

She screams again.

"You can scream as loudly as you like. No one will hear you. Now hold still. The more you struggle, the more pain you'll cause yourself. And we don't want that, do we?"

Alice chokes back a sob as he frees her from the trap. Then he grabs her under the arms. She barely feels the sharp rocks and pebbles cutting her back. Terror seizing her as he drags her across the forest floor.

He's taking her deeper into the woods.

In the distance, she can hear the faint gurgling of water.

He stops walking. Drops her arms. As she scrambles to her feet, she sees him walking toward a hillock overgrown with vegetation.

Now he's pushing aside branches and vines.

A small stone structure is nestled into the side of the low hill.

It has a door.

Panic closes up her throat. She turns and tries to run, but can't put any weight on her right ankle.

He grabs her from behind. The heels of her bare feet slide across the muddy earth as he pulls her backwards. Then he slowly turns her around.

The door stands open.

Beyond, all is darkness.

FORTY-TWO

A man bolts up from his bed, screams echoing in his skull.

He has lived in the woods for decades, and can distinguish between human and animal sounds. For many years, he has tracked a Hunter who stalks a different kind of prey. He has traversed hundreds of miles of forest, laying elaborate traps to catch him. But so far, this enemy has eluded him.

He's not sure when it was—he long ago lost all sense of time—that his search finally led him to a neglected, overgrown place that held the graves of the unknown soldiers. A short distance away, he saw a car parked. At first he thought it was someone burying their dead. Or it could be a hunter. Many hunters pass through the woods in search of wild game. Sure enough, a few days—weeks?—later, the car was gone. He marked certain trees to help him find the spot again. Then he made camp a few miles away—carefully camouflaged, of course—because a creek was nearby, a source of running water.

Weeks—months?—later, the woodsman heard a car and ventured the several miles from camp. He used his tree markings and the soldier graveyard as a guide. When he got there, he again saw the car parked in the same place. Hunters rarely return to the same hunting ground. This time, he came closer to inspect the vehicle. During the next few days, he kept stealth watch. One day, he saw a man get into the car. After the man drove off, he searched the area. He found no other camps or abandoned cabins. So where was the Hunter staying? Why had he laid the traps? And if he was a hunter, why hadn't he heard any gunshots?

The next time he heard a car, the woodsman was ready. He watched from his hiding place as the driver emerged from the car. Although he couldn't be sure, it looked like the same man he'd seen before. The man opened the trunk and pulled out a figure whose wrists and ankles were bound with rope.

This was no ordinary wild game hunter.

Was it the Hunter he'd been seeking for so long?

As the Hunter carried off his captive, she started screaming, which set off memories of screams in a country far away. The woodsman fled back to camp, where terror kept him captive for a long time. When he finally got up the courage to venture forth again, the car was gone.

For a long time after that, he didn't see the car. He wondered if he'd imagined it all—the car, the man, the bound figure. The screams.

Until today.

Determined to overcome his fears, the woodsman emerges from his camp and starts walking. About a quarter mile on, he once again sees a car a short distance from the soldier graveyard. He moves stealthily, in case the Hunter is near. When the coast is clear, he inspects the car, which isn't the same car he'd seen before. Inside the car, the blood-spattered body of a woman is hunched over the wheel. She is dressed in civilian clothes, but is wearing what look like soldier's shoes.

After determining that she's dead, he initiates a covert search of the area. But he sees no sign of the sniper. When he returns to the car, he lifts her head and gently lays her against the headrest. Then he closes the female soldier's eyes.

She should be given a proper burial. After giving up her life for her country, it's the least he can do for her.

And he knows exactly where her place of final rest should be.

He'll need a shovel to dig the grave.

He turns to head back to camp.

Stops in his tracks.

Sniffs the air.

Artillery fire.

There has been a skirmish recently. Not a lone sniper, then?

He surveils the area again. Sees no sign of life. But they could be concealed behind trees. Crouched in the underbrush.

He goes motionless. Listens. He can hear it now.

Movement in the brush.

How long before the enemy opens fire?

But how can he leave her unburied and unmourned? How many more are out there who can be counted among the dead? Whose bodies are yet to be discovered?

He may need to dig more than one grave.

He looks in on his dead comrade once more. In spite of her wounds, with her eyes closed, she seems more at peace.

I will come back for you.

The words remain locked inside his head. He has forgotten the sound of his voice, but he can hear his thoughts.

Sometimes, he can even see them.

He starts to leave when he hears it.

The sound of a twig snapping.

The enemy is getting closer.

He turns back to the soldier. He would have buried her with it, but he knows she'd understand. This is war. Armed with her weapon, he starts out on his mission. As he walks, he keeps an eye out for the enemy.

And more bodies.

He's up against a very cunning foe. It will take more than bullets to outmaneuver him.

He walks faster. Breaks into a run. When he reaches camp, he's out of breath and shaking.

He gets into bed and lies unmoving.

But his mind refuses to grow quiet.

He made a tactical error.

He should have never left.

No one knows about this place.

He can hide here until the enemy is gone.

Yet even as he lies trembling under the blanket, the gun clutched in his hand, a distant voice speaks in his head.

Telling him that there is a word for men like him.

Coward.

FORTY-THREE

Alexis can't believe she's still here.

She should have been on the train back to the city by now. The one that left over an hour ago. The 7:05 was the last train out of Lowood tonight.

Now she'll have to wait until tomorrow. If she catches the early train, she'll be home in plenty of time to make Saturday night's show. But Damien's got to chill. Since she got here Wednesday night, he sent like a dozen texts to remind her. Like she's really going to forget.

As soon as she finds out what she came here for. Which Damien doesn't know yet is a lot more important than a stupid music gig. That's why she switched off her phone after texting him that she was dealing with some personal stuff and would be incommunicado for a while.

She can't remember the last time she turned off her cell, maybe to fix a glitch. She was afraid she'd end up telling him where she was, and she doesn't want to talk about it until she's ready. It feels weird, though. It's only been, like, one day, but it feels like she's not connected. She wonders how people lived before cell phones and social media. Maybe it was better. She hates being so dependent on an inanimate object, so maybe this is a good thing. Healthier for the baby.

She wonders about her mother, though. Not that her mom calls much. And she never texts. But what if there's an emergency? What if something happens with Charles? She tells herself it's okay, she'll be home tomorrow.

But she didn't come all the way up here to leave empty-handed. That's why she's standing across the street from the diner, telling herself she'd better not wimp out like she did yesterday.

That was really dumb, going into the diner during breakfast. The place was wall-to-wall people. She spotted Constance Moore right away from the photo on her Facebook page. Her blond hair was up in a bun and she was sweating bullets as she ran from table to table because she didn't have enough waitstaff.

When Alexis first walked in and saw the red-and-white checkered floor and jukebox mounted on a wall that Damien would think very cool, it felt like she was in a time warp. The whole town felt that way. What there was of it.

On Lowood's main drag, just a couple of twisty streets, she passed a Walmart Supercenter, a furniture outlet, an appliance and repair shop, a tractor supply company, a video rental and liquor store that tripled as a laundromat, storefronts with signs offering landscaping and snow removal, guns and fishing supplies, and a record store with vinyl in the window that Damien would kill to own.

On the town's actual Main Street, where she's standing now, a Dollar General store and mom-and-pop tobacco shop are next door to a trendy jewelry store, a nail salon and a photography studio, home décor and computer repair stores, and the retro clothing shop she checked out that was a total waste of time because she couldn't afford to buy anything.

Her stomach's growling. It's almost eight-thirty, and the last thing she ate was the PowerBar she brought with her from the city. Skipping lunch couldn't be good for the baby. And before that, the breakfast pizza she picked up at a 7-Eleven for two bucks just made her miss the pancakes she splurged on at the diner yesterday. It was almost worth the trip up here just for that. Thank God she had her appetite back after those first horrible weeks of feeling nauseated all the time. Only now it feels like she's always starving.

The girl who waited on her looked like she could have used a stack herself, heavy on the butter and syrup. She was so skinny her collarbone stuck out and her arms were like two sticks. And her long, frizzy red hair looked like it hadn't been cut in months.

She was much too young to be able to tell Alexis anything—probably wasn't even born in 1989. Not that she even talked to Alexis, not one word. She just nodded as she took the order, her face scrunched up in concentration like she was afraid of writing it down wrong.

It was after Alexis finished wolfing down the pancakes that she noticed the tall man sitting at the counter. There weren't any empty stools, so his black hat was in his lap. He must have come in when she wasn't looking. Constance Moore was pouring him coffee like she and the town sheriff were really tight. While he ate, a bunch of customers came up to him. He probably knew everyone who ate here.

Which made her stick out like a sore thumb.

After Alexis paid her bill and got the hell out of there, she followed directions she'd Googled to Lowood High. She walked around the building, closed up now with classes out and summer school over. Then she sat for a while on the bleachers, trying to picture her mother going to school here. She checked out the street where her grandfather's hardware store used to be, now a home center that took up almost the whole block. That was followed by a high-calorie cheeseburger at a dive near her hole-in-the-wall motel on the outskirts of town.

She hated it there. It felt like the middle of nowhere, with woods all around that looked so dark after the bright lights of the city. No wonder her mom moved back to New York after college.

She stayed up too late watching TV.

This whole trip, which wasn't cheap, was so probably a waste of time.

Maybe this is like a sign or something, even though her mom doesn't believe in stuff like that and raised her to believe that everyone has to make their own destiny.

But why did her mother lie to her?

Across the street, a ton of people are coming out of the diner. Must be a lot of early-bird specials up here. Especially with night falling earlier now. She hates seeing summer end. The days are just going to get shorter and shorter.

Alexis waits a little while longer. No one else comes out. She's still standing there, wishing it wasn't so dark and the streetlamps were brighter and trying to get up the nerve to cross the street when Constance Moore comes outside. She's carrying two large garbage bags that she puts into a bin on the sidewalk.

Alexis waits until Moore goes back inside. Then she squares her shoulders and crosses the street.

If this isn't a sign, she doesn't know what is.

FORTY-FOUR

Connie frowns as she walks back into the diner.

She's worried about Mia.

In the five weeks she's been working here, Connie can't remember her ever not showing up.

Usually, she's early.

Maybe she forgot that she agreed to cover the dinner shift tonight.

Maybe she's sick.

That summer flu that's been lingering for months and hit some towns unusually hard has been an especially nasty one this year. Some think it's a harbinger of the cold winter to come.

Too sick to call?

Connie can't call her because when she hired her Mia refused to give a contact number.

Or an address.

At the time, Connie understood. She saw the other woman as a kindred spirit. That was why she agreed to pay her under the table.

What if Mia's on the run again? From whoever was abusing her?

Walt's probably right. Mia isn't her real name. And that red hair really does look like a bad dye job.

How do you find someone who doesn't want to be found?

Connie sighs. Tells herself that whatever's going on with her waitress isn't her problem. Mia's a grown woman. She's going to have to figure things out for herself.

But Connie has her diner to think about. If Mia's gone for good, she'll have to find a new waitress.

Again.

She just hopes Mia didn't do something stupid like go back to the son of a bitch who hurt her.

Connie goes over to the window, her mind still on the other woman.

She remembers that day a few weeks back when Mia stood right where she's standing now. Staring out the window, looking as if she might bolt at any moment.

Could Mia really be on the run again?

A thought hidden at the back of her mind tunnels its way to the front.

What if whoever Mia was running from has already found her?

She should have forced Mia to go to the sheriff's office. Walt would have gotten a local judge to issue an order of protection. The way he did for Connie before he ran Wade out of town.

She should have taken Mia there herself.

Just like she should taken Alice thirty years ago.

Even though by then it was too late for her friend.

It might not be too late for Mia.

Walt has resources. He'll get out a description and start a search. It's better than doing nothing.

Connie starts walking back to her office to retrieve her phone, which is still in her shoulder bag where she tossed it when she left her apartment to come down to work this morning. Between manning the counter for breakfast and lunch and then covering for Mia tonight, she hasn't had a minute to herself.

And she's starting to feel it.

The bell over the front door tinkles.

Connie frowns. It's almost quarter to nine. Dinner hour's over.

The door opens.

And Alice walks in.

FORTY-FIVE

Connie blinks.

She looks like an apparition appearing out of the mist.

Or a ghost.

A ghost from the past.

Alice is still standing in the doorway.

Connie's heart squeezes. She can't catch her breath.

Alice starts walking.

No. Not Alice.

Someone who looks a lot like her.

Except that Alice's eyes were brown.

Alice-Who-Isn't-Alice stops in front of her. "You're Constance Moore, right?"

Her voice echoes across the empty diner.

Alice's voice.

"I tried calling your home number, but no one answered."

She knows she's expecting her to say something, but the best Connie can manage is a nod.

"Did you get my email?" She chews her lower lip. Just like Alice used to do whenever she was worried or upset.

The email. Of course.

The email Connie never answered.

"I'm Alexis McKerrity."

She holds out her hand.

And still Connie doesn't move.

McKerrity's brows knit together in a frown, making her look more like Connie's old friend than ever.

Overcome by emotion, Connie reaches for the outstretched hand.

As she grasps Alexis McKerrity's smaller hand in her larger, calloused one, she finally finds her voice.

"How's your mother? How is Alice?"

FORTY-SIX

She feels bruised and battered.

Her back aches from sitting in the same position on the floor, her wrists bound behind her with her court officer's handcuffs. Her right ankle throbs from the long iron chain that manacles her feet to a metal ring in the floor. And she can feel a bruise forming on the back of her skull where her head hit the moss-covered stones as he dragged her down to this hellhole below the earth.

She must have lost consciousness then because the next thing she knew she was over his shoulder, her head lolling like a rag doll. Cold seemed to emanate from everywhere. The passageway grew narrower as they moved through, the air more frigid.

He stopped. Lowered her to the unforgiving cement floor. Her ankle gave way and she grabbed on to him to keep from falling. He smiled down at her.

"We've arrived. Home sweet home."

Alice looked over her shoulder.

She couldn't see anything. It was pitch-black. She had the sense of being in a vast, open space. Nothing but the impenetrable dark.

And the chill that was seeping into her bones.

As if the darkness and the cold had become one.

—m—

The candle on the floor next to her has begun to flicker.

Any minute now it will go out.

Panic quickens her breath.

She has no idea how long she's been here, the darkness and the cold her constant companions.

Is this the fate she escaped? Only to end up here thirty years later?

She doesn't know which is worse, the shackles tearing her skin. Or the biting cold that makes her feel as if she were inside a refrigerator.

But she welcomes the pain.

The pain is real. It reminds her that she's alive.

And as long as she's alive, there's a chance she can get out of here.

She has to believe that or she really will go crazy.

The hairs on the back of her neck prickle.

It was the way she felt in court when she'd catch him staring at her. Unable to look away, as if his will were stronger than hers.

As if he knew what she was thinking before she'd consciously formed the thoughts.

Or maybe he's always been there. In her mind.

He never left.

He's here now. She can hear his footsteps.

In the flickering candlelight, she sees him.

A shadow on the wall.

As he gets closer, the flames dance higher.

For a second, Alice sees the face that stared at her across the bar. Then the flames burn down and he's the defendant in her courtroom again.

The monster in the woods.

He kneels in front of her.

"Oh, Alice." Hearing the two syllables emerge from his mouth feels like an obscenity. "Don't you know that pulling on your chains will only cause more pain? You'd think you would have learned from the bear trap. The more you struggle, the worse it will be for you."

He smiles. The same smile she saw that night in the car when he turned to look at her.

"Where am I? What is this place?"

"It's called an icehouse. I found it purely by accident. I was looking for somewhere to squat for the night, preferably near a source of running water. Imagine my surprise when I saw something peeking out from brambles and vines next to a large tributary. Under all that overgrown vegetation was this stone structure that looked like it had been around for centuries. But it wasn't until I came down here and looked around that I realized where I was."

He chuckles. "You know the great thing about icehouses? Besides keeping food from spoiling? If you look carefully, you can see sawdust and straw in the walls. That's insulation. To keep the ice from melting. Do you know what else insulation is good for? It makes everything soundproof."

His words strike terror in her heart. And rage. "Why are you keeping me here? What do you want?"

"What everyone wants. Love. Respect. I'm really not a very complicated person. My physical needs are simple. A roof over my head, of course. Water. Food. Speaking of which."

He removes the lid from the pot he brought with him. The aroma of cooked salmon fills the air.

Her stomach turns over.

"You must be famished. Nothing like a hearty meal to chase away the Devil, like my mama used to say."

He slips a fork from his pocket. "Did I tell you how I caught the slippery critters? So desperate to make it upstream, they never saw me coming.

Didn't know what hit them until they got trapped in a wall of netting. An old fisherman's trick. Do you know what they used to call that? A kill box. Fitting, don't you think?"

He chuckles as he impales a piece of fish on the fork and holds it out. Alice clamps her lips closed.

"Open your mouth, Alice. I won't ask nicely again."

When she refuses to obey, he grabs her hair.

And pulls.

When she starts to scream, he forks the salmon into her mouth.

The fish is stuck in her throat. She chokes on a tiny bone. "Didn't your mama teach you proper dining etiquette? The food will never get digested unless you chew each bite slowly."

He stabs another piece of fish with the fork. With his other hand, he holds her mouth open. As he shoves it down her throat, she imagines stabbing him in the eye with the fork's sharp tines.

Over and over again.

When he reaches down for more, she spits out the uneaten salmon.

He doesn't say anything as he wipes off the fork and replaces the lid on the pot. "That was a mistake, Alice. Do you know the work that went into preparing this meal? Fishing in the dark. Then having to cook without electricity while keeping everything properly ventilated. Now you'll have to stay shackled instead of getting a proper night's sleep. Without even a blanket to keep warm. And I'll have to punish you. But you know all about punishment, don't you? It seems you and I aren't that different, after all."

"I'm nothing like you," she chokes out. "You're a killer."

"And you're not? I did my research. Nine times out of ten, you've sentenced defendants to the maximum. And if New York still had the death penalty, I have no doubt those poor slobs would end up with needles in their arms."

"Whoever I sentenced deserved it. Just like you deserve to die. A needle in the arm would be too good for you."

"So now you're judge, jury, and executioner?" He yanks her hair again. She bites back a scream. "You're in my prison now. And don't you ever forget it.

"A pity you didn't enjoy your supper," he says when he finally lets her go. "You really do need to keep up your strength." He picks up the still-flickering candle and gets to his feet.

"What are you doing?" The words out before she can stop them.

He smiles at her. "You're not afraid of the dark, are you?"

His grin widens. He starts whistling as he walks away.

At the door, he blows out the candle.

She listens to his footsteps dying away.

Chokes back a sob of despair, her earlier bravado gone.

She's never going to get out of here.

She's never going to see Alexis and Charles again.

She'll die in this freezing, God-awful place.

In the darkness just waiting to swallow her whole.

FORTY-SEVEN

"**A**nother slice?"

"I'm good, thanks."

Alexis McKerrity leans back against the red Naugahyde of the booth. Connie braces herself for the barrage of questions that brought the younger woman to Lowood on the eve of a holiday weekend. Instead, McKerrity asks for the ladies' room. "Must have been the tea." Her mouth widens in an apologetic smile.

Alice's smile.

After she tells her, Connie watches McKerrity walk across the diner. The offer of food seemed a natural way to break the ice. And to buy time while she figured out what she was going to say.

They hadn't talked much after Connie served the apple pie and took a seat opposite her. McKerrity had rejected her offer of tonight's special. Even with the diner at full capacity, there'd been quite a few fish dinners left over because of the proliferation of salmon and trout in the area this time of year.

As she watched Alice's daughter eat two generous slices of pie and look as if she could wolf down two more, Connie didn't miss the way the younger woman's hand rested on her belly over her loose, unflattering clothes. The way her skin seemed to glow from the inside.

She'd been pregnant enough times to recognize the signs.

That, and the fact that McKerrity turned down her offer of coffee and asked for tea. Decaf.

As she sips her coffee, Connie wonders who the father is. McKerrity isn't wearing a wedding band. No rings of any kind.

She wonders if Alice knows.

If that's the reason her daughter needs to fill in the blanks.

When McKerrity returns, Connie waits until she's settled back in the booth.

"When are you due?"

"Is it that obvious?" McKerrity rests a hand on her belly again. "February twenty-fifth."

"Boy or girl?"

"I don't know. I want to be surprised."

I. Not *we.* So there's no father in the picture. Is McKerrity planning to be a single mother?

Like Alice. Until Charles McKerrity adopted Alice's daughter.

"Ms. Moore?"

McKerrity's sitting up straight now, a questioning look in her blue eyes.

"Call me Connie."

"Okay." McKerrity heaves in a breath as if this were as hard for her to ask as it will be for Connie to answer. "I never heard back from you. Did you get my email?"

Connie nods. "Sorry about that. I've been really busy lately." Her voice trails off. She never was a good liar.

"But you read it, right?" Connie nods. "On the Lowood High Facebook page, you posted that you knew my mother. Were you friends?"

"Yes." The one word not nearly enough to express what Alice was to her. What they were to each other. "Your mother never mentioned me?"

When McKerrity shakes her head, Connie feels the old hurt surfacing. "She doesn't talk much about her past. And she doesn't have a lot of friends."

She never did, Connie thinks. *I was it.*

"I guess she has her hands full with Charles. He has Alzheimer's." McKerrity twists and untwists her hands in her lap. "My mom doesn't want anyone to know. It's why he had to quit being a judge. They met in court. After they got married, he adopted me." She looks at Connie. "I want to find my biological father."

Although she'd been expecting to hear this ever since McKerrity walked into her diner, Connie finds herself stalling for time. Then she asks the question that has been on her mind for weeks. Ever since she saw McKerrity's post and realized that Alice conceived a child here thirty years ago. "What did your mother tell you?"

"She said it was a one-night thing. He was a boy she met at a dance in a town called Renegade Falls. She wouldn't tell me his name." McKerrity's voice is tight with hurt and anger. "I don't believe her."

The moment of truth has arrived.

But how can she tell Alice's daughter what she now suspects?

When Connie ran out of her house that frigid Saturday morning in December, Alice was totally out of it. Swaying on her bare feet, as if the effort of getting there had sapped all her strength. If Connie hadn't caught her, she would have fallen. Her eyes were glassy and unfocused. There were cuts and gashes on her face from running through the woods. And red welts on her throat. The gold chain containing the three interlocking hearts that she never took off no longer around her neck.

"Everything's going to be okay." Repeating it over and over, Alice clinging to her for dear life. All Connie could think was she had to get her to the hospital.

Her car was in the driveway. She already had the keys in her pocket. She was still feeling the aftereffects of last night's party high and hoped she wouldn't be stopped for driving under the influence.

But Alice refused to get into the car. She started screaming. Connie was afraid she'd wake the neighbors. So she brought her into the house. Her folks were away at one of those weekend communes they and their hippy-dippy friends were always attending. A cut on Alice's face was bleeding. There was rubbing alcohol upstairs. And bandages. Then she'd call the sheriff's office and speak to the new sheriff, who'd take it from there. His name was Walter Church.

After she got Alice upstairs, she put her on her bed. Alice just lay there staring at the ceiling. Didn't resist as Connie undressed her.

Her clothing was torn, her panties gone. Her pubic area was bruised and bloody. Connie agonized over what to do as she cleaned and bandaged the wounds the best she could. Not thinking clearly enough to consider that she might be destroying evidence.

She waited until Alice was asleep. Shaking with fury at whoever did this to her as she headed for her parents' room to make the call.

She had the phone off the hook and was dialing when Alice started screaming again. When she ran back to her bedroom, she found her cowering in the closet. Alice screamed louder when she saw her, clawing at her with a strength Connie hadn't known she possessed. Scratched her face so hard she drew blood before Connie finally grabbed hold of her wrists. Still she kept screaming. Until Connie slapped her.

Alice's eyes rolled back in her head. Then she looked at Connie as if she were seeing her for the first time. She grasped her shoulders, her fingernails digging into Connie's skin. "Promise me." Her voice a hoarse whisper. "Promise you'll never tell."

Like they were twelve again and sharing secrets.

Connie didn't understand. "We have to go to the police. Tell them who did this to you."

"No." Alice's voice was hard and implacable. She looked older than her sixteen years. "You have to promise. On our oath."

What could she do?

They were sisters.

She fretted over what to do for hours. Long after Alice went limp in her arms.

She ended up falling asleep too, next to Alice.

When she woke up, her friend was gone.

When she called her house, Alice's father answered. Nathan Dunn's voice was cold and angry. He told her he knew about the late-night parties and he was forbidding his daughter to see her anymore. If she ever phoned again, he'd call the police.

At least she knew Alice had made it home.

In a clean set of clothes Connie found missing from her closet.

Then she sat down and cried.

Because she knew Alice was lost to her.

From the moment she let her walk out of her house.

Two months later, Alice left Lowood.

Pregnant with her daughter.

McKerrity's voice rouses her back to the present.

"I think she was lying to me. You were her friend. Were you and my mother close?"

As close as two sisters could be who weren't bound by blood. Until a couple of weeks before Alice was assaulted. When she stopped confiding in Connie and started keeping secrets.

McKerrity can see the answer in her eyes. "I know my mother moved away during her senior year. She never graduated. Do you know if she was dating anyone? Did she have a boyfriend?"

"No one that I knew about." Which is the truth. But Connie had been sure that Alice was seeing someone. She had no clue who he was and didn't know why Alice was being so secretive. Now that she thinks about it, Alice changed after that dance in Renegade Falls, where she told her daughter she was conceived during a one-night stand.

Connie was also at that dance. It was attended mostly by older kids. And a few teachers acting as chaperones.

She tries to think back. But it was such a long time ago, and she and Alice went to a lot of dances and parties. And bars, where they were underage but were let in with the fake IDs Connie got from the Lowood senior who sold her her pot.

Renegade Falls, though. They didn't drive to that village very often.

Luke wasn't at that dance, and she'd been glad to be away from him for once. He was so crazy jealous. She'd drunk too much—what else was new?—and was hot and sweaty after dancing on the packed floor with some guy she'd never see again. She remembers now that she lost track of Alice at some point.

Had Alice hooked up with someone at the dance?

McKerrity's looking at her as if she's trying to decide whether to believe her. "You don't have to worry about my mother finding out. Whatever you tell me will be in confidence. I swear."

"So she doesn't know you're here?" McKerrity shakes her head. "Does she know you're pregnant?" Another shake of the head. "What about the baby's father?"

"I haven't told him yet."

"Don't you think he should know?"

"He's in a rock band. I'm lead singer. We're this close to nailing a recording contract. The timing's just not right." McKerrity looks so miserable that Connie's heart goes out to her. "And I can't tell my mom. She's busy with this trial she's doing. But something's going on with her. She's been having nightmares. And smoking again after she quit a few years ago. She's also been taking sleeping pills. And a couple of weeks ago, she—"

McKerrity stops talking abruptly. After a moment, she shrugs. "I know my mom has a lot on her plate. Between work and Charles, it's got to be tough. It's not that I don't love my father. Even if he has no idea who I am anymore."

McKerrity clearly feels the need to talk. Something's weighing on her. Guilt?

"Do you think he was married?"

"Who?"

"My biological father."

"It's possible." That was the only reason Connie could come up with that Alice hadn't confided in her. Was it someone they both knew? One of the teacher chaperones at the dance? One of the married teacher chaperones? "Maybe she was trying to protect you."

"That's the problem. But she can't baby me forever. I'm not a child anymore."

She's wrong, Connie thinks. She'll find out when her own baby is born.

In her mother's eyes, she'll always be her little girl.

McKerrity chews on her lower lip as she leans forward. "I probably shouldn't be telling you this, but you know the nightmares I told you my mother's been having? They didn't just start now. They've been going on since I was little. She'd wake up in the middle of the night screaming. But she wouldn't talk about it. Not to me or my grandfather. She said they were just bad dreams. And she never, ever talks about Lowood. Like that part of her life didn't exist. It made me wonder. If something happened to her when she was living here."

The silence stretches out.

And still Connie says nothing, even though she's sure the younger woman can see her for the liar she is. She keeps thinking about the long-ago promise she made to her best friend. But Alice's daughter traveled all the way up here for answers. Maybe if Alexis McKerrity knew the truth, it would help her better understand her mother.

Connie's still grappling with what do when the bell over the front door tinkles.

Saved by the bell.

FORTY-EIGHT

"**D**oes it hurt?"

Alice bites down on her lower lip as his fingers press into her swollen ankle. She refuses to give him the satisfaction of showing weakness, which is exactly what he wants.

She didn't expect him back this soon. The sound of his footsteps roused her from wherever her mind had receded. She awoke to the same blackness she'd seen behind her closed lids. The light from the candle in his hand dispelled the dark. The light flamed brighter as he came toward her.

When he moved toward her, she braced herself as he brought a hand to her cheek. It was the merest brush of his fingers, but her skin felt branded wherever he touched her.

He shook his head and said he was disappointed in her. Said he could smell her fear the way he smelled it on the inmate he attacked with the shank he'd made in prison. That was the reason he wasn't in court that first morning of jury selection. Until Alice ordered a special bus to bring him to Manhattan from Rikers Island.

She'd watched him hobble into her courtroom in his shackles, thinking he wasn't any different from all the other defendants she sentenced.

He had been right about that—she wanted to punish them for their crimes against women.

Against humanity.

She tried not to flinch as he caressed her face, assuring her that she had no reason to be afraid.

Then he knelt once again at her feet and unshackled her ankles so he could inspect her wounds.

His sadistic way of keeping her off-balance?

As he now wraps a bandage around her ankle, Alice braces herself. She knows that this is his way of disarming her, of lulling her into a sense of false security.

He looks up. "It's all right, Alice. You don't have to put on a brave face. What is pain after all, but the Lord's way of letting us know we're alive?"

His words mimicking her earlier thoughts.

It isn't just her body that he's violating.

It's as if he's reaching into her mind.

He smiles, mistaking her indrawn breath for pain.

"There we are. All better now?"

His words bring her back.

They're the words she used to say to Alexis.

"Don't look at me like that, Alice. It's not the way you looked at me that night in the bar."

"That was before I knew who you were."

"You're wrong. I was who I always was. Maybe you saw what you wanted to see."

She flashes to that long-ago night, to the moment their eyes met across the bar. Remembering how instantly drawn she was to him, a feeling as emotional as it was physical.

Is he right? Had she been seeing merely a reflection of her own needs and desires in those blue eyes?

"You got into my car, didn't you? That was your choice. No one held a gun to your head." His voice has dropped to a whisper. "Admit it. You wanted me. As much as I wanted you."

She shakes her head. "No."

"Don't lie to me, Alice. Don't blaspheme even more by lying to yourself." She watches him pick up the bag, wonders what else is inside.

"Is this how you show your feelings? By chaining me up?"

"Is this how you show your appreciation? After I went to the trouble of bringing you a heater? Which wasn't easy to come by."

The propane heater sitting a few feet away that has dispelled some of the chill. "You said you wanted respect and love," Alice says as if he hadn't spoken. "Now who's the one deceiving himself? Whatever you think this is, it's not love."

For several seconds, he doesn't move. When he straightens, she can see a muscle twitching in his jaw.

"You think you have me figured out. You have no idea."

"Enlighten me."

He doesn't respond, zips the bag.

"Did you think you were showing love for your victims? How many did you keep captive here against their will? How many were raped and beaten to death in the name of love?"

"I think that's enough chitchatting for now."

"How many women did you kill? More than Ted Bundy?"

"Hell, yeah!"

Alice knew he wouldn't be able to resist the opportunity to brag. He wants the world to know. Just like he wanted her to know in court when he asked the bite-mark expert the total number of Bundy's victims.

Because he believes that he's the superior killer.

Young shakes his head. "Bundy couldn't even conduct a decent defense at his own trials. Bungled his one and only escape from that Florida courthouse. He deserved to fry in the chair. That man was an amateur next to me."

"They never found the bodies of all his victims, did they?"

"No. But they'll never find any of mine. Not a single one."

"Where did you bury them?" Again she sees herself in the woods, running from his car. Feeling as if she were passing over her own grave.

She shudders. Forces herself to go on. "Why do we have to wait? Can't you show me?"

"That would mean freeing you. After all the trouble I went to chaining you up. You must be patient. It will come to pass. All in the Lord's good time."

She tries to not flinch as he reshackles her ankles. She knows she won't be able to take a clean breath until he's gone.

But how can she let him leave? He's her only chance of getting out of here.

God help her.

"I was your first, wasn't I?"

He turns around. His expression changes again. It's the face she saw in the bar that long-ago night. But she knows that's an illusion. A trick of the candlelight.

"Why didn't you bring me here?"

"I would have liked to." His tone is filled with regret. "But I hadn't found this place yet."

Now she understood.

That was why he raped her in the woods.

She never had any doubt that he would have killed her afterward. If something hadn't startled him—she never knew what it was—and he hadn't run off and left her lying on the ground.

Brutalized.

But alive.

"You're here now. That's all that matters."

His mouth stretches into the smile that isn't a smile.

Her mouth goes dry. She forces herself to speak past the brushfire in her throat. "When did you realize who I was?"

His smile widens. It's a terrible thing to see. "That first day in court, I knew there was something familiar about you. I was sure we'd met before. You were so beautiful. With the same Devil-streaked hair."

Alice wills herself to remain motionless as he raises a hand to her head. "I couldn't get you out of my mind. Ever since that autumn afternoon I saw you walking home from school."

She was right. He had been stalking her. For months.

"In the bar, I kept waiting for you to look up and see me. I'd hoped you'd be the one to come for the drinks. Not your clueless blond friend, thrusting her cleavage at me as if that would get me into her bed. As if I wanted what all ignorant young males want."

Connie. She'd been so jealous, certain that her best friend was sleeping with him. How could she have been so blind? So stupid?

He starts stroking Alice's hair. "Do you remember that day in court? I'd just finished my cross-examination of that bite-mark expert. The moment I saw her seated in the gallery, I knew. It was His will bringing you and me back together. Coming full circle at last."

Her body freezes as she realizes who he's talking about.

Alexis.

That night, Alice dreamed about him.

"Looking at her was like seeing the past and the future all at once. What is she like? Your daughter?"

Rage rips through her, swift and fierce. "You'll never know because you won't lay eyes on her again. You'll never get anywhere near her."

"That's up to Him, isn't it? The Lord who sees, knows, and forgives all."

"He'll never forgive you. Why would He? God doesn't give absolution to monsters."

214

He yanks her hair so hard that she sees stars. Then his hands go around her neck. He starts squeezing.

She's on the ground underneath him.

His fingers press into her windpipe, cutting off her air supply.

The screams die in her throat.

She claws at his hands. He squeezes harder. She feels the gold chain around her neck ripping into her skin. Choking her.

"I could kill you now," he hisses in her ear. "But where's the sport in that? Especially with you at such an unfair disadvantage."

When he finally lets her go, she starts coughing until her entire body's wracked with it. She feels his eyes on her as she struggles for breath. Then he picks up the candle. And starts walking away.

Shadows dance on the wall.

"Wait!"

He keeps walking.

"Please."

He stops, turns. "What is it now?" His voice is hard and cold.

"You were right." Her throat feels raw and tender. It's an effort to talk.

"About what?"

"I need . . . to keep up my strength."

"Are you asking to be fed?" She nods. "I went to a lot of trouble preparing that meal. And look how you showed your gratitude."

"I know. I'm sorry."

He studies her for a long moment. "If I give you another chance, it will be your last. If you disobey this time, your punishment will be severe."

Again, she nods.

"You'll have to speak up. I didn't hear you."

Throwing back her own words to him in court.

"Yes," she says through gritted teeth.

The candle flickers. She feels the weight of the darkness about to descend, like a shroud.

"You really need to get over this childish fear of yours. Have you ever asked yourself why you're so frightened of the dark?"

Because that's where monsters like you live.

"You can't hide from the darkness, Alice. It's already inside you. You must learn to embrace it." He walks back toward her. "You were afraid that night. That was the reason you ran. But you need to ask yourself why. It couldn't have been me because you and I share the same darkness. That's why I chose you. But there was something else going on. I sensed it the moment you got into my car. Your mind was troubled. Your conscience wasn't clear. What were you really running from?"

She doesn't answer. When he steps closer, she shrinks back. "It's all right. Because you're making a sincere effort to atone, I've decided to bestow a gift on you. I'm allowing you to give into your fear. For just this one night."

He places the candle on the floor. "This will give you time to think about what I've said. You can blow it out at any time. If you're feeling brave."

After he's gone, she stares at the flickering candlelight and her mind spins back.

To a night nearly a month before she ever laid eyes on William Henry Young in a bar.

The night she attended a dance in Renegade Falls.

Sneaking away together while everyone was on the dance floor. Driving to his house on the outskirts of town. Determined that this was the night she would lose her virginity.

Later, wondering what all the fuss was about. A few minutes of groping in the dark, bedsprings squeaking, until his body writhed in one last, terrible contortion. Sliding off her, his face turning white when he saw the blood. Asking why she hadn't told him. Turning away, her own face hot with shame. Unwilling to tell him how much it had hurt. As if the insides of her body had been torn apart.

Afterward, feeling overwhelmed by guilt. Tallying up all the sins her father and their church would say she'd committed. Having sex before marriage. Being a minor. Using someone she'd known for years, then treating him like the dirt under her feet. Not knowing how badly she'd hurt him until the night of the party.

The same night compounding her sins by getting into a stranger's car.

The candle is burning down.

Soon darkness will envelop her again.

Young said the darkness was inside her.

He said they shared the same darkness. That was the reason he chose her.

He's wrong.

They don't share anything.

He's trying to manipulate her. Prey on her weaknesses to make her more afraid.

He's right about one thing.

It's time to get over her childish fears.

The terror of the dark is something Alice has in common with most children. It's the uncertainty; the fear of what we cannot see.

She's seen him now.

The monster of her worst nightmares.

She will find a way to escape this hellhole.

She can't let the monster win.

FORTY-NINE

"**I**s she okay?"

Connie follows Alexis McKerrity's gaze. "I don't know." She slides out of the booth. "I'll be right back."

Something's going on. She felt it ever since Mia walked into the diner without a single excuse for not showing up for her shift. Not that she ever says much even on the best of days.

When Mia went straight to the ladies' room, Connie didn't know what to think.

But she's been gone too long.

When Connie opens the door to the ladies', the other woman isn't at the sink or standing in front of the full-length mirror. Connie heads for the closed door of a stall. She knocks. "Mia? Are you all right?"

She tries the door. It's unlocked. Inside, Mia cowers in a corner.

Connie blinks. For a second she sees her best friend the night Alice was assaulted, cowering in Connie's closet.

"What is it, Mia? What's wrong?"

The other woman shakes her head violently back and forth. Her bottle-dyed hair falls like a curtain across her pale face. Mia knew her abuser wouldn't be looking for a redhead.

Looks like he found her, anyway.

"Is it him? The man you're running from?" Connie crouches next to her. "I can help you. Just tell me. Is he here? In Lowood?"

Mia hugs her body in closer to herself as she starts to whimper.

"It's okay. Shhh." Connie puts her arms around her. She can feel her trembling. It's like living what happened with her second husband all over again. The only difference is she didn't have anyone to comfort her.

"It'll be okay," Connie murmurs as she rocks her. "He's not going to hurt you anymore. I'm calling Sheriff Church."

"No!" Mia pulls away, her eyes wild.

Jesus. It's even worse than she thought. The bastard really has his hooks into her. Probably told her he'd kill her if she went to the police. Isn't that what all abusers do? Threaten their victims with physical force?

All it does is expose them for the bullies and cowards they are.

But we believe them, God help us. Like she believed Wade before she finally got up the courage to fight back. That earned her a broken arm and three cracked ribs before Church finally ran him out of town.

"Mia, listen to me. He's not going to stop. Wherever you go, he'll find you. Like he found you now. That's why we need to get the sheriff."

"NO!"

Mia lunges. Before Connie can react, she starts clawing at her.

. . . with a strength Connie hadn't known Alice possessed. Scratched her face so hard she drew blood before Connie finally grabbed hold of her wrists. Still Alice kept screaming. Until Connie slapped her.

Mia stops fighting; stops moving entirely. She stares at Connie as if she has no idea who she is. Connie remembers Alice reacting the same way. Then Mia raises her arm and touches Connie's cheek where she scratched her.

That's when Connie sees it.

The blood on Mia's sleeve.

She forgets what just happened as fury rises up in her. "Are you hurt? He did this to you, didn't he?"

Mia doesn't respond. But she doesn't resist as Connie rolls up the sleeve of her blouse.

There isn't a mark on her.

No scratches or bruises. No injury of any kind.

The blood isn't Mia's.

Which means she fought back.

Worst case scenario: he's dead.

Which would make Mia his killer. In self-defense, which Connie will swear on a Bible if it comes to that. But she doesn't know the circumstances. Her first instinct is to protect Mia, to see what happened for herself. Walt's a good man, but he's still law enforcement. And he might not understand.

Only women who have lived through this can truly understand.

"Where is he?" she asks. "Can you take me to him?"

Mia nods, but she's shaking again.

Which makes Connie wonder if he's still alive.

"Everything okay?"

Alexis McKerrity is outside the stall. Connie didn't hear her come into the ladies' room.

"It is now," Connie shouts through the closed door. Then she holds out a hand to Mia. "Come on." When Mia hesitates she says, "It's going to be okay, I promise. You have to trust me."

—⚬—

As the three of them pile into her SUV a few minutes later, Connie hopes she made the right call.

But she made a promise, and she never goes back on her word. She has no idea how long this is going to take, but she plans to be with Mia every step of the way.

As she shifts into drive, Connie glances in the rearview. In the back seat, Alexis McKerrity looks as frightened as Mia. Connie tried to stop her from coming with them. She didn't want her exposing her unborn child to potential danger. But McKerrity refused to be left behind. Connie hopes that wasn't another bad call. As they head down the street, she feels the weight of the shotgun across her lap. A legacy of her third husband, who taught her how to shoot.

Just in case the son of a bitch who has been abusing Mia is still breathing.

FIFTY

lice watches him wipe off the utensils he just used to feed her.

This time the fork was plastic, not stainless steel; as if he knew that she'd been fantasizing about stabbing him in the eyes with the fork's sharp tines.

He seems different, something in his demeanor altered that she can't put her finger on.

Or maybe it's her.

She's not the same person she was before he left her alone in the dark with only a dying candle for company. She has no idea how long he has been gone. It's impossible to measure the time in here with no natural light or windows to distinguish night from day.

She waits until he has replaced the lid on the pot that held the fish—trout this time—that was surprisingly tasty. "Thank you for giving me a second chance. Your mama was right. There's nothing like a hearty meal to chase away the Devil."

A shadow passes across his face that could be the wavering light of the candle he brought with him.

"What was your mama like?" she goes on as if he'd spoken. "You asked about my daughter. But I also had a mother. She died when I was ten. Where's your mother? Is she alive?"

He looks at her for a long moment, then shakes his head. "Do you think I don't know what you're trying to do? For a judge used to dealing with the criminal mind, you're pretty transparent. Too bad your psychological games won't work on me."

"I'm just making conversation. It gets lonely in here. We can talk about your father instead. In court, you asked Dr. Liu if she believed in God. Was it your daddy who taught you about religion?"

Young lets out a bitter bark of laughter. "He didn't teach me anything."

Alice pictures his rap sheet on her computer screen, the blank box where the names of his parents should be. His rage in court when he told Dr. Hannah Liu that the father of Angel Diallo's baby could have been any of the johns who paid for sex with her.

Whoever his own father is, he's the primary target of Young's rage.

"When I moved here after my mother died, my father dragged me to church every Sunday. But I'm not sure I ever believed in God. What's your God like? Does he speak through you? Did he tell you to kill all those women?"

"Sorry to disappoint you, but I don't hear voices. I'm not insane."

"Isn't believing you're sane the first sign of insanity? If it wasn't God, who was it? The Devil?"

The muscle in his jaw jumps again. "I think that's enough chitchatting."

"That's what you always say when you don't like the way the conversation is going."

Because he has to be the one controlling the narrative.

"The more you talk, the more severe your punishment will be."

"Is that how you show your strength? By threatening women who can't defend themselves? That doesn't make you someone worthy of admiration. That just makes you a bully. Is that what your father was?"

"Don't push me, Alice."

"I'm not afraid of you."

"You should be. You should be very afraid."

"Why? What can you do to me? I already know your endgame. And you're right. You do disappoint me. Because you don't play fair."

That gives him pause. He doesn't want to see himself as a monster.

"What do you mean I don't play fair?"

It's exactly the response she'd hoped for. She began with seemingly idle conversation designed to disarm and gather information while keeping him off-balance. Just the way he did with her.

Now she has to beat him at his own game.

He's right about one thing. She has been in a courtroom long enough to be able to read criminal behavior. And William Henry Young is no different from any other defendant. Their shared past clouded her judgment, made it impossible for her to be objective. But if she takes herself out of the equation, he's just another serial killer with a father who likely abandoned him and a mother he both loved and hated. The individual details may change, but the impulse driving them is always the same.

The need to feel powerful.

Admired.

In control.

She has to take that control away from him. Rewrite the narrative. But he has to believe that everything is being orchestrated by him. He's the one making the decisions.

But she'll make the first move. She'll start by tossing down the gauntlet.

Hurling his own words back at him.

"Aren't you the one who said where was the sport in killing me since I was at such an unfair disadvantage? Or was that a lie?"

"I never lie."

"Prove it."

"How? By liberating you? Nice try, Alice."

She was prepared for that too.

"You said we shared the same darkness. That that was the reason I got into your car." Something she'll regret until the day she dies. "Because we have a special connection. You said I wanted you as much as you wanted me. You still want me, don't you?"

"Now who's trying to take unfair advantage? I expected more from you, Alice. Using what was between us in the past is such an obvious ploy. And you've already let me know how you feel about me. But you're right. We do have unfinished business. After all, you're the one who got away."

The expression on his face chills her, but she soldiers on.

What other choice does she have?

She has one last card to play.

"You said that I was in your prison now. Which implies that you were in mine. But you were never shackled in my courtroom. I could have ordered you to be, but I chose not to. I gave you free rein during your trial."

She takes a breath and studies him. His face gives nothing away. "You said you wanted respect. I showed you respect by refusing to allow you to be shackled, which I thought would be too prejudicial for the jury. Why won't you show me the same respect?"

"Sorry, Alice. It doesn't work that way."

"Maybe it's because that's who you really are. A monster who chains up an unarmed, physically weaker woman even if there's no sport in that."

His blue eyes grow darker. That muscle jumps in his jaw. She can see the effort it's taking for him to tamp down the anger that, like hers, is never far from the surface. "For a judge with book smarts, you're not a very good judge of character. You think you can provoke me into freeing you. And you have it backwards. I give women what they want. You wanted the same thing that night. But you got scared. Only it wasn't me you were running from. It was yourself."

"You're wrong." No matter how upset and guilt-ridden she felt after leaving the party, it was what she saw in his eyes that made her run. Then she remembers something. "In the car, you said that deer should have run when she had the chance. Who were you really talking about? Your mother? Was your father the monster she should have run from?"

Her stab in the dark paid off. His mouth flies open. But instead of the rage she expects, he lets out a belly laugh that reverberates off the walls.

"Oh, Alice. You think you know me." He stops laughing abruptly. "Now I have a question for you. How far do you think you'll be able to run with that ankle? You don't have to answer. It was rhetorical. But just to show you what a good sport I can be and in light of what we once were to each other, I'm going to give you what you want. You'll see, Alice. I'm not the monster you think I am."

He smiles to let her know how magnanimous he's being. Winks as he picks up the candle and the pot. Whistles through his teeth as he walks to the door.

She listens to the sound of his footsteps dying away.

His face floats out of the void.

She sees that diabolical smile.

Hears that tuneless whistle.

He gave in too easily.

He's planning something.

And she played right into his hands.

She forces herself to focus.

Closes her eyes.

Once again hears him earlier. His footsteps. The shadows on the wall.

Watching him emerge in the wavering light of the candle he was holding.

Something seemed different about him.

She felt it as he removed the lid from the pot.

What was it?

An intensity. A single-mindedness of purpose as he fed her.

And something else.

He seemed pent-up. Like a little boy on Christmas Eve. Nodding with satisfaction after she finished every bite. As if he'd achieved some kind of victory.

Why was it so important to him that she eat the meals he prepared? What did keeping up her strength matter? She already knew his endgame. Did he have something else in mind?

Or was he just fattening her up for the kill?

Of course, she could be remembering it wrong. Projecting.

Maybe it was another trick of the light.

But she sensed those same emotions in him when he said he gave women what they want.

He said she wanted the same thing the night she got into his car.

She wanted to be desired. To feel loved.

He wants love. He admitted as much.

What did his father do to his mother?

Whatever happened between them, it wasn't about desire.

Or love.

It's all connected somehow.

The key to his pathology.

She has to figure out what that is.

Or she's going to die.

FIFTY-ONE

Connie shifts into park.

In the near distance, the headstones of Old Lowood Cemetery glow with an unearthly light.

They'll have to go the rest of the way on foot.

Good thing she brought the shotgun.

Just in case they run into a black bear.

But it isn't just black bears they have to steer clear of.

Next to her in the passenger seat, Mia stares straight ahead. In the reflection of the headlights, she looks like the proverbial deer. Barely moving; barely even breathing. As if one false move will shatter her into a thousand pieces.

Connie can almost smell her fear.

She kills the lights. The last thing she needs is to broadcast their arrival. It's so damn dark. You'd never know there's daylight on the other side of the trees.

Connie expected Mia to take her to wherever she's been living.

Not into the woods.

Maybe she should have called Church after all.

As if reading her mind, the other woman grabs her arm. She's shaking again.

"It's okay, Mia. Everything's going to be okay."

Connie wishes she felt as confident as she sounds. She picks up the flashlight she brought with her. "Can you take me to him?"

Mia nods.

"Wait in the car," Connie tells Alexis McKerrity. "After we're gone, lock the doors."

"I'm coming with you."

"Alexis—"

"You're not leaving me here alone."

Connie hears the finality in McKerrity's voice. If Connie's smart, she'll turn around and get the hell out of the woods.

Let Walter Church take it from here.

But she's never been one to back down from danger.

Or let an abuser get away with it.

No one says anything as they pile out of the car. The sound of doors closing shatters the stillness. It echoes in Connie's ears as she turns to Mia. "You ready?"

Mia nods. Hitches in a breath like she's trying to gather her courage.

"Stay close behind me," Connie tells McKerrity. She hands Mia the flashlight and hitches the sling holding the shotgun higher up on her shoulder as they start walking, the wavering yellow beam illuminating only a few feet in front of them. Now the forest seems to burst with sound, the cheeping and chattering of nocturnal creatures keeping them company as they walk. Then the noise dies down, as if the animals were all holding their breath.

The sudden silence spooks Connie even more.

She can't remember the last time she was here. It's got to be decades. She has a flash of Alice showing up at her house that Saturday morning, twigs and leaves clinging to her.

Now her daughter's here.

And she's pregnant.

Again, Connie chastises herself for not forcing Alexis McKerrity to stay behind.

A twig snaps.

There's someone behind that tree.

Connie has no idea how badly wounded he is, but she isn't taking any chances. Son of a bitch could be lying in wait to ambush them.

She aims the shotgun.

It hasn't been fired in years.

Doesn't mean she can't shoot.

Shoot to kill, if necessary.

Something darts out from behind the tree. It stops for a millisecond before scurrying off in the opposite direction.

Just a raccoon.

Connie lets out a relieved sigh. Then draws in her breath again.

There's a parked car up ahead.

She tightens her grip on the shotgun as she approaches the car.

Someone's in the driver's seat.

As she gets closer, Connie sees a figure behind the wheel.

A woman.

She isn't moving.

Connie keeps the gun aimed as she slowly opens the driver's door.

Alexis McKerrity lets out a gasp.

The woman is slumped back in her seat. The headrest is coated with dried blood.

She's wearing black trousers and a black blazer over a white blouse. Then Connie notices her shoes.

They're similar to the boots Walter Church wears.

Connie turns to Mia. "Who is she?" Instead of answering, Mia starts backing away. "It's okay. She can't hurt you anymore." As Connie studies the dead woman, she tries to put the pieces together.

This woman was Mia's abuser?

She was also a cop?

Maybe she has it wrong. The woman could have been a hired gun. Or a PI who tracked Mia to Lowood.

But who shot her?

Connie didn't see a gun on Mia. Doesn't mean she hasn't got one.

Before she can ask her, Mia starts walking again, the beams of Connie's flashlight wavering in the dark.

She's leading them deeper into the woods.

FIFTY-TWO

S he smells him first.

It's the same scent he was wearing the night she got into his car—*seeing only his shadowy form behind the wheel because he'd turned off the lights.*

His shadow dances down the wall.

Disappears.

She hears him breathing.

The *whoosh* of a match being lit.

She watches his silhouette touch the matchlight to the wick of a candle, which he then places on the floor.

He crouches down, touches flame to wick.

Over and over again.

She blinks as the light from a dozen candles fills her vision.

He rises.

Looks at her.

And she sees him.

Across the bar.

He smiles.

He's still smiling as he steps carefully around the candles he placed in a semicircle as if they were some kind of offering.

He walks toward her.

This time, it isn't a trick of the light.

He shaved off the mustache and beard.

Except for the gray in his newly cut hair, it's him.

The stranger in the bar.

The monster in the woods.

"You're remembering too, aren't you?"

His voice has dropped to a silky whisper. It crawls across her skin like an insect, burrowing deep inside her.

A soft voice.

A seductive voice.

A voice designed to disarm his unsuspecting victims.

The voice she never heard.

Until the day William Henry Young walked into her courtroom.

"I have another surprise for you, Alice."

She tenses as he reaches behind his back. His hand disappears into his left pocket.

He pulls out the Glock. Aims it at her.

"You should see your face." He laughs. "Just to show you that I don't take unfair advantage." He takes a tiny key from his coat pocket and crouches down. He unlocks her ankle chains. Then he slides out another key—Luiz's key—and leans closer. As he unlocks the handcuffs, his cologne overpowers her. And something else. That bestial odor that no amount of man-made ingredients can disguise.

When she's free, he hauls her to her feet. She totters, and he grabs her. Holds her close, a grotesque tableau of lovers locked in an embrace. Bile fills her throat as his lips brush her hair. When he finally lets her go, he takes her hand and rubs it across his clean-shaven cheek.

"Doesn't that feel good? I did it for you, Alice."

His words send an involuntary shudder through her.

Then she reminds herself that she's no longer shackled.

It's a first step.

"I remember." She forces herself to smile. "You look just like you did then."

It was the wrong thing to say. His hand drops as his blue eyes darken. "Don't lie to me, Alice. I can't abide falsehoods. Especially from you. If we can't have the Lord's honest truth between us, what's left?"

"Love."

He looks at her, then nods as if it this were a test and she finally gave the correct answer. "Ah. Yes." He cocks his head as he studies her. "Who do you love, Alice?"

She doesn't respond. It's another trick. A trap.

"I know you loved your mother. I could tell from your voice when you talked about her. Which is as the Lord intended. What child doesn't love his mother? She's the first person in our life. The one we trust to protect us. To keep us safe. But your mother didn't do that."

He shakes his head. "She died and left you all alone. And you hated her for that, didn't you? You never forgave her for leaving you and forcing you to live with your father. The man who dragged you to church every Sunday. You said you weren't sure you believed in our exalted Father. I bet that made your daddy angry. Turning your back on the Lord."

Still, she says nothing. She knows what he's trying to do. Manipulate her into showing weakness. She refuses to engage. She won't take the bait.

"But that's all in the past. Although we both know the past is always with us. Sometimes masquerading as truth. Sometimes as something else." He leans closer. She fights the urge to gag. "Tell me about your husband."

At the mention of Charles, Alice feels a rush of emotion. She flashes to the last time she saw him. When she came home to retrieve the gun to shoot William Henry Young. Charles's once-handsome face a mass of worry lines. Now she's sure that he knew what she had planned.

She blinks away tears. Will that be her final memory of him?

"If you really want to know, he has early onset Alzheimer's." In spite of herself, it feels good to finally speak aloud the secret she's been keeping to herself for two interminable years. "And if you really aren't a monster, you'll let me call home to find out how he is."

They'd barely driven away from the courthouse when Young reached into the pocket of her robe and grabbed her phone. He removed the SIM card, which he cut into tiny pieces with the scissors the court officer handed him from her handbag. He then smashed the phone to smithereens under his shoe.

He'd overlooked nothing.

Young is shaking his head. "You know I can't let you do that. But I'm truly sorry to hear about your husband. A human brain reduced to rubble. How hard that must be to live with. I can only imagine how angry that must have made you. Yet you still care about him even though he can't love you the way the Lord created man in His exalted image to love a woman. Maybe he never could."

Once again, Alice feels him reaching into her mind. Seeing herself on her wedding night. A frightened twenty-eight-year-old who'd married an older man because she thought he was safe. Giving up passion and intimacy for what became an essentially sexless marriage.

How could Young know that?

He isn't insane. Just a sadistic bully who takes pleasure in other people's pain.

"You don't have to tell me. I can see the answer in your face. A pity. You and I could have known real love. Now it's too late."

Panic overtakes her anger.

She can't allow all this to have been for naught.

"Now who's the liar?" That gets his attention. "If you believed that, you wouldn't have gone to all this trouble." When he remains silent, she presses her advantage. "You said we had unfinished business. Maybe your walking into my courtroom was a sign. What the Lord intended. That we'd end up here where it all began. It's our destiny. Coming full circle."

Still, he says nothing. But he hasn't shackled her again. She inches closer. Lowers her voice to a whisper. "Think of it as a second chance. Not everyone gets that."

She brings a hand to his face. Forces herself to caress his skin even as her own flesh starts to crawl.

"You said I was still beautiful. Maybe that's true. Or maybe you're seeing what you want to see." Throwing back his own words at him. "Neither of us is who we once were. How can we be? But we're still the same inside, where it counts. You said you wanted love. I want it, too."

Is it her imagination, or does his gaze soften?

For a moment, she sees the stranger in the bar again.

So much hope and promise in that blue gaze. At least, to a naïve, conflicted sixteen-year-old.

Young raises a hand to her cheek. "Your skin is so soft. Like velvet."

His touch brings her back. She goes cold inside. Feels her body start to shake. He doesn't seem to notice as he takes her hands and tenderly strokes the raw, red skin of her wrists.

She forces the words past the thickness of her tongue. "We can start over."

That seems to resonate. "Yes. It will be as if the past never existed. We'll begin with a blank slate. The way children come into the world. That is why the Lord in his infinite wisdom has seen fit to reunite us."

She hears it in his voice again. Sees it in his eyes. That air of excitement. Of anticipation. She can't let herself dwell on what that means. He grasps her hands and starts inching backwards.

He stops. "Are you sure? This is a big decision. You have to be ready."

She nods, even though she has no idea what he's talking about.

He smiles. The torn, matted material of her robe trails behind like the train of a gown as he continues to move them backwards. As if he were leading her onto a dance floor, swaying to music only he can hear.

Alice pretends to stumble on her injured ankle. As she starts to go down, she tries to wrench free. But he grasps her arms tighter and yanks her to her feet.

Her bare feet slide across the floor as he drags her toward the open space in the semi-circle of candles. She's still struggling to get away when he pulls her against his chest. Grasping her under the arms, he lifts her into the air.

And throws her down.

The back of her skull collides with the hard, damp earth.

Her vision blurs.

She sees double.

When she opens her eyes, there are two of him.

Two sets of blue eyes staring down at her.

"You think I didn't know what you were up to? But how could I resist letting you believe you could escape?" His laugh echoes in her head. "No one deceives William Henry Young. Not even my mama, may she rot in hell. Where you're going after you give me what I want."

Hands close around her neck.

The screams die in her throat as fingers squeeze her windpipe.

She claws at his hands. He squeezes harder. She struggles to pry his fingers away. Her fingers become entangled in the gold chain around her neck. She feels it start to give way. Her skin burns as the chain breaks.

It's sliding off her neck. Her blurred vision conjures the trio of entwined hearts dangling from the gold chain that she never took off. It was her mother's final gift, a symbol of her love for her daughter; hers and the father Alice couldn't remember. Her last coherent thought as her vision tunnels into darkness that she'll finally see her again.

"Don't fight it, Alice."

She's still awake.

The sounds of the forest engulf her. Sharp pebbles and rocks press into her back.

She opens her eyes and sees an owl perched on a high branch, tracking her with its ancient yellow eyes.

She feels eyes all around.

And something moving at the edges of her vision . . .

Candlelight dances on the walls.

It hypnotizes her.

He just removed the skirt she was wearing underneath her robe.

Now her panties are ripping.

He's got them in his teeth.

The flames flicker higher. She can feel their heat.

Seeping into her sluggish mind.

He pushes up her robe and settles himself on top of her.

She's pinned beneath him.

But her arms are free.

"Bill?"

She's never called him by that name before.

He lifts his head, as she knew he would.

She shoves the candle in his face. He screams as the flame singes his skin. He grabs frantically at her wrist, tries to push the candle away.

She lets the candle drop. He rears back, presses his hands to his face.

Adrenaline surges through her. She scrambles to her feet.

It's agony to run, but she can't stop now.

Behind her, she hears the monster. Roaring in pain and rage.

Her ankle gives out and she stumbles, for real this time.

She forces herself to keep moving. She has no idea where she's going or what direction leads out of this hellish maze.

It's getting colder.

His footsteps thunder behind her.

Then she sees it.

A door.

She pushes it open.

And barricades herself inside.

FIFTY-THREE

"**W**ho is she?"

Alexis McKerrity is shaking so hard she can barely get out the words.

"I'm not sure." But Connie is sure they should get the hell out of here while they still can. Except there's a dead body in the car. If Mia is the shooter—and Connie can't believe she is—how can she say it was self-defense when the victim was shot in the back of the head?

"She wants us to c-c-c-come," McKerrity says through chattering teeth.

In the distance, Mia is waving the flashlight in the air. "Stay close to me," Connie tells McKerrity. Since she can't be sure who killed the cop, she can't risk leaving the younger woman behind. Not that McKerrity would listen.

She keeps her shotgun aimed as they walk.

When they reach Mia, she's staring at the ground. "Be careful," Connie warns McKerrity as she edges closer to the open bear trap.

There's something inside.

Connie crouches down and lifts out a woman's shoe.

It can't belong to the dead cop. She's wearing both her shoes.

And this isn't a black boot. It's a low-heeled brown pump.

Alexis McKerrity gasps.

Connie shoots to her feet. "What is it?"

"It looks like m-m-my mother's shoe . . ."

Connie's mind spirals back. To Alice when she showed up outside her window that long-ago Saturday morning. She was barefoot, the stilettoes Connie loaned her to wear to the party nowhere to be seen.

But even if this had been the mate to the pair Alice wore that freezing December night, how could her daughter think she recognized the shoe thirty years later?

Connie crouches down again.

There's blood in the trap. It looks fairly fresh.

Her head spins. What could this mean? Alice was here? Recently? But she lives in New York City. Hours away from Lowood. She hasn't come anywhere near this town in thirty years.

She studies the shoe. It looks like any other brown pump. "Do you really think this belongs to your mother?"

McKerrity doesn't answer. She's sliding out her phone. After she turns it on, she lets out a scream.

Connie gets to her feet, looks over McKerrity's shoulder.

Several missed texts, emails, and social media posts are on the screen.

Including a news flash at the bottom.

It came in twelve hours ago.

FIFTY-FOUR

Darkness surrounds her.

And the cold that now feels as if it's a part of her.

He's pounding on the door. She ignores him as her eyes adjust to the dimness.

She has experience now.

All those hours alone in the dark.

"UNLOCK THIS DOOR!"

His rage ignites her own as she tries to figure out what kind of room this is.

But there's something in the corner.

She hobbles over.

It's caked with dust.

She touches it, and it starts to rock.

Back and forth.

"YOU'RE NOT ALLOWED IN THERE!"

She barely hears him now as she realizes where she is.

A space he converted into a primitive nursery.

She almost trips over something next to the wood crib.

A mattress on the floor. Covered by a light film of dust.

Which means that someone slept here at one time.

Her blood chills.

"YOU FUCKING BITCH! NOW YOU'RE GOING TO DIE!"

A deafening noise pierces the air.

He shot out the lock.

Alice grabs the ends of the crib. It's heavier than she thought, but she finally gets it moving. She slides it across the room and shoves it against the door.

He jiggles the doorknob.

The door doesn't budge.

As he curses at her through the door, she frantically tries to piece it together.

Whoever slept on the mattress had to be one of his victims.

Was he keeping some of the women here? Why?

He's pushing against the door. She can hear his animal grunts.

As Alice pushes back, her face presses up against the wooden bars of the crib.

She stares into its eerie emptiness.

"It will be as if the past never existed. We'll begin with a blank slate. The way children come into the world. That is why the Lord in his infinite wisdom has seen fit to reunite us."

She's in the other room.

He's feeding her.

Telling her that she has to keep up her strength.

For what? Why did she need to keep up her strength if he was planning to kill her?

Because killing wasn't his endgame.

Or maybe it was.

Once his victims were no longer useful.

"No one deceives William Henry Young. Not even my mama, may she rot in hell. Where you're going after you give me what I want."

Alice isn't sure how his mother figures into this.

But she knows what he wants.

God save them all.

Another ear-splitting sound shatters her eardrums.

The doorframe shakes. The wood in the door splinters.

The crib starts to move.

Alice puts all her body weight behind it. Stumbles back as the door flies open.

She shoves the crib at him.

He pushes it aside as if it weighed nothing.

Her ankle starts to give out as she backs up.

"I know why you're bringing them here."

He doesn't answer.

He's a shadowy silhouette across the room, but she can see the silver gleam of Luiz's Glock.

"You weren't feeding them to fatten them up for the kill. You were trying to make them pregnant."

She feels the wall against her back. There's nowhere left to go.

"Where are they? Where are the children?"

FIFTY-FIVE

Supreme Court Judge Alice D. McKerrity was abducted from a Manhattan courthouse a few hours ago by William Henry Young, the defendant who was on trial. The judge has brown eyes and ash-brown hair and was last seen wearing her judicial robe. Young has blue eyes, gray hair, a mustache, and a beard. He was last seen wearing a blue suit and a red tie. He is armed and extremely dangerous. It is believed that Young kidnapped McKerrity and made his escape in a black sedan driven by a third person. No other information is currently available.

Connie's mind reels as she reads. Next to her, McKerrity stares at her phone in open-mouthed shock.

Alice was kidnapped?

Connie looks at the brown pump in her hand. If this really is Alice's shoe, that means—

She's here. In Lowood.

Connie can't wrap her mind around that.

Alice gets assaulted in the woods and thirty years later she's abducted and brought back to the same place?

What are the odds of that happening?

Unless—

Her kidnapper is the same man.

How is that possible?

Alexis McKerrity grabs Connie's arm. "Where did he take her?"

"I don't know." She didn't know back then either. She always assumed that Alice's assailant had raped her in the woods.

But where? The woods go on for hundreds of miles.

The news flash saying Alice was abducted a few hours ago came in at one o'clock this afternoon.

It's now almost ten-thirty.

Nearly half a day.

Alice could be anywhere by now.

On McKerrity's phone screen, there are two photos side by side. The one on the left is of Alice. She looks older, but there's no doubt that it's Connie's old friend.

Connie studies the photo on the right.

It's the man who abducted Alice.

William Henry Young.

The name means nothing to her.

With her finger, she enlarges the photo.

Now she can see his features.

She looks at his eyes.

Merciful God in Heaven.

She knows those blue eyes.

She looks up.

McKerrity is running toward Mia, who has stopped next to an overgrown knoll.

Connie wonders if she's seeing things as the younger woman pushes aside some of the vegetation, revealing a low, squat building that had been hidden from view.

FIFTY-SIX

Her eyes follow the Glock as he advances. He's still on the other side of the nursery. He moves slowly, and there's an odd shamble to his usual purposeful stride. He stumbles here and there, as if he were drunk.

Through the thin material of her robe, Alice can feel the coldness of the stone wall against her spine. And the throbbing of her ankle. She shifts her weight to the other foot. "Where are the children?" she asks again. "You must have dozens by now."

"They are with Him."

The room throws back echoes of his voice.

"They're dead?" She shudders as she pictures the women he raped and murdered in their graves under the earth, their lifeless babies next to them. "All of them?" Alice sees the shadowy silhouette of the crib that now stands unmoving on the other side of the room. She's picturing that thick coating of dust.

From years of disuse.

Perhaps decades.

"How did they die?"

Again, he doesn't answer. But the Glock is no longer moving toward her. Because he's no longer moving. Her gaze is drawn back to the bed that stands just a few feet away, covered by only a thin layer of dust.

Because someone slept there recently.

His latest victim.

Not Angel Diallo. She never got into his car. The working girl before her?

She tries to visualize the scenario:

Young abducts a woman in New York City and brings her to Lowood, where he enslaves her. Feeds her. Rapes her. When she conceives, he brings her into the nursery to await the birth of their child.

But something goes wrong.

Alice keeps Young in her line of vision as she creeps toward the bed.

She looks down at the mattress. Now she can see the dark red stains under the layer of dust.

Sweet Jesus.

The crib is covered in dust because it was never occupied. No newborn baby was ever laid in there.

Their remains aren't in the graves because they didn't leave this room. Didn't take their first breath outside their mothers' wombs.

They were never born.

FIFTY-SEVEN

The rusted iron door swings slowly back on its hinges.

Connie takes a step closer. Through the opening, she sees a series of cracked stones. It takes a few seconds to find her voice. "What's down there?"

Her question goes unanswered. Mia looks like she's in a trance. So does McKerrity. Then Connie remembers that she still has McKerrity's phone. She holds it out to Mia, points at the photo of Alice. "Did you see her?" Mia's head bobs slowly up and down. "When?"

"Before." Mia's eyes are huge with fear as she whispers the word.

Was that why she didn't show up for work? "What about him?" Connie indicates the photo of William Henry Young, again feels that jolt of recognition as she looks into his blue eyes.

Mia is making mewling noises in her throat. Connie tries to keep the alarm out of her voice. "Did you see him take the judge down there?" The mewling sounds get louder. Connie again studies the decrepit stone steps that lead down to God knows where.

Is Alice down there?

Merciful Lord in Heaven.

Connie pulls out her phone. There's no reception. "Alexis, give me your cell." When she doesn't respond, Connie takes her phone. No reception on her device, either.

She could go back to the spot where they were standing earlier. But that would waste precious time. And she can't be sure she'll even be able to get out a call.

"Mia." The mewling noises stop. "Take my car and drive to the sheriff's office. It's on Main Street. You know Sheriff Church. He comes into the diner every day for breakfast. Key's in the ignition. Do you hear me? Mia?"

The other woman blinks as if she just woke up.

"I need you to get the sheriff. Now. Mia!"

The younger woman nods as if she were a dog, responding to the sound of her name. Anger bubbles up in Connie. She can only imagine what Mia's abuser did to her. And she has no idea what she was doing in the woods in the first place.

None of that matters now.

Mia's looking at her, as if waiting for her next command. "Go," Connie says. Mia takes a step, then another. Connie turns to Alexis. "Go with Mia."

"I'm not leaving my mother!"

"Please, Alexis—"

"No!"

"Okay." The last thing Connie needs is for McKerrity to get hysterical. "Then stay here. Wait for Mia to come back with the sheriff." Connie hands McKerrity's phone back to her, then hitches her shotgun higher on her shoulder.

The alert called William Henry Young armed and dangerous.

He's the one who killed the woman in the car that matches the description in the news flash.

She was probably the getaway driver.

Connie's armed too. And she has something on her side that son of a bitch doesn't.

The element of surprise.

She failed her old friend once.

She won't fail her again.

FIFTY-EIGHT

"What did you do to those women?"

"They had to be punished."

The reverberation of his voice makes him sound closer than he is. He's still across the room, but she knows how fast he can move.

"Why did they have to be punished? What did any of them ever do to you? What did Angel Diallo do?"

"She was just like the others. Having sex with anonymous men in the parking lot. The father of her child could have been any one of them."

That was what he said when he cross-examined Dr. Hannah Liu.

Now she understands. He didn't murder Angel Diallo and her unborn child because he hated pregnant women. Just the opposite. "That's why you killed her in that abandoned lot. She was carrying another man's child."

"We can never fully fathom what The Lord in His infinite wisdom sees fit to do. We are only His human vessels, after all."

She can barely contain her fury. "Was it the Lord who beat Angel Diallo's belly until her child bled out of her? What about your other victims?"

"What happened to them was not at my hand. They were sinners and they paid the price."

"Are you saying those women miscarried? They lost their babies?" She can barely get out the words.

"You shouldn't have come in here."

The Glock starts moving as Young advances toward her, his gait unsteady.

Because he can't see in the dark?

Or because of where they are?

The key to his pathology is here.

In this room.

Where he turned the miracle of life into something dark and twisted. Unspeakable.

"Why do you want a child so badly?"

He doesn't answer. Curses as he stumbles over something in his path.

"I read your rap sheet. You have no birth certificate. It's as if you'd never been born. Just like all those dead babies."

He makes a guttural sound in his throat as he keeps advancing.

"But you had a father and a mother. Did you know your daddy? Or was he gone before you were born?"

She watches his shadowy form weave across the room, her eyes on the Glock.

"What did your daddy do to your mama?"

"Why didn't she run when she had the chance?"

"Why should she rot in hell?"

The Glock is swaying wildly in his hands. He stumbles against the crib, which starts rocking.

"She didn't keep you safe, did she? The person you trusted to protect you." Throwing back his own words at him.

"CUNT!

"DECEIVER!

"WHORE!"

His voice bounces off the walls, the words echoing over and over.

She was wrong.

His father isn't the target of his rage.

It's his mother.

He picks up the crib and hurls it across the room.

Alice creeps down the wall.

He trips over the bed. Shoves it out of his way.

He stops.

"I know you're there, Alice. I can hear you breathing."

He takes a step. Another.

She edges farther down the wall.

He stops again. Cocks his head to listen.

Alice keeps moving, certain he can hear her heart thundering against her ribs. She shrinks into herself as if she could will her body into invisibility.

He's almost at the wall. She has reached the end. There's nowhere else to go.

She can feel him smiling in the dark.

He's enjoying this.

She holds her breath as he comes nearer.

Stops a few feet away.

Her eyes move from the gun in his hand to his face.

Her breath whooshes out of her.

Even in the dimness, she can see it.

The puckered skin where she burned him with the candle.

And above his cheekbone.

Dear God.

The candle flame didn't sear only his skin.

His right eye is a red-rimmed ruin.

As she watches, the eye begins to ooze. The viscous liquid runs down his withered cheek, and she experiences the strangest sensation. It's as if the outer layer of his skin were dissolving. His face disintegrating before her.

Revealing yet another.

The real William Henry Young?

The other eye is twitching now. She stares into the unmarred blue of his intact left eye. Tears have formed at the corners. His lashes are wet.

It's an illusion, of course; one eye compensating for the ocular devastation of the other.

The blue eye twitches again. He blinks. Moisture drips from the eye. He wipes it away with his sleeve. The eye fills again.

He's blinking rapidly now, the water in his left eye blurring his vision.

She creeps back down the wall.

He doesn't react.

She's on his blind side.

She pushes off the wall.

And runs.

"YOU FUCKING BITCH! YOU'LL NEVER ESCAPE!"

She can hear the Glock's safety latch releasing.

The first shot goes wild.

The next one hits the doorframe seconds after she makes it through the doorway.

And almost collides with the barrel of a shotgun.

FIFTY-NINE

The tall blond holding the shotgun looks as shocked as Alice feels.

"Alice! Are you all right? Are you hurt?"

She shakes her head. She hasn't heard that voice in thirty years. "Get behind me."

Alice does as she says, a dozen questions racing through her mind. She can't believe she's here. She touches the other woman's arm as if to reassure herself she's real, that this isn't a dream.

Connie gives her a brief smile. She turns back to the open doorway, but all is silent within. "Maybe he's conserving his bullets."

"Or he can't see." Alice tells her quickly what happened.

"That took guts." Her familiar green eyes search Alice's. "Is this where he kept you?" Alice shakes her head, knowing her old friend is picturing that long-ago Saturday morning when Alice showed up at her house. "Okay. Here's the deal. Start backing up. When I give the signal, we run."

Alice barely breathes as they move away from the doorway, praying her ankle will hold up.

They stop at a sound. Look at each other.

"That'll be the police," Connie whispers.

Alice goes weak-kneed with relief. Then she realizes.

If they heard footsteps, so did Young.

The footsteps stop.

A woman with a mane of wild red hair materializes out of the dark.

"What are you doing here? Where's Sheriff Church?"

The woman looks at Connie as if she has no idea who she is. Then she hangs her head. "I've been a bad girl."

"Mia," Connie whispers, her eyes on the doorway. "Go get the sheriff. Hurry!"

The woman snaps to attention. But instead of going back the way she came, she starts walking toward the nursery.

"Don't go in there."

The redhead ignores Connie. She moves as if she were in a trance. She stops a few feet from the open doorway and spins around, her face contorted in rage. "No one's allowed in this room. It's against the rules. And you know what happens when you break the rules. You get punished."

She turns back to the doorway. Startles as if she heard something. Then she squares her shoulders and steps across the threshold.

"What are you doing in the nursery?" She cocks her head. "I'm sorry I wasn't here to welcome you home. Please don't put me in the Ice Room. I won't do it again, Daddy. I promise."

Daddy?

This woman is Young's daughter?

Next to Alice, Connie is staring in open-mouthed shock.

The woman starts backing out of the room. "What happened to your face? Why do you have a gun?"

A shadow crosses the doorway.

Connie aims the shotgun.

No one moves. No one breathes.

Then everything explodes in sound.

Footsteps pounding down the hall.

The red-haired woman yelling "Daddy" over and over.

A figure stampeding toward them.

Connie shouting a warning because Alice has no voice.

The figure running into Young's immediate line of vision.

Howls erupting from Alice's throat as Young backs out of the nursery, the Glock against her daughter's head.

SIXTY

A lice runs after them, her ankle on fire.

They disappear through a narrow passageway.

It's darker here, the uneven, rocky ground cutting her bare feet.

She can no longer see her daughter or Young.

But she can hear him.

Surefooted, now. No tripping or stumbling.

No missteps.

Even with his impaired vision, he has the advantage. He knows the way blind.

It's his exit strategy.

He orchestrated his courthouse escape too carefully to not have an escape route from the icehouse.

"Mama!"

Her heart nearly stops.

"Let her go," Alice cries. "Take me. I'm the one you want."

Young's laugh reverberates around her, making it impossible to pinpoint where he is.

Rage drives Alice forward.

She stops. Hears something else.

The sound of someone breathing. For a second Connie's face looms, her green eyes gleaming in the dimness.

Now she's moving away.

A shot rings out.

Alexis screams.

Alice rushes blindly ahead, oblivious to everything but reaching her daughter.

She's in another passageway.

The ground is flooded here.

The hem of her robe drags in the water, which rises higher with every treacherous step.

And it's getting brighter, as if she were moving closer to a source of light.

Illuminating the arched dome of the low ceiling and curved stone walls that feel as if they're closing in on her.

She hears the sound of water splashing behind her.

"Daddy!"

The red-haired woman wades past Alice as if she weren't there.

"We don't need her," Mia shouts. "We can make things like they were before you left. Just the two of us. Together forever."

The crack of another gunshot echoes through the tunnel.

Mia wobbles on her feet, then falls.

Now Alice sees them.

Young is still pointing the Glock as he inches backward through the water toward the mouth of the tunnel, holding Alexis in front of him like a shield.

She's still screaming.

"You bastard! Let her go!"

She ducks as he fires.

Shouts at her daughter to run as he again takes aim.

She drops to her knees.

SIXTY-ONE

S he doesn't move.

Barely breathes as she kneels in the water.

"Mama!"

Alice rises unsteadily to her feet, not sure if she's awake or dreaming. There's a buzzing in her head, and her ears are ringing.

The water splashes up around her as Alexis runs into her arms.

Alice is unprepared for the heaviness of her daughter's limbs under the bulky sweater. As if she were expecting the child she bore and not the woman Alexis is now.

She's whimpering. Alice holds her closer. She hasn't held her like this in decades, when Alexis would wake up screaming from a nightmare.

As if the terror inside of Alice had been reborn in her.

Her mind goes dark.

Back to a time before she held her daughter.

When her child emerged from her ravaged womb on an unusually cold, early September night, kicking and screaming her bloody way into the world. Barely able to look at her as the newborn was placed in her arms.

Alice's mind spins further back.

To another night.

In the woods.

Her rapist on top of her.

Tearing apart her insides.

The last few minutes come rushing back.

The blast of the shotgun still reverberates in her head.

She tries to cover her daughter's body with her own as she looks around. After the deafening noise of earlier, everything feels so quiet.

Too quiet.

A few feet from the mouth of the tunnel, she sees Connie.

Her back is to her.

Alexis clings to her as Alice wades through the water.

When they get there, Connie is aiming her shotgun at Young. The red-haired woman lies a few feet away.

Young is on the ground, the lower half of his body submerged in water that's rapidly turning red.

His eyes are closed.

"Is he—?"

Connie shakes her head. "The son of a bitch is still breathing. I was aiming at his heart. I got him in the leg. But I might have hit his femur."

That would account for all the blood. "How long do you think he has?"

"No idea. And I could be wrong. The water could make it look like there's more blood than there really is."

"So he might not be dying?"

"Maybe not."

Alexis turns away from the sight. Buries her face in her mother's chest.

Alice can hear Young moaning now as he presses down on his thigh in a vain attempt to stem the flow of blood. "I don't see the Glock."

"It's probably under the water somewhere," Connie says. "But I wasn't taking any chances. The bastard missed me by a hair."

Alice remembers seeing Connie's face in the dimness earlier, seconds before the first shot rang out.

If Young had killed her, Alice would probably be dead now too.

Her old friend saved her life.

"I want to go."

Her daughter's voice is muffled against her chest, but Alice hears the words.

She could do as Alexis asks. Leave here and go to the police.

Something she should have done thirty years ago.

She knows how that scenario would play out.

Young would be arrested. If he survives, he'd likely stand trial again. If convicted, he'd spend the rest of his life in prison.

But he'd still be alive.

Alice remembers her plan to kill him in her chambers, only to be deprived of the chance.

"Mama?"

She should leave. Now. Before it's too late.

Before she does something she'll regret for the rest of her life.

It's already too late.

Thirty years too late.

Over her daughter's head, Alice's eyes meet Connie's. "Take her out of here," she whispers.

Connie knows.

She also knows there can be no witnesses.

Especially Alice's daughter.

"You and Alexis were never here."

Connie nods, starts to remove the sling holding the shotgun from around her neck.

Then Alice thinks of something.

The police will be looking for the weapon that matches the bullet in Young's leg. A weapon that could be traced back to her friend.

Alice looks around, her mind scrambling for a solution. A few feet away, the red-haired woman lies unmoving in the water. She turns back to Connie. "How do you know Mia?"

"She was a waitress at my diner." Connie's voice breaks on the last words. "She's the one who led us here."

Us?

Alexis lifts her head. Alice reads the guilt there before her daughter averts her face.

Now isn't the time to ask questions. Like what Alexis was doing in Lowood.

"Where do you keep the shotgun?" Alice asks Connie.

"In my apartment."

"Where's your apartment?"

"Above the diner."

Alice doesn't need to say anything more. With a last look at Young, who's barely moving now, Connie goes over to Mia and places the shotgun in her hands.

To the law, it will look like a daughter who tried to kill her father.

"I know who he is."

Connie's face is stormy with anger. That's when Alice realizes. Her friend must have recognized him from that night in the bar. Even after three decades. Did she notice Young and Alice staring at one another while she flirted with him? Did she wonder at the coincidence of him turning up in Alice's courtroom all these years later?

Not coincidence.

Karmic destiny.

Alexis clings tighter, as if she knows what's in her mother's mind. As she gently disengages Alexis's hands from around her neck, Alice sees the gold chain that her daughter never takes off. The rest of the chain isn't visible where it disappears into the vee of her sweater. But Alice knows that the chain holds the three entwined hearts she bought Alexis for her eighteenth birthday.

It was the closest Alice could find to matching the necklace that had been torn from her neck that night in the woods.

A gift from her own mother.

The gold chain containing the triple hearts was all Alice had had left of her.

That won't happen to her daughter.

But first she has to reclaim the part of her that has been lost for so long.

Alexis looks at her, blue eyes full of fear. And questions that Alice can never answer.

Alice watches as Connie puts her arm around Alexis and leads her through the water. Once they're out of the tunnel, she looks down at Young.

Her eyes never leave him as she goes over to Mia's body and picks up the shotgun.

SIXTY-TWO

The water swirling around him has become a blood pool.

Did Connie's shot hit his femoral artery after all?

She could let him bleed out.

It would be an agonizing end.

But he'd be dead.

Only not at her hand.

Where's the justice in that?

In her mind's eye, she sees Mia. Hears the entreaty in her voice as she tells Young that they can make things like they used to be. When it was just the two of them.

Now it's the two of us, Alice thinks. *Him and me.*

She thinks about the confluence of events that led her here.

Back to where it all began.

She thinks again about justice.

And revenge.

The instinct that reduces us to our most primal impulses. Exposing us for the bloodthirsty beasts we are.

Young's eyes are open now. He knows what she's going to do. He tries to crawl away, like the coward he is.

Alice watches him struggle, his movements growing more and more frenzied. His arms chop through the water like propellers as he tries to drag the dead weight of his body out of the line of fire.

She hears it now.

Under the sound of the water.

It reverberates in her head, drowning out everything else.

A plaintive wail that rips at her heart.

Alice knows she's gone, that she's hearing only the echo of her voice.

There is another primal impulse.

A mother's need to protect her child.

She looks down.

Young's hands are no longer chopping the water. He's getting weaker. Losing blood.

She doesn't have much time.

There won't be a second chance.

Slowly, she lowers the gun until it's level with his heart.

Her vision wavers.

She's on the ground, staring up into a pair of blue eyes.

Her mind has become a thing apart from her body as he pounds into her. She feels pain as she's never known before. Now there's a stickiness between her legs. She can feel blood running down the insides of her thighs. But she's too weak to fight.

She closes her eyes. When she opens them, she sees the owl on the high branch, its ancient yellow eyes watching.

Always watching.

Something moves at the edges of her vision.

Just below the owl.

She blinks.

Her double vision clears.

The sea of blue dissipates.

Resolves into a single blue eye.

She shifts her gaze so that she's staring into the ruin of his right eye.

Once again, he becomes the faceless monster of her nightmares.

She grasps the shotgun tighter.

There will be no mistakes this time.

No more lost chances.

Revenge isn't going to slip through her fingers.

All that's left is to pull the trigger.

SIXTY-THREE

"I read that the icehouse was there since before the Civil War."

". . . had to bring in law enforcement from two counties over just to deal with all the dead."

". . . Last I heard, the body count was close to thirty."

"If he hadn't killed them, they would have died from hypothermia."

Connie catches snippets of conversation as she waits on the last few tables of the breakfast rush. She still has the lunch and dinner shifts to get through, which means she'll end up having been on her feet for most of the day and night.

She's done more business in the past week than in the whole last month.

"Can you believe he was trying to force those women to have his babies?"

Connie glances over her shoulder at the table she just passed. A family of four, the teenaged son talking about something he can't understand and hopefully never will. Only a woman could comprehend the true horror of what Young had done.

She still has nightmares after seeing photos of the obscenity of a nursery he'd created out of a room once used to store food and ice.

And she'd known who he was. Before he raped Alice. Before he went on to rape and murder so many women. When she saw his photo on

Alexis McKerrity's phone, she couldn't believe it. Decades older, but it was the same man.

As she picks up two orders, Connie's mind slips back. Going up to the bar for a second round, her sexual antenna on high alert when she spotted him, even though she'd been seeing Luke for six months by then. She was only sixteen, too young to be tied to one boy.

The guy with the sexy surfer looks hanging out at the bar was a charmer. Until she got close to him.

She might have had lousy judgment in men, but she knew evil when she was standing next to it.

That must have been when Young targeted Alice. That night at the bar.

Thirty years later, he walked into Alice's New York City courtroom.

Connie's still trying to wrap her mind around that. She wasn't brought up to believe in the Almighty—her folks were agnostic—but it makes her wonder.

Was it just a coincidence?

Or some higher power?

"Did one of his victims really work here?"

She just placed two heaping plates of flapjacks in front of the couple in the first booth. The husband's looking at her with the same expression she has seen on the faces of everyone who has come into her diner lately. Tourists and reporters are still swarming the town. Not to mention state troopers and the FBI, who have set up shop in the old municipal building next to the courthouse on Main Street. And it doesn't look like they'll be leaving any time soon, not with all the evidence still to be sorted. There isn't a room to be had at the local motels in Lowood or her two sister towns.

A rarity in Lowood, especially with Labor Day over and the school season starting.

Bad news travels fast. Human tragedy even faster.

The man's waiting for her answer.

The bell over the door tinkles.

Saved by the bell.

"Excuse me."

Everyone turns at the sight of the Lowood sheriff walking into the diner.

Walter Church looks as exhausted as Connie has ever seen him.

She leads him to a booth in the back she just cleared. There's a stool open at the counter where he usually sits. But the last thing he needs is to be barraged with questions.

"I don't need a whole booth to myself, Con. You can fit a whole family here."

Trust him to think about her bottom line in the middle of everything.

"Don't worry about it. Your eggs will be out in a few minutes."

"I think I'll skip it today. Just some coffee."

Connie's raises an eyebrow. He hasn't missed breakfast in over two decades. "You have to eat. You need your strength."

"Don't have much of a taste for food right now."

She can't blame him. She feels the same way. "Be right back." She puts checks on the remaining tables, tops up someone's half-empty mug at the counter. A couple just got up and are heading to the register, where two people are waiting to pay their bill.

Church is reading something on his phone when she returns with his coffee.

"I haven't seen you in three days. Besides skipping breakfast, you getting any sleep?"

"Not really." He looks up from his phone. "You look pretty worn out yourself. Haven't found a replacement yet?"

Connie shakes her head, wondering when her mind's going to stop replaying Mia getting shot in the tunnel. Walt was right. That wasn't her real name. And her red hair did come out of a bottle.

If there really is a God, what possible reason could He have had for allowing that to happen? Connie has thought a lot lately about the courage it took for her to leave that prison, only to end up losing her life at the hands of the man who held such power over her.

Connie still regrets not having tried to do more. Like found out who Mia really was. Protected her.

"Don't beat yourself up, Con. You can't help someone who doesn't want to be helped. What I want to know is why he didn't kill her like all the others."

Or why she called him Daddy.

Connie keeps that particular thought to herself.

"Breakfast crowd's thinning out. Why don't you take a break? Join me in a cup of coffee."

Connie looks around. Most of the other tables are paid up. Only a few lingerers left at the counter. She gives them their checks, then grabs the coffee pot and a clean mug.

She didn't realize how tired she was until she slides into the booth opposite Church. An exhaustion she feels in her bones.

His phone chirps.

When he looks up again, his face is grim. "They found another one."

Will this ever end?

The guilt that's never far away digs its claws in deeper as Connie sips her coffee.

Another death that could have been prevented if she'd forced Alice to tell Church what William Henry Young did to her.

Alice was lucky. She survived. After Young raped her, he didn't kill her and dig her grave.

That was why the search almost three decades ago never turned up the bodies of the two local girls who disappeared.

Because Young didn't bury his victims in the woods.

They were found in the ice chamber, a section of the icehouse that Young had turned into a separate room. Like the nursery. Connie remembered Mia calling it the Ice Room when she begged Young to not punish her.

The room Young turned into his own mass graveyard.

The IDs in the wallets that have been recovered so far belong to New York City working girls.

There are rumors that the bodies of his victims before Angel Diallo have been preserved as they were when they died because the extreme cold delayed decomposition. Young's twisted version of cryogenics.

DNA is being analyzed from older remains. One set of bones could belong to Ela Comstock, the sixteen-year-old Cannonville resident who vanished while walking home from a bingo game at the United Methodist Church.

Another is likely the remains of Kimberley Evans, the troubled seventeen-year-old who disappeared after leaving a party in Renegade Falls.

The body found lying on the floor of the tunnel has been identified as Megan O'Sullivan. Like Angel Diallo, she was a working girl. Connie has no idea why, out of all his victims, Young spared her. Or why she called herself Mia. Early tests indicate that she had given birth. What happened to her baby is anyone's guess. In the nearby woods, graves have been uncovered containing tiny skeletons that might have been stillborns or infants who didn't live beyond a few weeks or months.

All casualties of the serial killer whom the media has dubbed the Monster in the Icehouse.

"Con? I need to ask you something."

Church is looking at her strangely. Maybe he didn't buy her story that Megan O'Sullivan must have stolen the shotgun from Connie's apartment above the diner.

"It's about Teddy."

"What about him?"

Church flinches at the sharpness in her voice. "Town wants to throw a parade in his honor. And in honor of the war he fought, they want to rebury the remains of Young's victims that go unclaimed in Old Lowood Cemetery. Next to the soldiers' graves."

"No."

"Connie."

"They can rebury the remains." She thought Teddy would like that. "But no parade. Town doesn't get to make him a hero after everyone was so quick to point fingers back then. They're not going to turn my brother into a spectacle to ease their consciences."

And yours.

"I'm sorry."

Too little, too late.

"He doesn't have to go on living there, you know. There are legal ways."

"You mean force him to leave? Don't you think he's been through enough?"

"I thought you'd want him home. At least his name has finally been cleared."

His words only fuel her anger. "I told you back then he was innocent. That he didn't have anything to do with the disappearances of Evans and Comstock. But did you listen? Did anyone?"

"I won't insult you by saying I was young. Under pressure. Those are just excuses. That's something I have to live with for the rest of my life."

Connie says nothing, her anger gone as quickly as it appeared. Now she just feels drained.

"I'd better get a move on. Thanks for the coffee. And Con? Don't give up hope. Maybe he will come home. Now that it's over."

She says nothing as Church puts on his tall black hat. She watches him walk out. He looks as if he's aged ten years.

At the cash register, Sean as usual is texting on his phone.

Life going on.

Except nothing can ever be the same.

She'll never be the same.

She still can't believe Teddy has been here all these years, right under everyone's noses.

Like William Henry Young.

Teddy was ID'd from the dog tags he kept in a box in his shelter in the woods. He'd apparently been living there a while, though remnants of other camps were discovered. He'd kept constantly on the move so he wouldn't be found.

Not that anyone was looking.

She was stunned when she first saw him. She wouldn't have recognized him if she hadn't been prepared ahead of time. The grizzled, silent stranger was a world away from the twenty-one-year-old idealist who fled Lowood almost thirty years ago.

Champion of the soldiers who fought for their country. Defender of their burial ground.

Her protector.

And Alice's.

Teddy was the one who led law enforcement to the icehouse.

Connie always suspected her older brother had a crush on her best friend. She used to fantasize that Teddy and Alice would get married and the three of them would be entwined forever, like the triple hearts on Alice's necklace.

Then she and Alice would have been sisters in every way.

Instead, Teddy left town under a cloud of suspicion. She didn't hear from him again. It was as if he'd vanished off the face of the earth.

Until her parents received a letter from the United States Army a little over a year later.

First Lt. Edward Michael Wilcox had been honorably discharged after being wounded in battle.

Nobody even knew he'd enlisted.

Her family prepared for his return.

He didn't come home.

Two men living in the woods.

Two men with blond hair and blue eyes.

One was an angel.

The other was the Devil.

At least Young got what he had coming. He'll never be able to hurt another woman.

If it were her, she would have emptied her whole damn shotgun into the bastard.

But no one's ever going to know because she'll never tell.

She swore on the blood vow they made long ago.

She kept Alice's first secret.

And she'll keep her last.

SIXTY-FOUR

A lice clasps her hands in her lap as the onslaught begins.

"Judge McKerrity, I'd like to take you back to August twenty-ninth of this year."

Her tone isn't confrontational or accusatory.

It's measured. Respectful.

Because of who Alice is.

"On that particular morning, how long had the jury been deliberating?"

"A week."

She peers through her glasses at notes she doesn't need. "Please tell us what happened when you took the bench that morning."

"The court clerk brought a note to me."

"Who was the note from?"

"The defendant."

"Is that unusual?"

"Yes."

"Can you tell us why?"

"The jury was out. We had already received a few notes, which is why I assumed the note was from the jury."

"What did you do next?"

"I ordered that the defendant be brought into my chambers."

"Where was the prosecutor at that time?"

"In the courtroom." Alice knows where she's going, but there's nothing she can do.

"Just to be clear, the defendant was allowed in your chambers because he was representing himself?"

"Yes."

"Did you assign a court officer to escort the defendant out of the courtroom and into your chambers?"

"Yes."

Luiz survived Young's attack. But she's responsible. She put him at risk.

"Let's backtrack a moment. When you allowed the defendant to go pro se, why didn't you assign shadow counsel to sit at the defense table?"

"I can't answer that."

"Can't or won't?"

"I don't know why." It's true. Even now, she isn't sure. Or is she? Wasn't she looking for a way to bring William Henry Young into her chambers, ever since the first day of jury selection? She takes a sip of water. "I was dealing with stress at home. My husband isn't well. I know that's not an excuse, but I'm trying to explain my state of mind at the time."

Her questioner looks at Alice over her glasses. "You didn't order the defendant to be shackled during trial. Please tell us why."

"I made that ruling before the first day of jury selection."

"You could have reversed your earlier ruling for the safety of your courtroom."

"Looking back in hindsight, yes, I could have. But I stand on my ruling. I felt then and I feel now that it's too prejudicial for the jury to see a defendant in chains."

She's back in the icehouse. Her hands bound behind her with her court officer's handcuffs, ankles shackled to a metal ring in the middle of a cement floor.

Alice closes her eyes.

She's given a moment before the questioning resumes.

"You are aware, are you not, that it's forbidden under the law to have an ex parte communication, without both attorneys being present?"

"Yes."

"Yet you told the prosecutor to remain in the courtroom because you had to make a phone call, according to the statement you gave the police."

"Yes."

"Were you planning to make a phone call?"

"No."

"So you lied?"

"Yes."

Like any good attorney, she pauses to let her words sink in. "You instructed your court officer to remain in the hall, knowing that that would leave you alone in your chambers with the defendant."

"Yes."

"Please tell us what was written in the note from the defendant."

Alice sits up straighter in her chair. Of all the lies she has told, this is the one that matters.

The lie that must be accepted as truth.

She has prepared for this as well.

"The defendant threatened my family and me if I didn't give him a deal."

"A plea arrangement is the province of the District Attorney's office, isn't it?"

"Yes. But the defendant knew that it was within my power to accept or reject a plea. He wanted to ensure that I was on board before he attempted to contact the DA."

"Is the note still in your possession?"

"No."

"Do you know where the note is?"

"No."

More lies. Alice discovered the note in the pocket of her robe weeks after she'd returned home.

She reread what Young had written, reliving the shock of knowing that she'd been right.

The monster of her worst nightmares had been in her courtroom all along.

Although it was still summer, she tossed some logs into the fireplace.

She watched the note ignite, the five words that had nearly stopped her heart—I KNOW WHO YOU ARE—the last to burn.

Another member of the panel has taken up the questioning.

"What did you think you would accomplish by calling the defendant into your chambers alone?"

On the bench, she leans forward as if she really wanted to know.

"I thought I could reason with him."

"Reason with a killer?"

Alice doesn't answer.

She sees him lying there, the waters rising over him.

"Why didn't you bring the note to the chief administrative judge? Or the Manhattan DA?" another judge asks.

"I thought if I told him I'd give him what he wanted, he might back down. I know it was foolish and reckless, but I was terrified and not thinking straight. Panic overrode rational thought."

That wasn't true either.

Not when she sat on the bench after getting over her initial shock, the note clutched in her hand.

And not in the tunnel as she pointed the shotgun at William Henry Young, her mind clearer than it had been in weeks.

—₥—

In the end, the panel of judges who sit on the Commission on Judicial Performance didn't deem her behavior egregious enough for further action to be taken. Which meant their findings were never sent up to the state judicial oversight panel that has the power to remove her from the bench for judicial misconduct. Her actions that morning were found to be sanctionable, meriting a possible suspension.

Alice saves them the trouble of deciding a just punishment by stepping down, citing personal reasons.

That isn't a lie.

Although Charles has shown some slight improvement as a result of the new medication, he still needs her.

So does her daughter.

But there's one thing she has to do before the past can be laid to rest.

Something she should have done thirty years ago.

SIXTY-FIVE

The headstones of Old Lowood Cemetery rise out of the darkness like phantoms from a long-ago past.

Alice looks around and tries to put things in perspective, her surroundings both familiar and unfamiliar all at once.

Or perhaps she's the one who has changed.

The woods have lost their power over her. She has confronted the worst horrors a human being can endure.

And survived.

Twice.

She flexes and unflexes her gloved fingers as she walks, keeping the headstones in her sights. It's cold; the same bone-chilling cold she felt that Friday night in December, three days before Christmas.

It's thirty years, almost to the day.

A sense of inevitability settles over her. The feeling has gradually been growing stronger, as if everything in the past three decades had been leading up to this moment in time.

It's getting colder. She can hear the wind whistling through the treetops.

Just as it did that night.

Shivering underneath her coat in the impractical short, slinky dress her best friend had picked out for her. Unsteady in Connie's borrowed stilettos as she teetered down unlit streets. The alcohol she'd consumed making her light-headed. Her mind unable to let go of what happened at the party that she never wanted to attend in the first place.

Never dreaming that the worst was yet to come.

Alice forces herself to keep walking. Even with her phone light illuminating the ground a few feet ahead, her eyes have grown accustomed to the darkness. She's moving through the same terrain that she did three decades ago.

Everything that happened here took place in the dark.

In these woods.

She was never taken to that hell beneath the earth.

That night, as she fled the monster in the car, she remembers running over the graves of the dead soldiers and feeling as if she were running over her own grave.

Running deeper into the darkness waiting to swallow her whole.

Alone with her terror.

And the man who was about to rape her.

She feels it again, that sense of things moving inexorably forward, relentless and inescapable, as she continues navigating through the woods. She inches ahead slowly to avoid overhanging branches, the forest animals chittering and chattering around her.

The cold is creeping into her bones. In spite of the insulated gloves, her fingers are getting numb.

A sound stops her in her tracks.

The hoot of an owl.

A vision dances behind her eyelids. The same disturbing vision that lately has been occurring with more and more frequency.

She's on her back.

Her rapist is on top of her, his blue eyes locked on hers.

She has to look away.

She gazes up.

Sees an owl perched on the high branch of a nearby tree.

Something moves at the edges of her vision.

Just below the owl.

She blinks.

The headstones are still in her line of sight. Which means that the place where she was assaulted isn't far from here.

The high branch is empty.

But she still sees the unblinking yellow gaze of the owl glowing in the blackness.

She remembers the feeling of eyes all around her.

As if she were being watched.

A twig snaps.

She lets out her breath.

Just a raccoon scampering out of the brush, its long fingers fisted into its front paws giving it an unsettling human aspect.

It has something in its mouth.

It darts past her, the dead mouse between its teeth.

Alice sniffs the air.

The inky sky seems to brighten.

Now she can see the flickering of firelight.

She slides a rolled-up paper from her pocket. Shines the phone light on the map.

The camp isn't far.

She starts walking again.

SIXTY-SIX

U p ahead is a large tree.

Even from here, Alice can see the claw marks on its massive trunk.

A sign of the black bears who have always lived here.

She thinks of the bear trap that ensnared her as she ran from Young's car for the second time, almost thirty years after he raped her in these woods. Praying that a hunter would hear her screams.

Never dreaming that someone had.

The icehouse was demolished last month after county officials deemed the structure unsafe due to its deteriorated condition. Over time, after more than a century of disuse, water from the collapsed riverbed that had never been shored up backed up into part of the tunnel.

Ironic, because the icehouse had originally been carved next to the tributary in order to transport salmon and other frozen fish down the river to sell in New York City.

A place built to help people survive. That one man used for his own evil ends.

Now it's as if the icehouse never existed.

But it will always live in the memories that are never far away.

Along with other memories moving closer with every step that takes her deeper into the woods.

The darkness brightens as she approaches the camp, which Alice can see now is little more than a wood hut. It looks smaller and more primitive than it did in the photos that were taken more than three months ago.

The light is coming from a firepit. Next to the pit is a bucket, a shovel, and several logs of wood.

A fishing rod lies next to a bicycle missing its rear wheel. Nearby is a hammer, a pile of nails, and a rusted ax that must have been used to chop down the trees to build the shelter.

A short distance from the camp is a partially frozen-over creek.

A clothesline is suspended between two trees. Hanging from one end is a pair of mismatched socks, a T-shirt, and a pair of threadbare pants. On the other end are tarnished pots and pans. All flanking an American flag given pride of place in the center.

Alice knows from what she read that he fought in the Gulf War.

She had no idea what happened to him after she and her father moved away.

She cut all ties to her past.

Including him.

A once-white laundry bag lies on the ground near the clothesline. Stacked under a tree is a mini-fortress constructed out of milk crates. Alice sees something flapping on a branch.

The tattered sleeve of a coat.

What must it have been like to live in isolation all these years, cut off from the world? Was it the PTSD that the media dissected for weeks until the story was no longer front-page news and he was finally left alone?

Alice had no idea he was a suspect in the two disappearances that William Henry Young was responsible for.

Was that why he enlisted?

Or was there another reason?

She walks back to the camp. When she reaches the hut, she hesitates. Maybe this was a mistake. So much time has gone by. He has been to Hell and back. A soldier fighting his own private war. Maybe it's better to keep the past in the past, where it belongs.

But it's too late for that now.

Or has it always been too late? Hasn't the past been incrementally moving forward for decades? Encroaching on the present minute by minute, hour by hour, every day for the last thirty years?

Keeping it buried would be like trying to stop time itself.

Alice takes a steadying breath. As she starts to lift up a section of the protective tarp, she can't help but feel that she's invading the privacy he fought for years to keep.

No longer the recluse living in the forest, anonymous and unknown.

His secret is out.

Now it's time to heal old wounds.

She steps inside.

He isn't asleep under the torn blanket on top of a sagging mattress.

He isn't seated on one of a pair of rusted beach chairs around another stack of milk crates that doubles as a table. A few feet away, stained gray tarps cover the open spaces between branches in an effort to keep out the elements. An enormous tree shoots up incongruously through the middle of the hut. An old transistor radio and a rotary phone missing its cord lie next to yet another set of milk crates mounted against a crude door fashioned out of wood. Next to the crates is a pair of newish-looking space heaters.

She almost trips on a dead car battery as she walks over to the heaters to warm her hands.

In her mind's eye, she sees the heater Young placed in front of her cell in the icehouse, a concession to prove to her that he wasn't a monster.

A sound makes her jump.

The pots and pans clanging against each other on the clothesline.

The wind must be picking up.

Now Alice can hear something else.

Someone breathing.

She turns around.

He's standing next to the tree.

And he's got a gun.

SIXTY-SEVEN

She never heard him coming.

He must have learned that in the war. How to move by stealth.

He makes a sound in his throat. He's trying to speak.

"Alice?"

Hearing the two syllables of her name sends her back to that mid-August morning. The day after she first laid eyes on William Henry Young in her courtroom. Charles saying her name in those rare moments of lucidity before the light went out of his eyes for the last time.

But his voice is deeper, huskier; as if he weren't used to speaking.

He doesn't move, but she can feel his tension.

"Yes," she finally answers. "It's me."

Alice is trying to reconcile this guarded, white-haired stranger in threadbare trousers and a coat missing several buttons with the boy with the laughing face and bright blond hair she met the summer before she turned eleven.

His golden head was the first thing she saw. Rising from the headstones as if he were a reborn spirit of the Revolutionary War soldiers that she'd heard were buried there.

She'd moved to Lowood in June. Angry and lonely and still grieving for her dead mother, whom she missed every second of every day.

She hated living with her father. Hated this awful place so far from the city. Where she had no friends. Where her mother wasn't.

She hated the woods most of all. The trees that seemed to be everywhere and cast their long shadows on every street. Shutting out the light. Turning day into night. A darkness that could swallow you whole if you weren't careful.

It was on a hot August day that she made up her mind. She'd put away her night-light when she moved here, and now she was determined to overcome her fears.

Even with a flashlight, the minute she walked across the dirt road leading into the woods, she could feel the darkness closing in. She forced herself to keep walking, wielding the flashlight as if it were a weapon and imagining monsters hiding behind trees the same way they hid under her bed or lurked in the closet.

As Alice went deeper into the woods, she felt invisible eyes following her. Everything around her took on sinister meaning.

The hooting of an owl.

Two squirrels fighting over a scrap of food.

The endless drone of crickets.

Then she heard it: a high-pitched screech, followed by a sound like thunder. When she looked up, she saw something spreading across the treetops. They were the most enormous wings she'd ever seen. She was sure they were about to swoop down and carry her away.

She turned and ran. It wasn't the way she'd come because headstones suddenly filled her vision. Rising out of the darkness like silver ghosts.

She stopped to catch her breath.

That was when she saw him. Coming out from behind one of the headstones.

"You okay?"

She didn't answer. She was staring up at the sky, where what looked like a long plume of smoke was streaking across the clouds.

"You're not from around here, are you?"

She shook her head.

He was tall, with broad shoulders and eyes the color of a turquoise sea.

He pointed to the sky. "That was a hoary bat. Did you know bats are the only mammals that can fly? But don't worry. They only eat insects, not people." He smiled; it lit up his face. "The animals of the forest live together in peace. They would never hurt you. You're safe here. Trust me. There are no monsters in the woods."

Alice wanted to believe that. Wanted to trust him.

But she wasn't convinced.

When the assistant principal brought her into Constance Wilcox's fifth-grade class at Lowood Elementary a month later, she had no idea that he was Connie's older brother.

His name was Edward Michael Wilcox.

Everyone called him Teddy.

When Connie introduced them, Alice didn't tell her that they'd already met. Neither did he.

That late-summer afternoon in the woods remained their secret.

It was the first secret Alice kept from her best friend.

It wasn't long before she had another secret.

Teddy liked her. More than just as his kid sister's best friend.

Several years later, she took advantage of those feelings to shed herself of something she wanted desperately to lose.

He still hasn't moved. He stands motionless next to the tree, the gun in his hand.

Once again, Alice is overcome by a sense of inevitability.

And something more.

As if time were both advancing and retreating.

Contracting and expanding.

She's running.

She sees the headstones rising out of the darkness.

Sharp pebbles slash her bare feet as she stumbles over rocks and tree roots. Low-hanging branches stab her face.

She runs faster. A car door slams. The sound echoes in her head. Now she's running between the headstones.

Footsteps crash through the underbrush.

Just when she thinks she can't go any farther, she sees an enormous tree. She wills herself to be invisible as she crouches behind the gnarled trunk, trying to blend in with the darkness.

In the sudden silence that falls, the sounds of the forest seem magnified.

The chainsawing chirp of crickets.

The growls and shrieks of owls.

And most terrifying of all, the sound that still echoes in her nightmares: A high-pitched screech, followed by the deafening flapping of wings as a red bat flees its perch.

Then all is quiet again, as if the animals are holding their collective breath.

That sound of a car door slamming once again echoes through the forest.

Has he given up?

So easily?

She peeks out from behind the tree.

She takes a tentative step. Then another.

Too late, she sees him. A silhouette in the blackness.

Just waiting to ambush her.

She hears it again. The echo of a car door slamming.

She runs from the figure next to the tree, only to be grabbed moments later and thrown to the ground so violently that her vision divides . . .

Teddy is no longer next to the tree. He makes no sound as he walks over to the milk crates piled against the wood door. He places the gun on the top crate. Then he walks toward her.

He stops a few feet away. Reaches into the pocket of his coat.

Alice stares in shock and disbelief at what rests in his open palm.

A gold chain.

That holds a trio of entwined hearts.

SIXTY-EIGHT

"**W**here did you find that?"

She barely recognizes her own voice.

Her mind hurtling back to the last time she saw the necklace.

As she tried to pry her rapist's fingers from her throat.

Feeling the chain ripping, then sliding off her neck.

But this chain is intact. It looks almost new.

And the three hearts are immaculate, as if the necklace had been maintained with loving care.

With his other hand, Teddy rubs his fingers over the necklace. Caressing the hearts that are almost swallowed up in his large hands.

She has seen him do that before.

Once again, she has the unsettling sense of moving through time.

Every step forward a step back.

He turns away, but not before Alice see acknowledgment in his eyes.

And something else.

Shame.

And guilt.

He shakes his head violently back and forth. "I'm . . . sorry."

He said those words to her before.

The night they had sex. After they left the dance in Renegade Falls. When he saw the blood after he'd taken her virginity. His blue eyes fixed on her as he caressed the entwined hearts that nestled between her naked breasts.

Afterward, overcome with guilt, all she wanted was to put that night behind her. Pretend it had never happened.

But he wouldn't let her.

Everywhere she went, there he was.

Although he'd graduated from Lowood High three years earlier, he started hanging out at school. He followed her around like a lovesick puppy, always when she was alone, which happened more and more after the night they had sex. She knew Connie was hurt because they used to always walk home from school together. If she suspected, she never said. And Alice couldn't tell her.

It felt like she had a stalker, even though she told herself this was Teddy, the boy who told her there were no monsters in the woods. But she was starting to feel frightened, wondering if she'd met the monster after all.

A monster with a human face.

All she wanted was to get away from him.

Especially once she saw William Henry Young in the bar.

Another man with blond hair and blue eyes.

But where Teddy was boring and clingy, Young was exciting and dangerous.

She wanted him.

As badly as Teddy wanted her.

She didn't know how badly until the night of the party.

He's watching her in that still way of his. Nothing moving but his eyes.

Is he waiting for her to accept his apology? For what? Hurting her during sex, which wasn't his fault? Or for what happened afterward?

Is he remembering that night, too?

Accosting her in the hall as she tried to leave the party. Demanding to know why she was ignoring him after the night they'd spent together. That was when she realized that it was worse than she thought: He'd fallen in love with her. She agonized over what to do. Thinking how he could ruin everything she'd fantasized about doing with the stranger from the bar who now consumed her every waking thought.

Finally making it out the front door, afraid that Teddy was going to grab her again.

That he'd never let her go.

SIXTY-NINE

*O*utside, the cold hits her right away.

She feels it through the skimpy dress. She thinks of the long walk back to Connie's house, which only gets the guilt going again. She wonders if Connie witnessed the scene Teddy made in the hall, and if she did what on earth Alice was going to tell her.

Her toes are starting to get numb in the impractical open-toed heels she's wearing. She feels dizzy and a little nauseated and wishes she hadn't drank so much at the party.

She hears the sound of an engine as she walks.

She stops. Turns.

It's too far away to see the make or model. She has no idea if it's the same car Teddy drove when he took her to his house the night of the dance.

She lets out her breath when the car disappears around a corner.

As she continues walking, she starts to feel angry. Just because they had sex once doesn't mean that he owns her.

She hears it again. This time when she turns around, she's blinded by the glare of headlights.

She puts up a hand to shield her eyes.

The car cruises slowly down the street.

Pulls up next to her.

The passenger window rolls down.

Excitement replaces the anger. It's him. Her stranger from the bar. It was his blond head she saw behind the wheel the night she walked home from choir practice. His car that she just saw disappear around the corner.

He's playing games.

She forgets all about Teddy and what happened at the party as she steps off the curb, almost tripping in her heels and ignoring the voice warning her to not get into the car.

Feeling the first stirrings of alarm as she hears the locks click into place. Alarm turning to fear when he drives into the woods. Fear mushrooming into terror as she bolts from the car. Hiding behind a tree. Sneaking out when she thinks the danger's past, only to see someone standing there. Hurtling past him, afraid her legs are going to give out. Running blind, moving so fast that she doesn't see the arms reaching out until it's too late . . .

Young hadn't given up. He hadn't left the woods.

It wasn't the echo of his car door slamming a second time that she heard as she crouched behind the tree.

She wasn't seeing double as she was being raped.

Someone else was in the woods that night.

"You were there, weren't you?"

He doesn't answer. He doesn't have to.

Her mind races, trying to put the pieces together.

He must have left the party soon after she did.

That was the car she saw just before it disappeared around the corner. It was too far away to see the make or model.

Not William Henry Young playing games.

Teddy. As she'd initially feared.

Teddy all along.

"You followed me."

Which meant he saw her get into Young's car.

He must have thought she had a secret assignation. That would have enraged him even more. He was probably right behind them as Young drove into the woods.

That was the second car door she heard.

Two cars.

Two men in the woods.

And one of them knew the terrain better than anybody.

He's trying to speak. Her necklace glitters in his open palm.

Alice once again sees his hands as they lovingly caressed the entwined hearts after they had sex that night.

Then she's on the ground, seeing the headstones rising out of the darkness, the gold chain cutting into her skin as she claws at her own neck to pry the fingers of her rapist loose . . .

"Forgive me."

He's holding out his hand.

As if the necklace were an offering.

Or an act of contrition.

SEVENTY

The screams echo through the silent house.

Alice sits up and reaches for the robe that she keeps at the foot of the bed. Although the clock on the nightstand reads two A.M., she had only just begun to drift off.

She doesn't sleep so well these days, either.

The screams have diminished to anguished cries when Alice goes into the hall. She looks in on Charles, who's asleep, undisturbed by the noise two doors down. Next to her husband's bed, Larry looks up from his reading, concern in his eyes. Tonight isn't the first time this has happened.

Alice gives him what she hopes is a reassuring smile, then continues down the hall. She stops at the last room on the right. The door is always left open, so that she can hear her in the night.

All is quiet now. During the day, when Alice brings her meals and tends to her needs, she almost misses the loud music that used to blare from her room. Now there's mostly silence broken only by her cries and screams, a result of the night terrors that Alice fears now may never leave her.

Her bedroom is spotless. No magazines litter the floor. No clothes strewn across the bed that now seems too large for her. She lies there with the blanket pulled up to her chin, staring at her mother with eyes like saucers. It's exactly how she looked when she was little and afraid of the bogeyman.

Alice would get into bed with her, just like her mother did when she was a frightened young girl. Alice would hold her until the fear abated and she finally drifted back to sleep.

Alexis watches her mother now as Alice goes to the partially open window, where a chilly breeze flutters the curtains. A branch from the tree outside is knocking against the glass, which could be what set her off tonight.

The wind is picking up. An early January snowstorm is predicted overnight. Alice closes the window, starts to draw back the curtains.

"Did you lock it?"

As Alice secures the window, she sees herself moving through the house back in August, during those hellish weeks of the trial. Not feeling safe until she'd bolted every door and window.

"Mama?"

She turns from the window. "Yes, sweetheart?"

"It's so dark."

Alice looks at her. Shadows from the old night-light plugged into the wall next to her bed play across Alexis's pale face. Alice brought the night-light back into her room after her daughter came close to losing her life in the tunnel.

That was when the nightmares started.

A little over four months ago.

Alice flips a switch on the wall, and the room is suddenly ablaze with light.

The shadows disappear. Every corner of the room is illuminated.

Her daughter's eyes are still full of fear.

Because she knows now that real monsters exist?

"Would you get under the covers with me?"

This, too, has become a nightly ritual. Alice forces her mind away from the darkness that she still feels pressing down on her like a shroud as she pulls back the blanket and slides in next to her daughter. Alexis's hands rest protectively on her belly.

Her baby is due next month.

Alice hadn't even known she was pregnant.

Alexis started bleeding two weeks after she came home.

She has been on bed rest ever since.

Her doctor examines her frequently to check for blood clots and decreased bone mass as a result of a prolonged period spent in bed, which is as dangerous to her as it is to her unborn child.

Another consequence of the ordeal she endured.

Alice has so much to make amends for.

Alexis has her head turned toward Alice, her gaze watchful. Maybe it's because they spend so much time together since she has been confined to her bed, but she seems attuned to her mother's every mood.

They've never talked about what happened.

Someday, perhaps they will. Although Alice hasn't decided yet what to tell her.

Right now the only thing that matters is that she has a safe delivery.

One day at a time.

She puts her hands over her daughter's. As she moves her hands in concentric circles, gently kneading the warm mound of her belly, Alexis starts to relax. "Have you and Damien decided on a name?" Alice asks.

A few weeks ago, they found out the baby's gender. Alexis hadn't been sure she wanted to know, but her boyfriend prevailed.

Damien comes to visit every day. When Alexis first told her mother about him, Alice expected someone with long hair dressed in a KillJoy sweatshirt with emblazoned knives dripping blood like the ones Alexis used to wear. Not the clean-cut, respectful young man who kept addressing her as "Your Honor" until she finally told him to call her by her name.

Lately, Damien has been talking about getting a job and keeping the rock band as a side gig.

Alice has a feeling he's going to propose soon.

"We're going to call him Nathan. After Grandpa. And Charles for his middle name."

Tears prick Alice's eyes. For a moment, she can't speak. "Your father would like that."

"I hope he looks like Damien. He has the most beautiful green eyes."

"He'll be beautiful no matter what." Because he'll be loved. "We'll talk more tomorrow. You and Nathan Charles both need your rest."

Alice is almost in the doorway when her daughter's voice stops her.

"What did he look like? My biological father?"

SEVENTY-ONE

Alexis is asleep.

Alice hasn't seen her look this much at peace in months. Maybe years.

She turns out the overhead light as she tiptoes out of her daughter's room. She leaves on the night-light, hoping that someday soon she will no longer need it.

She'll put it away with her childhood things.

As Alice once did.

Only to take it out again after William Henry Young walked into her courtroom.

She closes her eyes and takes a calming breath. Continues down the hall.

As she runs a bath, her mind circles back to her daughter.

When she asked about her father, Alice thought her heart would stop.

It wasn't as if she didn't know that this day would arrive. When Alexis was young, Alice became very adept at circumventing her questions when she used to ask. And she asked all the time. When did she stop? Alice can't pinpoint exactly when, but she remembers the relief she felt. As if she'd somehow been let off the hook.

What she did was to allow a lie to fester for decades.

A lie she knew her daughter didn't believe.

She knows that was the reason Alexis went to Lowood. To dig up the missing pieces of her mother's past.

She needed to find her father because she was soon to become a parent herself.

Alice thought about that, as her daughter waited to hear the words that would tell her to whom she belonged. The words that would make her feel whole.

As she lowers herself into the tub, Alice wonders which is worse: Not knowing who your father is? Or knowing who he is, but that he didn't want you? Didn't love you enough to stay.

She was around the same age Alexis was when she first asked why her father left them. Her mother said it had nothing to do with her. That it wasn't her fault. But Alice believed it was. Just as a part of her believed that what happened to her in the woods was her fault too.

Isn't that the first thing victims do? Blame themselves?

As time passed, she stopped asking why. Convinced herself that bad things could happen to good people.

She never told her father what happened to her.

Or who the father of her unborn child was.

After they left Lowood and moved farther north, her father shocked her by deciding that they wouldn't put up the baby for adoption. Especially after he'd abandoned her when she was a baby. She had thought he'd left because he didn't like children.

Then her daughter was born.

Perhaps it was because he was a generation removed, but Nathan Dunn adored Alexis.

And she adored him until the day he died.

But a grandfather isn't a father.

She had the right to know whose blood flowed through her veins. After all these years, she deserved the truth.

But how was Alice to tell her? Knowing what she now knew?

She began with the part Alexis had heard many times before.

The story about a lonely young girl whose mother had just died.

She had no sisters or brothers, no cousins, uncles, or aunts. With no one to take her in, she was forced to move to a strange new town hundreds of miles away, to be raised by a man she had never met.

Then she continued the story.

"*She had always been a fearful child. Afraid of her own shadow. One day, not long after she'd arrived in Lowood, she made up her mind that she was going to conquer her fears. On a hot summer afternoon, she gathered up her courage and went into the woods . . .*"

When she got to the part about the bat that struck terror in her ten-and-a-half-year-old heart, Alexis listened with the same rapt expression Alice used to see when she'd read to her from one of the books she loved as a child.

"*It was there, on a hot summer afternoon in the woods, that she first met him. He was the one who eased her fears . . .*"

As she talked, she saw him again. Not the white-haired, guilt-ridden recluse in the woods. But the boy who rose up from behind the headstone in the cemetery like a hero out of a fairy tale. The impossibly handsome boy with the blond hair and blue eyes who was going to save her from the monsters that she still believed existed even though he assured her they didn't.

"*His name was Teddy. They became the closest of friends. That friendship gradually blossomed into love. They met in secret because he was older and his sister was her best friend. They would meet wherever they could be alone. It didn't matter as long as they were together. Sometimes they even met in the woods. Then she discovered she was pregnant . . .*"

Here Alice paused. Then took a deep breath and resumed.

"She was afraid to tell him about the baby because she didn't want him to get into trouble. Or maybe he'd feel he had to do the honorable thing and marry her when he was still so young himself. She didn't want to ruin his life. She thought she was doing the right thing, not saddling him with a family before he was ready.

"Her father couldn't live with the stigma of having an unmarried, pregnant daughter. He sold the hardware store that had been in his family for generations and they moved to Jonasville, a village near the Saint Lawrence River that was a lot like Lowood. That was when she realized her mistake, that it was wrong to keep the truth from her lover. That somehow, together, they'd find a way to make it work. But she was too late.

"He had left town to fight in the Gulf War . . ."

She spun a fiction of clandestine romance and star-crossed love.

And fate.

". . . It was Fate that brought them back together. He had returned to Lowood, but no one knew. Until the day he set out to rescue her from the monster . . ."

Alice told her daughter that he was the one who led police to the icehouse.

She told her that her father was a hero.

When she was finished, Alexis didn't say anything for a long time.

Then she asked why he lived in the woods.

Alice said that the war had left him with a severe case of PTSD that affected his mind and his memory.

"Like Charles?" she asked.

"Yes," Alice said. "Like Charles."

She told her daughter that she needed to sleep now. That they'd talk again in the morning.

Just before Alexis drifted off, she asked one last question.

Would her father know who she was?

Alice saw herself in his camp again. Heard him speak her name.

She told her that she thought he would.

Her daughter is almost her mirror image.

Except that she has his blue eyes.

The water has gone cold.

Alice sits up and releases the drain and thinks about the things that Alexis will never know.

Alice will not tell her about the night she was raped.

She will not tell her the real reason her father lives in the woods.

Thirty years ago, she told her daughter a lie because she wanted to protect her.

She's still protecting her.

SEVENTY-TWO

When Teddy held out the necklace that she had lost so long ago, Alice's head spun.

Was it possible?

Could she have gotten everything wrong?

Not seeing things as they were? But as something else?

What was it William Henry Young had said?

Something about the past masquerading as the truth.

Sometimes as something else.

Had her mind been playing tricks, turning what happened that night into fact that she eventually transmuted into memory?

False memory?

Her mind raced back.

To the trial.

The way William Henry Young looked at her in the courtroom.

As if he knew a secret about her that no one else knew.

Testing her.

Taunting her.

Letting her know that she was his first victim. Not Angel Diallo, the woman he was on trial for killing.

Could she have misread him so badly?

Then she remembered the note.

I KNOW WHO YOU ARE.

Five words that had convinced her that she was right.

Five words that proved nothing.

They could have merely meant he'd recognized her as the girl who got into his car.

He talked about that in the icehouse.

How she got into his car that night because she wanted him as much as he wanted her.

She tried to remember the other things he said.

Choosing her because we shared the same darkness.

Saying there was unfinished business between them.

That she was the one who got away.

Being reunited.

And something about a second chance.

But he never actually confessed to raping her.

Then she looked into Teddy's eyes.

She saw him clearly. For the first time since that long-ago night.

Standing next to the tree. Under the owl.

That was when she realized what had happened.

It was Teddy who startled Young.

Teddy who made Young realize that they weren't alone.

There was a witness.

That was why Young ran. If Teddy hadn't been there, Young likely would have killed her after he finished raping her.

Just like he killed his other victims.

Teddy saved her life.

But he didn't save her from a savage assault.

"Why didn't you do something?" she asked him as they stood across from one another in his shelter in the woods, her voice shaking with emotion. "Why didn't you try to help me? Get the police?"

He just bowed his head.

Forcing her to draw her own conclusions.

She thought back to the terrible scene in the hall before she left the party.

The way he begged her to tell him what he'd done wrong. Pleading for another chance to prove his love.

How his hurt and rejection only made her feel guiltier. Telling him if he didn't take his hands off her, she'd scream.

A dozen emotions raging inside her as she fled into the night.

Maybe he didn't think she was being assaulted in the woods.

Maybe he thought she and Young were playing some kind of sex game.

Maybe he was in shock.

Or maybe she was just making excuses for him.

He'd been seething with anger at the party.

He must have been so jealous when he saw her get into Young's car.

Was this his revenge?

Did he think that she got what she deserved?

But no one deserves to be raped.

"Forgive me," he said again.

His voice an entreaty.

Or a prayer.

—⁂—

In the end, Alice granted him the absolution he asked for.

What else could she do? He was a shattered husk of a man who'd suffered unimaginable horrors.

Before she left, she told him he had a daughter. That was the reason she'd made the trip back to Lowood in the dead of winter.

He was stunned.

She waited for him to put together what that meant. They had slept together only that one time.

He started to cry. She knew he was back in the past, seeing what she was seeing, watching the present fold in on itself like a movie spooling backward, until he came to the reel where he stood next to the tree. A silent witness to another man raping her. Doing nothing to stop William Henry Young or to protect the mother of his child that neither of them knew was growing inside her.

He was still crying when she left his camp and walked out of the woods for the last time.

SEVENTY-THREE

Winter is once again upon them.

It has been almost a year since Alice made her final pilgrimage to the woods to heal the wounds of the past and tell the father of her child that they had miraculously created a life together.

Before she left his camp, she told him to keep the necklace with the three entwined hearts that he'd repaired and preserved with such care.

—⁓—

Two men in the woods.

One raped her.

The other loved her.

—⁓—

She still tortures herself with the *what ifs*:

What if she hadn't gotten into William Henry Young's car that night?

She might have married Teddy.

He wouldn't have left Lowood and come back with half his mind gone.

Her daughter would have grown up with her biological father.

—⚋—

She knows it's time to move on.

But the past still weighs on her.

Alexis, on the other hand, is thriving.

Alice likes to think it's because she's now a mother herself.

Her child's birth was relatively easy and painless, given the risks and dangers of her pregnancy. Alice was with her every step of the way, a part of her marveling at the four-hour labor that was far easier than hers.

For weeks, all anyone could talk about was the color of her grandson's eyes. Alexis and Damien have placed bets that his eyes will change color, as babies' eyes often do. His mother is hoping for the emerald green of his father's. Or perhaps it will reach back a generation and his eyes will become the deep brown of his grandmother's. But it has been ten months since he was born, and they haven't changed. They stubbornly remain the color of Alexis's eyes.

Blue.

Her daughter is turning out to be a good mother. Far better than Alice was, at least in those hellish early years. She and Damien have chosen a wedding date: next spring, to commemorate their child's first year of life. Alice likes the symbolism of that.

Spring as a time of rebirth and renewal. Life beginning again.

The chance to start over. To correct the sins of the past.

As William Henry Young once said to her:

"It will be as if the past never existed. We'll begin with a blank slate. The way children come into the world."

The nuptials will take place at home, so that Charles can attend. He'll be there in body, if not in mind and spirit. The guests will include the band members of KillJoy and a few friends. Alexis never had many friends. Like her mother.

Constance Moore will be invited, of course. She and Alice reconnected after the events of two summers ago brought them back together. She told Alice about the email correspondences between her and Alexis.

Connie was delighted to find out she was an aunt. Alice knows that once Connie met Alexis, her old friend believed that the man who brutalized Alice was Alexis's father. If that man had been Teddy, he could have put the life of his own unborn child at risk.

He continues to live in the woods. It was, after all, the place he had always loved best. Still, his sister never gives up hope that one day he'll come home.

In the past few months, Alexis hasn't asked about her father.

Whom she has yet to meet. That, too, may come in time. Or not. Maybe she prefers to imagine him as her mother described him to her, the day Alice first saw him rise up from behind that headstone like a hero out of a Greek myth.

Alexis seems truly happy now. She has more compassion for Charles, whom Alice has vowed to never put in a care facility no matter what happens. A place where he'd be surrounded by strangers instead of those who love him.

She and her daughter still haven't talked about what happened in the tunnel. That remains the elephant in the room.

It could be her imagination, but a few times in the last month—and just the other day, as they were decorating the magnificent evergreen that Damien brought for Christmas—Alice has caught Alexis looking at her.

Even after Connie had taken her out of there, she would have heard the blast.

Alice remembers how her daughter clung to her while a few feet away William Henry Young lay in a pool of bloody water, wounded and unarmed.

In her own way, had Alexis been trying to stop her?

Alice sees herself running from Young's car in a terrifying replay of what happened thirty years earlier.

Was that Teddy's way of atoning for what he couldn't—or wouldn't—do before?

When he led police to the icehouse, did he believe he was saving Alice? From herself?

SEVENTY-FOUR

Young's eyes are open.

His arms cut through the water as he tries to drag the dead weight of his body out of the line of fire.

She hears it now.

Under the sound of the water.

It reverberates in her head, drowning out everything else.

A plaintive wail that rips at her heart.

Alice knows she's gone, that she's hearing only the echo of her voice.

There is another primal impulse.

A mother's need to protect her child.

She looks down.

Young has stopped moving. He's getting weaker. Losing blood.

She doesn't have much time.

She won't get a second chance.

Slowly, she lowers the gun until it's level with his heart.

Her vision wavers.

She's on the ground, staring up into a pair of blue eyes.

Her mind has become a thing apart from her body as he pounds into her.

She feels pain like she's never known before. Now there's a stickiness between *her legs. She can feel blood running down the insides of her thighs. But she's too weak to fight.*

She closes her eyes. When she opens them, she sees the owl on the high branch, its ancient yellow eyes watching.

Always watching.

Something moves at the edges of her vision.

Just below the owl.

She blinks.

Her double vision clears.

The sea of blue dissipates.

Resolves into a single blue eye.

She shifts her gaze so that she's staring into the ruin of his right eye.

Once again, he becomes the faceless monster of her nightmares.

She grasps the shotgun tighter.

All that's left is to pull the trigger . . .

—⚉—

Afterward, she thought she'd feel exultant.

Vindicated.

Avenged at long last.

All she felt was numb.

The opposite of feeling. The absence of emotion.

The reverberation still echoed in her head.

Then silence.

Until the tunnel once again exploded in sound.

Voices shouting.

Footsteps pounding.

It was as if an army were advancing.

When she turned around, she saw guns pointed at her.

She heard a voice telling her to put down the shotgun. Slow and easy because no one could be sure of her mental state, and that made her unpredictable.

She just stood there, swaying a little on her feet, when one of them finally walked toward her. Alice's eyes were on the weapon in his hand as he spoke words meant to reassure and disarm her.

She offered no resistance as he carefully took the just-fired shotgun from her hands.

She hadn't spoken when a police jacket was placed over her shoulders, as if that could obliterate the chill she felt in every part of her body.

She closed her eyes against the glaring lights that turned night into day.

She closed her mind against the horrific images she saw behind her lids.

When she opened her eyes, someone was taking the pulse of the red-haired woman.

He shook his head.

A group of them were gathered around William Henry Young, who lay unmoving in the swirling scarlet waters.

Someone wearing a jacket with a *CSU* insignia was placing the Glock into an evidence bag. Alice's gaze lingered there for a moment.

She still hadn't uttered a word as she was led out of the tunnel.

How could she?

She was in shock.

The hospital kept her there several days for observation, less for the physical injury to her ankle, which would heal, than for her unseen wounds. Doctors wanted to evaluate the psychic damage from her having been abducted and imprisoned for more than seven hours by a serial killer whom she then shot.

To Alice, it felt more like seven days.

After Lowood doctors released her into the care of her doctor who had prescribed the antianxiety medication she'd taken during the trial, with a directive to follow up with the hospital, Alice was driven back to the city in a police cruiser to find more members of the media camped on her front doorstep.

Inside her town house, Connie was waiting.

When she heard the sirens after leaving Alice in the tunnel, Connie had had only moments to make a decision. She couldn't wait for Alice. She had to protect Alexis, knowing that was what her friend would have wanted. She told Alexis that her mother had to stay behind to tell the police about her abduction. She got McKerrity into her car just in time. As she sped out of the woods, she saw the headlights on the other side of the road. An army of them.

She kept driving and didn't stop until she reached Manhattan.

With the help of Larry and Edith, Charles's two aides, Connie looked after Alexis, who still hadn't spoken a word when Alice arrived home. After promising Alice that she'd never tell anyone about Charles's condition—another secret she'd keep—Connie left. She steered clear of the press by taking backstreets to the garage where she'd parked her SUV several nights earlier.

—៣—

In deference to her status as a Supreme Court judge, the Lewis County District Attorney put in a call to the Manhattan District Attorney, who claimed jurisdiction over the case because William Henry Young had abducted the Honorable Alice D. McKerrity from a courthouse in New York City.

A week after she returned home from Lowood, Alice met with the Manhattan DA.

She stated how the defendant had chased her into the tunnel after he shot out the lock in the door of the room where she'd barricaded herself to escape from him.

Near the entrance to the tunnel, where the water was almost knee-deep, she heard someone.

She saw a woman with red hair holding a shotgun.

She saw the defendant backing up, aiming the Glock.

She heard shots ring out.

Heard the woman scream.

Saw her fall.

Then she saw the defendant on the ground.

Aiming her court officer's Glock at her.

That was when she grabbed the shotgun that had fallen from the red-haired woman's hands as she fell.

After she finished, the DA grasped both of Alice's hands in hers in a rare display of emotion.

A few details in her story were true.

The most important detail.

The Glock was in Young's hand when law enforcement arrived at the scene.

The Manhattan District Attorney's office declined to prosecute, believing that Alice had acted in self-defense.

She was never charged.

SEVENTY-FIVE

When Alice heard the voices in the tunnel, she knew she had only minutes.

Maybe less.

Young wasn't moving.

Then his right arm shot out of the water.

Her finger froze on the safety. She started to duck, but not in time.

The shock on his face mirrored her own.

She was still on her feet when he tried to pull the trigger again.

She could have held the shotgun on him until the police arrived, knowing the odds of the Glock firing the third or fourth or even fifth time.

—ᴍ—

As she climbs the stairs after locking up for the night, Alice is thinking about water.

If the tunnel hadn't been flooded, the Glock would not have sunk beneath the surface after slipping out of Young's hand when Connie shot him. That was the reason he'd been frantically chopping through the water. Not to escape the line of fire, but to find the gun, which would

322

have barely been visible in the sludge-filled water made even murkier by Young's blood.

According to ballistics, it wasn't the fact of the gun being submerged that might have rendered it inoperable. Not only do Glocks have the ability to fire when wet, they can sometimes fire underwater.

It wasn't sand, silt, or other debris in the water that could have lodged in the Glock, causing it to jam.

Or a malfunction that prevented the bullet from loading into the chamber.

The explanation was much simpler.

The weapon had run out of ammunition.

God's hand?

Karmic destiny?

Justice?

Upstairs, Alice looks in on Charles, who is fast asleep. Next to his bed, Larry looks up from his reading.

Alice smiles at him and continues down the hall.

Her daughter is also asleep.

A few feet from his mother's bed, ten-month-old Nathan Charles rests peacefully in his crib.

As she watches the gentle rise and fall of her daughter's chest that reassured her that Alexis was breathing as a baby, Alice thinks again about karmic destiny.

And revenge.

When she pulled the trigger, she neglected to take into account that karmic destiny cuts both ways.

For every choice, there is a cost. Consequences to our actions.

She took the law into her own hands.

What sentence did she deserve? She, who spent more than a decade meting out punishment to fit the crime. What justified committing the ultimate act? How can you quantify the incalculable cost of taking a human life?

Maybe that's her true punishment.

The guilt she'll feel until her dying day.

She thinks about all the women who would still be alive if she'd gone to the police that long-ago night.

For a while, she was sure that a reporter would uncover the fact that she'd once lived in Lowood. And moved away two months before William Henry Young abducted Kimberley Evans, his second victim. A coincidence, but something Alice should have mentioned at the time of the shooting. One thing the law doesn't like is coincidences.

So far, it hasn't happened.

That doesn't mitigate her culpability.

If she'd told her daughter the truth, Alexis wouldn't have traveled to Lowood in search of answers. Alice put her life at risk as well.

She has so much to atone for.

And yet, if she could go back, would she make the same choices?

These are the hard questions Alice asks herself in the dead of night when sleep refuses to come.

Sensing her mother's presence, Alexis stirs.

She slides over to make room.

Alice's eyes fill. Then, as she did throughout the latter stages of Alexis's pregnancy, she gets under the covers with her.

She can feel her daughter's warm breath against her skin as Alexis places her head close to hers.

As if she knows.

And is absolving her.

All her sins forgiven.

ACKNOWLEDGMENTS

As writers, we live for that exhilarating, transformative moment when everything we have imagined, plotted and planned, sweat and wept over into recorders and onto blank pages, coalesces into a story ready to be shared with the world.

It's a wild ride fraught with fits and starts, joys and frustrations, transcendent moments and agonies of self-doubt, lightning flashes of brilliance and dark nights of the soul before our vision sees the light of day. With *First Victim*, it was Luisa Smith who helped me fully realize that vision and make Alice McKerrity into so much more than a voice in my head. Thank you, Luisa. You are truly an editor without equal!

Speaking of people who believe in me: Otto Penzler, Charles Perry, Jacob Shapiro, Will Luckman at Mysterious Press, Penzler Publishers, and Scarlet Suspense. Thank you all from the bottom of my heart for making my author journey exciting, eye-opening, and so much fun. Special thanks to Kathy Strickman, who did an outstanding job on copy edits, and Amy Medeiros for making some good catches.

I thought they wouldn't be able to top the astonishing cover they created for *Saving Grace*. But Faceout Studio did it again with *First Victim*!

No book would be complete without the behind-the-scenes folks who help with the bane of many an author's existence: getting the technical details right so that no one can tell us later that we got it wrong. Shout-outs to:

Jason Kolowski, forensics expert extraordinaire who cut his teeth (couldn't resist) at the New York City chief medical examiner's office and told me more than I ever wanted to know about bite marks, DNA, and how, yes, it is physically possible to beat someone to death with your fists.

Dr. George Sanchez, DDS of Delray Beach, Florida, who gave me the idea for a perfect lethal weapon that can be smuggled into a courtroom.

My agent Doug Grad, who knows his way around a publishing deal, and can also tell you a thing or two about upstate New York, abandoned forts and tunnels, and whether (spoiler alert) Glocks can float. For additional help with firearms, I owe a debt of gratitude to former Pennsylvania state trooper and retired Air Force vet Michael Huffstutler, Steve Philson and Steve Palincsar of the Gun Club, and a pair of NYPD officers I stopped to ask questions as they cruised around Manhattan's Central Park.

My husband Ted, trial litigator par excellence, who gave me invaluable insights into the interstices of criminal law. He brings so much more than legal expertise to the table. Which is why he will always be my first reader. (Ask me about the slow burn.)

First Victim is in memory of Philip Spitzer, who said I was a natural, and explained how time has no meaning for an artist. And told me one day my writing would be recognized.

I can't say enough to the authors, bloggers, Instagrammers, and reviewers who are never too busy to read a new novel. I marvel at your unflagging enthusiasm, perspicacity, and how you always seem to get it!

Finally, dear readers—I leave you with one last question: If you had to make the choice between justice and revenge, would you pull the trigger?

Debbie Babitt was Copy Director for two major Manhattan publishing companies. She has worked as an actress, playwright, and drama critic. Debbie is the daughter of a former federal judge and is married to a criminal defense attorney. Her first novel, *Saving Grace*, was selected by *Suspense Magazine* as one of the best debuts of 2021. She and her husband divide their time between New York and Florida.